THE FALL
OF A NATION

A SEQUEL TO
THE BIRTH OF A NATION

BY

THOMAS DIXON

AUTHOR OF "THE CLANSMAN," "THE SOUTHERNER,"
"THE FOOLISH VIRGIN," ETC.

ILLUSTRATED BY
CHARLES WRENN

Fredonia Books
Amsterdam, The Netherlands

The Fall of a Nation:
A Sequel to the Birth of a Nation

by
Thomas Dixon

ISBN: 1-4101-0787-6

Reprinted from the 1916 edition

Fredonia Books
Amsterdam, The Netherlands
http://www.fredoniabooks.com

TO

MY FRIEND

JAMES B. DUKE

TO THE READER

This novel is not a rehash of the idea of a foreign conquest of America based on the accidents of war. It is a study of the origin, meaning and destiny of American Democracy by one who believes that the time is ripe in this country for a revival of the principles on which our Republic was founded.

THOMAS DIXON.

LOS ANGELES, CALIFORNIA

LIST OF ILLUSTRATIONS

THE FALL OF A NATION

PROLOGUE

OVER a bleak hillside in Scotland the sun is sinking in the sea. A group of humble men and women stand before the King's soldiers accused of disobedience to Royal command. They have been found guilty of worshiping God according to the dictates of their own conscience and not according to the ritual of the Church of England.

The sheriff appeals in vain that they yield and live. The grim prelate advances, reads the death warrant, and offers pardon if they renounce their faith. With quiet smiles they lift their heads and pray.

The King on his throne has failed. The King within the soul of man is rising to reign.

The martyrs are bound to a stake, the fagots piled high, the torch applied. Above the crackle and roar of flames over the hills by the western sea rises their song —the battle hymn of a coming republic of freemen.

The women they reserve for kindlier treatment, these gallant servants of the King. Beside old Margaret

1

McLaughlin stands a beautiful girl of nineteen with wide eyes hungry for the joy of living. The poor father, faithful to the Church, has bought the life of his younger daughter for a hundred pounds in gold. He offers more for his first born. The older one they refuse to sell.

With generous chivalry the soldiers drive their stakes within the tide line of the sea. Drowning they say is an easy death. Old Margaret sinks quickly beneath the waves. Life has been hard for her. There's a far-off eager look in the old eyes as they are lifted to the sky.

The young girl fights for life with the instinctive will to live that beats in every mother soul. The prelate watching smiles. He sees a convert to his forms and signals to the guard. The girl is loosed and dragged ashore. Bending over the prostrate figure on the sands he offers life for an oath.

"Your King commands it!" the minion urges.

The girl answers in gentle tones:

"I am Christ's child—I follow Him!"

The prelate frowns, rises and gives the sign to his executioners. The soldiers tie her again to the stake, and the red shadow of the flames on the bleak hill fall across the white young face and mingle with the scarlet of the setting sun.

Every dungeon groans throughout the realm with

the madness of the King. The gentlest and the noblest are held as common felons. John Milton, brooding within his soul his immortal song, is gripped by prison bars. Roger Williams, his friend and fellow dreamer, sits by his side reading to the blind poet the principles of liberty proclaimed by their Dutch brethren across the channel.

From every dark port the ships lift their wings and sail westward. From the decks of one our Pilgrim Fathers land on Plymouth Rock and pray. Strange mixture of fine and common clay these ancestors of ours! They land first on their knees and then on the aborigines. The pilgrim becomes the invader. And he wins every battle for the simplest possible reason. He carries a weapon superior to the one in the hand of the untutored Indian. The bow and arrow goes down before the death dealing bolt hurled by gunpowder.

The simple aboriginal had made no preparation against invasion. His wigwam is burned, his land and goods taken, his children slain.

On other ships come nobler men who lift high the light of a new civilization.

Roger Williams, exiled from England and driven from Massachusetts by the Pilgrims, lands on Narragansett Bay, and proclaims religious liberty as the first principle of human progress. William Penn in

Pennsylvania and Roger Williams in Rhode Island at least atone for some of our early sins. The light they kindle on our shores streams across the sea to far-off king-ridden Germany whose men and women starve and freeze on snow-wrapped hills and mountains while crowned heads, aping the Court of the Grand Monarch of France, dance and drink in their palaces. As the snows melt an endless line of human misery pours along the banks of the Rhine to Rotterdam—with eyes fixed on the far-off new western world.

From the green hills of Ireland leaps another stream toward the western sea. An absentee landlord, wearing a coronet and loafing at the Court of Royalty, needs more money for his games. He decides to double his income by raising his rents. The Marquis of Donegal promptly evicts all tenants who cannot pay. The lordly example is followed by his landowning neighbors and thirty thousand Irish immigrants flee to America in a single year.

But strangest sign of the ages, the children of the Inquisition themselves at last feel the thumbscrew, rack and torch and turn their frightened faces westward to the new free world! Lord Baltimore leads his Catholic exiles to the shores of the Chesapeake and builds in new-found wisdom a free state with religious liberty its cornerstone.

4

PROLOGUE

From a rose bower in the Royal gardens at Fontainebleau the blackest cloud of a bloody century rises to darken the skies of sunny France. A gayly dressed page places a cushion and footstool and prostrates himself as before approaching divinity. A courtier enters, examines the cushion, kneels, kisses the footstool and stands at attention. The Grand Monarch, Louis XIV, approaches leaning heavily on the arm of his bespangled attendant. The King is bent with the consciousness of a life of sin. His fat legs totter, and there is a haunted look in his feverish eyes. Remorse for a brutal career is gnawing at his fear-stricken soul. The white hand of Death is beckoning and he sees.

Madame de Maintenon, his evil genius, hovers in the background, a black-robed priest whispering in her willing ear.

The King is seated by his courtiers. He roughly commands that they call his mistress-wife and waves them aside with imperious gesture.

De Maintenon's keen eye catches the order, the priest disappears and the harlot who rules a world approaches with cat-like tread, her face a study of quiet triumphant cunning. She protests her undying love and with pious eloquence points the way by which his gracious majesty may yet earn his heavenly crown. A million industrious Huguenots have unfortunately survived the massacre of St. Bartholomew. If the King would win eternal salvation he can by ordering their death or submission to the dishonor of denying their soul's faith in God. She presents the fatal document. The old roué with trembling hand signs the revocation of the Edict of Nantes. France is again deluged in blood and two hundred thousand of her noblest children driven into exile.

The sun of the new day rises on fields of flowers strewn with the bodies of dead mothers and babes. As the night falls, terror-stricken refugees creep across the dark sands of the beach, enter the little boats and push off from their beloved motherland for the long exile, their saddened faces turned westward.

The sea is wide but not so wide that the English King's hand cannot reach the throats of exiles and their children. By royal command Captain Preston orders his soldiers to shoot the people down in the streets of Boston on the night of March 5, 1770. Unarmed men shout defiance and the troops are withdrawn to hush the turmoil.

The frontiersmen of the wilderness of North Carolina are not so easily tamed. They seize their muskets and give the first armed resistance to the might of kings the New World has dared. The Royal Governor defeats the rebels in the Battle of Alamance on May

16, 1771, and hangs six of their leaders. As young James Pough stands with his arms pinioned behind his back he turns to his executioners and shouts: "My blood will be seed sown on good ground!"

Our fathers in Boston hear the shout and when the King attempts to enforce his stamp act they board his ship and throw the cargo into the sea.

The Colonies are at war with the King. The big bell in Philadelphia is calling all to unite in common defense and Thomas Jefferson reads his immortal Declaration of Independence to the assembled leaders. His voice rings with a strange prophetic elation:

"We hold these truths to be self evident—that all men are created equal!"

The startled kings of the earth hear the new heresy in sullen wrath and join hands to crush the rebels. The German rulers hire to George III more than thirty thousand Teutonic soldiers with which to stamp out the threatening conflagration. The Hessians land on our shores and join hands with the scarlet ranks of the King of England.

To mock their shame a noble Prussian, trained in the school of Frederick the Great, offers his sword to Washington and becomes the Inspector General of our ragged half-starved army.

Steuben stands beside Lafayette and Rochambeau

while Lord Cornwallis surrenders the British army at Yorktown.

Through ten years of defeat and anguish, of blood and suffering God leads the American Colonies at last into the sunlight of victory. George Washington, first president of the established union of free sovereign democratic States, delivers his inaugural address. A free nation rises from blood-red soil to haunt the dream of kings.

The rulers of earth are not slow to note the signs of the times. Democracy must be crushed. The handwriting on their palace walls is plain. He who runs may read. Imperialism challenges Democracy for a fight to the finish. The kings of Austria, Russia and Prussia meet in Paris and form the Holy Alliance. The purpose of their treaty is expressed in plain language. It has the ring of a bugle call to arms. They do not mince words:

"The high contracting parties, well convinced that the system of representative government is as incompatible with the monarchical system as the maxim of the sovereignty of the people is opposed to the principle of Divine Right, engage in the most solemn manner to employ all their means and unite all their efforts to put an end to the system of representative government wherever it is known to exist in the States of

Europe and to prevent it from being introduced into those States where it is not known."

Alexander I of Russia, Frederick William III of Prussia, and Francis I of Austria sign the solemn compact and fix their Royal seals. In due time the Bourbon King of France joins the Alliance against the rising Democracy. They would first crush the spirit of the French Revolution in Europe and halt the spirit of 1776 in America. They must re-establish the Crown over the revolting colonies of Central and South America and establish Russia's claim to Northwestern America.

James Monroe, president of the United States, answers this challenge with the doctrine of a free America ruled by her own people. The leader of world democracy does not mince words. His message rings also with the note of a bugle call to arms:

"The political system of the Allied Powers is essentially different from that of America. To the defense of our own, which has been achieved with the loss of so much blood and treasure, this whole nation is devoted and we should consider any attempt on their part to extend their system to any portion of this hemisphere as dangerous to our peace and safety. It is impossible therefore that the Allied Powers should extend their political system to either Continent of North or South America without endangering our life."

9

PROLOGUE

Imperial Europe has flung down the gantlet. American Democracy accepts the challenge and the fight is on to a finish.

The King of Prussia wins the first skirmish and strangles with iron hand the murmurs of the people of Germany for freedom. Karl Schurz, Franz Siegel, Jacobi and their fellow students crawl through the sewers, elude the Prussian soldiers, and reach our shores to swell the rank of militant Democracy. All Europe rings with the headsman's ax and from a thousand hilltops the ropes of hangmen swing in the stark heavens.

> Those corpses of young men,
> Those martyrs that hang from the gibbets—those
>   hearts pierced by the gray lead,
> Cold and motionless as they seem, live elsewhere
>   with unslaughtered vitality.
>
> They live in other young men, O kings!
> They live in brothers, again ready to defy you!
> They were purified by death—they were taught
>   and exalted.
>
> Not a disembodied spirit can the weapons of
>   tyrants let loose,
> But it stalks invisibly over the earth, whispering,
>   counseling, cautioning.

Democracy hears these invisible councilors and sets her house in order for the coming world crisis.

The old Federal Union of sovereign states has proven too frail for the strain of the new era. A stronger Union must be laid with new and deeper foundations. "Liberty and Union one and inseparable now and forever" ceases to be merely the eloquent prayer of a great statesman. It has become the first necessity of the political system of Democracy. Abraham Lincoln realizes this in his soul stirring cry from the great battlefield:

"That Government of the people by the people and for the people shall not perish from the earth!"

From her baptism of blood and tears the New Nation, strong, free, united, rises at last to face a hostile world, her house in order, her loins girded for the conflict.

Imperial Europe hastens to test her mettle. A princeling is proclaimed emperor of Mexico in a palace in Vienna, Austria, and sails for our shores. His reign is brief.

A few short months and Maximilian stands beside an old Spanish wall in a Mexican village and bids farewell to his friends. He is allowed to embrace Miramon and Mejia. With imperial gesture he throws his gold to the soldiers and bids them fire straight at his heart. The three fall simultaneously and the smoke

11

lifts once more on a Western nation ruled by the people.

Europe has not forgotten. She is busy for the moment setting her own house in order for the supreme conflict which her leaders foresee with the advance of the dangerous heresy of people claiming the right to govern themselves.

The Emperor of Germany sounds the keynote in an address to his magnificent army—The Divine Right of Kings was never so boldly proclaimed by any ruler of the world. He speaks the last word of Imperial Culture to Modern Democracy:

"We Hohenzollerns hold our crown from God alone. Who opposes me I shall crush to pieces!"

The American Republic is but a lusty youth of untried strength among the nations of earth. The real battle between the Crown and the People for the mastery of the world is yet to be fought. Eternal vigilance is the price of liberty today as yesterday and forever.

CHAPTER I

THE liveried flunkey entered the stately library and bowed:

"You rang, sir?"

He scarcely breathed the words. In every tone spoke the old servile humility of the creature in the presence of his creator the King. He might have said, "Sire." His voice, his straight-set eyes, his bowed body, did say it.

His master continued the conversation with the two men without lifting his head. He merely flung the order with studied carelessness:

"Lights, Otto—the table only."

The servant bowed low, pressed the electric switch, and softly left the room, walking backward as before royalty.

The two men with Charles Waldron in his palatial house in New York passed the incident apparently without knowledge of its significance. An American-born boy of fourteen, seeing it twenty-five years ago, would have wondered where on earth the creature came from. Of one thing he would have been certain—this flunkey could not have been made in the United States of America. Within the past quarter of a century, however, the imported menial has become one of our institutions and he is the outward sign of a momentous change within the mind of the class who have ruled our society.

The crown-embossed electric lantern above the massive table in the center of the room flooded the gold and scarlet cloth with light.

Waldron with a quick gesture of command spoke sharply:

"Be seated, gentlemen."

The two men instinctively brought their heels together and took seats within the circle of light. The master of the house paused a moment in deep thought before the stately Louis XIV window looking out on the broad waters of the Hudson.

His yacht, a huge ocean greyhound whose nose had scented the channels of every harbor of the world, lay at anchor in the stream along the heights of upper Manhattan, her keen prow bent seaward by the swift tide.

The strong face of the master of men was flushed with an inward fire. His gray eyes glowed. His jaws suddenly came together with decision. He turned from the window as if to join the two at the table and paused in his tracks studying the face of Meyer, the tall angular fellow who was evidently impatient at the delay.

Waldron had suddenly made up his mind to trust this man with a most important mission. And yet he disliked him. He was the type that must be used, but held with an iron hand—the modern enthusiast with scientific knowledge.

The smaller man, Mora, was easy—the nose of a ferret, coarse black cropped beard and thick sensuous lips. He could be managed—yes. He could be trusted —yes.

The other—he studied again—the strongly marked angular features, the large brilliant eyes, big nostrils and high forehead. He could be used for the first steps—it might be necessary to hang him later. All right, he would use him and then let him hang himself —suicide was common with his type.

Waldron smiled, quickly approached the table and took his seat. He nodded to Meyer and spoke suavely:

"Your invention has been perfected?"

The deep lines about the thinker's mouth twitched. He suddenly thrust his hand in his pocket, drew out a box and placed it under the light.

"I have it with me."

Mora bent close and Waldron watched keenly as

Meyer opened the leathern case and exposed the new device which he had promised to perfect.

"Examine the mechanisms," he said, passing it to Waldron. "It's perfectly harmless at present. The clockwork inside is as delicate as a Swiss watch."

The master of the house placed the smooth round surface to his ear, listened, laughed softly and passed it to Mora.

Meyer spoke with the certainty of positive knowledge, holding Waldron's eye with a steady gaze.

"I guarantee to stop the trade of this money-grabbing nation with all belligerents. I'll sink a ship from inside her hold as slick as that torpedo ten days ago got the *Lusitania*—"

Waldron made no reply. His jaw merely closed tightly.

The throb of an automobile climbing the steep roadway from the river drive struck the window. Waldron rose, listened a moment, walked to the casement and looked out.

A tall, distinguished-looking man with deep-cut lines in his strong face, who moved with military precision, opened the door of the tonneau without waiting for the chauffeur and leaped out.

The flunkey in the hall was evidently expecting his arrival. Villard whispered to the servant who closed the door quickly and led the way to the library.

The new guest was evidently nervous in spite of his well drilled manners. In his right hand he gripped an extra edition of a New York sensational evening paper.

Villard himself brushed the flunkey aside and rapped on the library door. Waldron opened and closed it instantly on his entrance. There was no mistaking the fact that the newcomer bore an important message. His deep, cold, blue eyes glowed with excitement and his hand visibly trembled. He drew his host to the window, opened the crumpled copy of the paper and pointed to its huge head lines:

CONGRESSMAN VASSAR OF NEW YORK INTRODUCES BILL DEMANDING A GREAT NAVY AND A MILLION TRAINED MEN FOR DEFENSE!

"This is a serious business"—Villard said curtly.

Waldron smiled:

"Serious—yes—unless we know how to meet the crisis. I happen to know—"

"It can be defeated then?"

"It will be defeated," was the quiet reply. "Many bills are introduced into our supreme law-making body,

Villard—but few are passed. This is one that will die an early and easy death—"

"You are sure?"

"As that I'm living. Come—sit down." Waldron moved toward the table and Villard quickly followed.

Waldron handed the paper to Meyer without comment and quietly watched him explode with excitement. Mora, too, was swept from his feet for the moment.

"It means—sir?" Meyer gasped.

"That we will move a little more quickly—that is all," Waldron answered.

The three men leaned close, each awaiting with evident deference the word of the master mind.

There was no mistaking the fact that one mind dominated the group. The high intellectual forehead of the man of millions marked him at once as a born leader and master of men. There was a consciousness of power in the poise of his big body and the slow movement of his piercing eyes that commanded attention and respect from his bitterest foe.

"Of course, gentlemen," he began calmly, "if we had in this country an intelligent and capable government we would be up against a serious situation. We have no such government. The alleged Democracy under which we live is the most asinine contrivance ever devised by theorists and dreamers. It never makes

18

an important move until too late and then will certainly
do the wrong thing in the moment of crisis. There is
but one thing you can always depend on at every session of Congress. They will pass the bill dividing the
Pork Barrel among the Congressional Districts. The
average Congressman considers this his first duty—the
rest is of but slight importance—"

Villard laughed heartily. The two others joined
feebly. They were not so sure of the situation. Their
knowledge of Waldron's power and the accuracy of his
judgment was not so clear as the older man's.

"Not only have we the most corrupt and incompetent
government of all history," Waldron went on, "but
to add to its confusion and weakness we have lately
thrust the duties of the ballot upon millions of hys-
terical women utterly unfitted for its responsibilities.
It is an actual fact that the women now enfranchised
in the Middle and Western states hold the balance of
power—"

Villard suddenly leaped to his feet.

"And they will vote solidly against every programme
of preparation!"

Waldron nodded.

"How fortunate at this moment!" Villard went on
enthusiastically, "that the women rule American men.
I begin to see the reason for your confidence. You

19

will enlist of course the eloquent young leader who addressed the mob in Union Square last week?"

"At once," Waldron answered quickly. "Virginia Holland is one of the feminine gods at the moment. It's amazing with what blind worship her disciples follow—"

"She's a stunning young woman, sir!" Villard broke in gallantly. "By Jove, she stirred me. You can't neglect her—"

"I shall cultivate her at once," was the quiet answer. "In the meantime, Meyer"—Waldron paused and held the enthusiast's eye for an instant and went on rapidly —"we will forget the ships—"

Meyer frowned in surprise but had no time to answer before he received the curt order in an undertone.

"Wait for me—I've more important work for you." Waldron rose and drew Villard and Mora aside.

Without ceremony he placed five yellow-backed one hundred dollar bills in Villard's hands and a single one in Mora's.

"We hold a great Peace rally to launch the popular movement against this bill to establish militarism in the United States. The classes who cherish varied theories of peace will join us. The Honorable Plato Barker is at the moment the leader of the peace yodelers. He is a professional lecturer who loves the sound of his own voice. He knows you, Villard, and prizes your opinions on Peace—"

Villard gave a dry little laugh.

"You will personally see the Honorable Plato and secure him as our principal speaker. And you, Mora, happen to know the Reverend A. Cuthbert Pike, D.D., President of the American Peace Union. His church maintains some missionaries in your benighted native land. His office is at the Bible House. I want him to introduce the Honorable Plato Barker—"

Mora smiled and bowed, and the two hurried to execute their orders. Villard's car was waiting. The master of the house took Meyer's arm, led him to the corner of the library and for half an hour gave explicit instructions in low tones.

Before showing Meyer to the door another roll of bills was duly delivered for defraying the expenses of his important work. The enthusiast brought his heels together with a sharp click, saluted and hurried down the broad stairs. He declined the offer of an automobile. He didn't like millionaires. He only used them.

Waldron watched him go with a curious smile, drew on his gloves and called for his hat and cane.

The flunkey who hovered near obeyed the order with quick servility and stood watching his master go by the broad porte-cochère, wondering why the order had not been given him for the car.

Waldron signaled his night chauffeur, and the big limousine darted to the stoop. As the driver leaned out to receive his orders, Waldron spoke in low tones:

"To Miss Virginia Holland's on Stuyvesant Square—"

The driver nodded and closed the door of the limousine. He had been there before.

CHAPTER II

VIRGINIA HOLLAND, at her desk preparing an address on the Modern Feminist Movement, dropped her pencil and raised her head with a look of startled surprise at the cry of a newsboy in the street below. The whole block seemed to vibrate with his uncanny yell:

"Wuxtra! Wuxtra!"

A sense of impending calamity caught her heart for a moment. It was a morbid fancy, of course, and yet the cry of the boy kept ringing a personal warning.

Work impossible, she opened her door, called and asked her brother Billy to get a copy of the paper.

Before he returned her anxiety had increased to the point of pain. She rapidly descended the stairs and waited at the door.

Billy entered reading the headlines announcing Vassar's new programme of military preparation. Virginia flushed and gazed at the announcement with increasing excitement. The name of John Vassar had caused a flush before the announcement of his bill had made an impression. Her handsome Congressman neighbor, though they had never formally met, had for some months past been a disturbing factor in a life of hitherto serene indifference to men. That he should have antagonized in this bill her well known position as the uncompromising advocate of peace and of universal disarmament was a shock. His proposal to arm the American Democracy came as a slap in her face. She felt it a personal affront.

Of course she had no right to such feeling. John Vassar was nothing to her! She had only seen him pass her window three times during the year. And yet the longer she gazed at the announcement the more furious she became. At least he might have consulted her as the leading public-spirited woman in his district on this measure of such transcendent importance. He had not done so, for a simple reason. He knew that she opposed militarism as the first article of her life faith. Her hand closed on the paper in a grip of resentment. She made up her mind instantly to force his hand on the suffrage issue. She would show him that she had some power in his District.

Her mood of absorbed anger was suddenly broken by Billy's joyous cry:

"Hurrah for John Vassar, sis. Me for West Point! Will you make him appoint me?"

She turned in sudden rage and boxed her young

brother's ears, smiled at his surprise, threw her arms around his neck and kissed him. She boxed his ears for crying hurrah for Vassar. She kissed him for the compliment of her supposed power over the coming statesman.

To hide her confusion she began at once a heated argument over the infamies of a military régime. The quarrel broke the peaceful scene of a game of checkers between the father and mother in the sitting-room, and brought the older people into the hall:

"In heaven's name, Virginia!" her father exclaimed. "What is the matter?"

"Read it"—she answered angrily, thrusting the paper into his hand.

The Grand Army veteran read with sparkling eyes. "Good!" he shouted.

"That's what I say, father!" Billy echoed.

"It's absurd," Virginia protested. "War on this country is impossible. It's unthinkable—"

The old soldier suddenly seized her hand.

"Impossible, is it? Come with me a minute, Miss!"

He drew her into the library followed by Billy—the mother striving gently to keep the peace.

Holland led his eloquent daughter to the rack above the center bookcase and took from its place his army musket.

"That's what they said, my girl, in '61. Here's the answer. That's what your grandmother said to your grandfather. That's why we've bungled every war we ever fought and paid for it in rivers of blood!"

The family row started anew—the father and boy for preparation against war, the daughter and mother for peace—peace at any price.

The quarrel was at its height when Waldron's car arrived.

Old Peter, the stately negro butler of the ancient régime, closed the folding doors to drown the din before ushering the distinguished guest into the parlor. Waldron was a prime favorite of Peter's. The millionaire had slipped him a twenty-dollar gold piece on a former occasion and no argument of friend or foe could shake his firm conviction that Charles Waldron was a gentleman of the old school. Besides, Peter was consumed with family pride in Virginia's hold on so distinguished a leader of the big world.

The old butler bowed his stateliest at the door of the parlor with the slightest hesitation on his exit as if the memory of the twenty-dollar gold piece lingered in spite of his resolution to hold himself above the influence of filthy lucre.

"I tell Miss Virginia, right away, sah—yassah!"

Waldron seated himself with confidence. Virginia

Holland lingered a few minutes merely to show the great man that she was not consumed with pride at his attentions. That she appreciated the compliment of his admiration she would not have denied even to John Vassar. Waldron had made the largest single contribution to the Woman's Movement it had received in America. She had gotten the credit of winning the great man's favor and opening his purse strings.

That the millionaire was interested in her charming personality she had not doubted from the first. He left no room for doubt in the eagerness with which he openly sought her favor.

And yet it had never occurred to her to think of him as a real lover. There was something so blunt and material in his personality that it forbade a romance. She could imagine him asking a woman to marry him. But in the wildest leap of her fancy she had not been able to conceive of his making love. In her strictly modern business woman's mind she was simply using her influence over the great man for all it was worth in a perfectly legitimate way and always for the advancement of the Cause.

She greeted him with a gracious smile and he bowed over her hand after the fashion of the European courtier in a way that half amused her and half pleased her vanity.

He held a copy of the evening paper.

"You have read it?"

Virginia nodded.

Waldron went straight to the point in his cold, impersonal but impressive way.

"You are the most eloquent leader of American women, Miss Holland. Your voice commands the widest hearing. You stand for peace and universal brotherhood. Will you preside at a mass meeting tomorrow night to protest against this infamous bill?"

Virginia Holland had given her consent mentally until he used the word "infamous." Somehow it didn't fit John Vassar's character and instinctively she resented it.

She blushed for an instant at her silly inconsistency. But a moment ago she had herself denounced the young statesman with unmeasured violence. In the next moment she was resenting an attack on him.

Waldron watched her hesitation with surprise and renewed his plea with more warmth than he had ever displayed.

Virginia extended her hand in a quick business-like way.

"Of course I'll preside. We are fighting for the same great end."

Waldron made no effort to press his victory. He rose at once to go, and bowed low over her hand.

"Au revoir—tomorrow night," he said in low tones.

Virginia watched him go with a mingled feeling of triumph and fear. There was something about the man that puzzled and annoyed her—something unconvincing in his apparent frankness. And yet the truth about his big life purpose never for a moment entered her imagination.

CHAPTER III

WHEN Meyer reached the quarter of the East Side where eager crowds surge through a little crooked thoroughfare leading from the old Armory on Essex Street he encountered unexpected difficulties.

He ran into a section of John Vassar's congressional district saturated with the young leader's ideals of a new Americanism. He was coldly received.

Benda, the Italian fruit-dealer on the corner, Meyer had marked finally as his opening wedge in the little clannish community. The Italian was the most popular man on the street, his store the meeting-place of the wives and children for three blocks.

Meyer entered the store and to his surprise found it deserted. The sounds of laughter in the little suite of living-room and kitchen behind the store told of festivities in progress. He waited impatiently for the proprietor to return.

Benda was presiding at a function too important to be interrupted by thoughts of trade. With Angela, his wife, and the neighbors, he was celebrating the fifth birthday of their only boy, Tommaso, Jr. The kids from far and near were bringing their little presents and Pasquale, his best friend, who was returning to Italy by the next steamer, had generously given his monkey and hand-organ. Benda himself had escorted Pasquale into the room and had just sprung the big surprise on the assembled party.

Pasquale was putting the monkey through his tricks amid screams of laughter when Meyer's dark face clouded the door leading from the store.

He beckoned angrily to Benda.

"May I see you a minute?"

Benda sprang to meet the unexpected apparition in his doorway while Angela led Pasquale and the children into the street for a grand concert. Meyer's tense face had not passed without her swift glance.

She left the children dancing and entered the store from the front. Meyer had just offered Benda good wages for his services in the cause and the Italian was tempted and puzzled.

Angela suddenly confronted Meyer. His suave explanation that the alliance which he had invited Benda to join was a benevolent order for self-protection was not convincing.

The wife swung her husband suddenly aside and

stepped between the two. She fairly threw her words into Meyer's face.

"You go now! My man stick to his beesness. He mak good mon. We got our little home."

Meyer attempted to argue. Benda tried to edge in a word. It was useless. Angela's shrill voice rose in an endless chorus of protest.

Benda threw up his hands in surrender and re-entered the store. Meyer angrily turned on his heel and crossed the street to see Schultz, the delicatessen man on the opposite corner.

Schultz proved impossible from the first. His jovial face was wreathed in smiles but his voice was firm in its deep mumbling undertone.

"No—mein frient—no more drill for me—I fight no more except for the flag dot give me mein freedom and mein home!"

The two men held each other's gaze in a moment of dramatic tension. The menace in Meyer's voice was unmistakable as he answered:

"I'll see you again!"

CHAPTER IV

JOHN VASSAR'S triumphant return to his home on Stuyvesant Square, after the introduction of his sensational bill in Congress, was beset with domestic complications. Congratulations from his father, nieces, and Wanda had scarcely been received before the trouble began.

"But you must hear Miss Holland!" Zonia pleaded.

John Vassar shook his head.

"Not tonight, dear—"

"I'd set my heart on introducing you. Ah, Uncy dear—please! She's the most eloquent orator in America—"

"That's why I hate her and all her tribe—"

A rosy cheek pressed close to his.

"Not all her tribe—"

"My Zonia—no—but I could wring her neck for leading a chick of your years into her fool movement—"

"But she didn't lead me, Uncy dear, I just saw it all in a flash while she was speaking—my duty to my sex and the world—"

33

"Duty to your sex! What do you know about duty to your sex?—you infant barely out of short dresses! Your hair ought to be still in braids. And it was all my fault. I let you out of the nursery too soon—"

He paused and looked at her wistfully.

"And I promised your father's spirit the day you came to us here that I'd guard you as my own—you and little Marya. I haven't done my duty. I've been too busy with big things to realize that I was neglecting the biggest thing in the world. You've slipped away from me, dear—and I'm heartsick over it. Maybe I'll be in time for Marya—you're lost at eighteen—"

"Marya's joined our Club too—"

"A babe of twelve?"

"She's going to be Miss Holland's page in the suffrage Pageant—"

John Vassar groaned, laid both hands on the girl's shoulders and rose abruptly.

"Now, Zonia, it's got to stop here and now. I'm not going to allow this brazen Amazon—"

His niece broke into a fit of laughter.

"Brazen Amazon?"

"That's what I said. This brazen Amazon is my enemy—"

The girl lifted her finger laughingly.

"But you're not afraid of her? John Vassar, a

descendant of old Yan Vasa in whose veins ran the royal blood of Poland—ten years in Congress from this big East Side district—the idol of the people—chairman of the National House Committee on Military Affairs"—she paused and her voice dropped to the tensest pride—"my candidate for governor of New York—you positively won't go to the meeting in Union Square tonight?" she added quietly.

"Positively—"

"Then, Uncy dear, I'll have to deliver the message—"

She drew a crumpled note from her bosom and handed it to him without a word.

He broke the seal and read with set lips:

HON. JOHN VASSAR, M. C.,
   16 STUYVESANT SQUARE,
     NEW YORK.

   DEAR SIR: Our committee in charge of the canvass of your congressional district in the campaign for woman's suffrage have tried in vain to obtain an expression of your views. We are making a house to house canvass of every voter in New York. You have thus far side-stepped us.

   You are a man of too much power in the State and nation to overlook in such a fight. The Congressional Directory informs us that you are barely thirty-six years old. You have already served ten years in Washington with distinction and have won your spurs as a national leader. A great future awaits you unless you incur the united opposition of the coming woman voter.

I warn you that we are going to sweep the Empire State. Your majority is large and has increased at each election. It is not large enough if we mark you for defeat. I have sincerely hoped that we might win you for our cause.

I ask for a declaration of your position. You must be for us or against us. There can be no longer a middle course.

I should deeply regret the necessity of your defeat if you force the issue. Your niece has quite won my heart and her passionate enthusiasm for her distinguished uncle has led me to delay this important message until the introduction of your bill for militarism has forced it.

Sincerely,

VIRGINIA HOLLAND,

Pres't National Campaign Committee.

John Vassar read the letter a second time, touched the tips of his mustache thoughtfully and fixed his eyes on Zonia.

"And my little sweetheart will join the enemy in this campaign!"

A tear trembled on the dark lashes.

"Ah, Uncy darling, how could you think such a thing!"

"You bring this challenge—"

"I only want to vote—to—elect—you—governor—"

The voice broke in a sob, as he bent and kissed the smooth young brow.

She clung to him tenderly.

"Uncy dear, just for my sake, because I love you so —because you're my hero—won't you do something for me—Just because *I* ask it?"

"Maybe—"

"Go to Union Square with me then—"

He shook his head emphatically.

"Against my principles, dear—"

"It's not against your principles to make me happy?"

He took her cheeks between his hands.

"Seeing that I've raised you from a chick—I don't think there ought to be much doubt about how I stand on the woman question as far as it affects two little specimens of the tribe—do you?"

"All right then," she cried gayly, "you love Marya and me. We are women. You can't refuse us a little old thing like a ballot if we want it— can you?"

She paused and kissed him again.

"So now, Uncy, you're going to hear Miss Holland speak just to make me happy—aren't you?"

He smiled and surrendered.

"To make you happy—yes—"

He couldn't say more. The arms were too tight about his neck.

He drew them gently down.

"This is what I dread in politics, dear—when the women go in to win. We've graft enough now. When the boys run up against this sort of thing—God help us!—and God save the country if you should happen to make a mistake in what you ask for! Well, you've won this fight—come on, let's get up front and hear the argument. I hate to stand on the edge and wonder what the hen is saying when she crows—"

Zonia handed his hat and cane and, radiant with smiles, opened the door.

"I suppose we'll let Marya stay with Grandpa?" he asked.

"They've been gone half an hour!"

"Oh—"

"I had no trouble with Grandpa at all. He agreed to sit on the platform with me—"

"Indeed!"

"But I don't think he really understood what the meeting was about—"

"Just to please his grandchick, however, the old traitor agreed to preside at my funeral—eh?"

"He won't if you say not—shall I tell him to keep

off? Marya will be awfully disappointed if we make them get down——"

"No—let him stay. Maybe he can placate the enemy. They can hold him as hostage for my good behavior."

The hand on his arm pressed tighter.

"It's so sweet of you, Uncy!"

"At what hour does this paragon of all the virtues, male and female, harangue the mob?"

"You mean Miss Holland?"

"Yes."

"Oh, they'll all be there tonight. Miss Holland is the principal speaker for the Federated Women's Clubs of America—she's the president, you know——"

"No—I didn't know——"

"She won't speak until 9:30. We can hear the others first. There'll be some big guns among the men too—the Honorable Plato Barker and the Reverend A. Cuthbert Pike, the president of the American Peace Union —and Waldron, the multi-millionaire, he presides at Miss Holland's stand——"

"Indeed——"

"Yes—they say he's in love with her but she doesn't care a rap for him or any other man——"

John Vassar had ceased to hear Zonia's chatter. The name of Charles Waldron had started a train of ugly thought. Of all the leaders of opinion in America this man was his pet aversion. He loathed his personality. He hated his newspaper with a fury which words could not express. It stood squarely for every tendency of degenerate materialism in our life, a worship of money and power first and last against all sentiment and all the hopes and aspirations of the masses. He posed as the Pecksniffian leader of Reform and the reform he advocated always meant the lash for the man who toils. His hatreds were implacable, too, and he used the power of his money with unscrupulous brutality. He had lately extended the chain of banks which he owned in New York until they covered the leading cities of every state in the Union. His newspaper, the *Evening Courier,* was waging an unceasing campaign for the establishment of an American aristocracy of wealth and culture.

Vassar was cudgeling his brain over the mystery of this man's sudden enthusiasm for woman suffrage and the Cause of Universal Peace. It was a sinister sign of the times. He rarely advocated a losing cause. That this cold-blooded materialist could believe in the dream of human emancipation through the influence of women was preposterous.

Zonia might be right, of course, in saying that he had become infatuated with the young Amazon leader of the Federated Women's Clubs. And yet that would hardly account for his presence as the presiding genius of a grand rally for suffrage. There were too many factions represented in such a demonstration for his personal interest in one woman to explain his activity in bringing those people together. His paper had, in fact, led the appeal to co-ordinate Demagogery, Labor, Peace Propaganda, Socialism, and Feminism in one monster mass meeting.

The longer Vassar puzzled over it, the more impenetrable became Waldron's motive. His leadership in the movement was uncanny. What did it mean?

CHAPTER V

I T was barely seven when they reached Union Square. It was already packed by a dense crowd of good-natured cheering men and women. Seventy-five thousand was a conservative estimate. The air was electric with contagious enthusiasm.

"We'll hear the apostle of peace first," Vassar said to Zonia, pushing his way slowly through the crowd toward a platform with three-foot letters covering its four sides:

PEACE! PEACE! PEACE! PEACE!

The Reverend A. Cuthbert Pike, president of the Peace Union of America, was delivering the opening address as the chairman of his meeting. He was a funny-looking little man of slight features, bald and decorated with a set of aggressive side whiskers. His manner was quick and nervous, electric in its nervousness, his voice in striking contrast to the jerky pugnacity of his body. The tones were soft and dreaming, as if he were trying to subdue the tendency of the flesh to fight for what he believed to be right.

42

He leaned far over the rail of the platform and breathed his words over the crowd:

"Two great powers contend for the mastery of the world, my friends," he was saying. "The spirit of Christ and the spirit of Napoleon. The one would overcome evil with good. The other would hurl evil against evil. One stands for love, humility, self-sacrifice. The other stands for the hate, pride and avarice of the militarism of today—"

Vassar lost the next sentence. His mind had leaped the seas and stood with brooding wonder over the miracle of self-sacrifice of a thousand blood-drenched trenches and battlefields where millions of stout-hearted men were now laying their lives on the altar of their country—an offering of simple love. They had left the selfish pursuit of pleasure and wealth and individual aggrandizement and merged their souls and bodies into the wider life of humanity—the hopes and aspirations of a race. Was all this hate and pride and avarice? Bah! The little fidgety preacher was surely crazy; the thing called war was too big and terrible and soul-searching for that. Such theories were too small. They could not account for the signs of the times.

The preacher was talking again. He caught the quiver of hate in his utterance of the name of the great German philosopher.

43

"In Nietzsche's words we have the supreme utterance of the modern anti-Christ in his blasphemous rendition of the Beatitudes. Hear him:

" 'Ye have heard how in olden times it was said, Blessed are the meek for they shall inherit the earth; but I say to you, Blessed are the valiant, for they shall make the earth their throne—' "

"Militarism, my friends, is the incarnate soul of blasphemy! It is confined to no country. It is a world curse. The mightiest task of the times in which we live is to cast out this devil from the body of civilization. We demand votes for women because we believe they will help us in the grim battle we are fighting with the powers of Death and Hell—"

Vassar turned with a sigh and pressed toward the next platform. The Honorable Plato Barker, silver-tongued orator of the plains, was soaring above the heads of his enraptured listeners. His benevolent bald head glistened in the sputtering rays of the arc light. He was supremely happy once more. He had resigned the cares of office to ride a new hobby and bask in the smiles of cheering thousands. He had ridden Free Silver to death and grown tired of Prohibition. He had groomed a new steed. His latest hobby was Peace. He too was demanding votes for women because they would save the world from the curse of war.

44

Vassar listened to the man whom he had once cheered and followed with growing wonder and weariness. With pompous pose and high-sounding phrase he inveighed against arms and armament. In the next breath he denounced his old opponent for the attempt to abolish armaments by an international organization to enforce peace through a central police power. He demanded that America should stand alone in her purity and her unselfish glory. He believed in America for the Americans. But he would not fight to maintain it—nor would he permit an entangling alliance with any nation which might make safe the doctrine without a fight. We would neither fight nor permit anyone else to fight for us. He demanded that we should not arm ourselves for defense and in the next breath declared that he was not in favor at present of dismantling the forts we now possessed or of disbanding the army. He denounced all arms and all wars and yet favored being half armed and half ready for an inadequate defense. He asked that we stand absolutely alone in the world and half armed maintain the guardianship of the Western Hemisphere against the serried millions of veteran soldiers of armed Europe. He demanded that we uphold international law and order and yet ridiculed any organization for that purpose.

Each empty platitude the crowd cheered. Each preposterous demand for the impossible they cheered again with redoubled power.

His last proposition was evidently his favorite. He dropped his voice to low persuasive tones:

"Even suppose the unthinkable thing should happen. Suppose that some misguided nation in an hour of madness should send a hundred thousand soldiers across three thousand miles of sea and attempt to invade this country—what then? This country, mark you, peopled by a nation of vastly superior numbers, equal intelligence, mechanical genius and political organization—"

He paused and thundered:

"What would happen?

"Those hundred thousand invading soldiers would never see their old homes again—"

Tremendous cheers rent the air.

"And what's more, dear friends, they would never desire to see their homes again. We would march out to meet them with smiles and flowers. We would bid them welcome to our shores. We would give to them the freedom of our city and greet them as brethren!"

Again the cheers leaped from the throats of thousands.

To John Vassar with the bitter memories of the might of kings that yet shadowed the world the scene was sickening in its utter fatuity. He mopped the perspiration from his forehead and hurried on.

He passed the platform on which Jane Hale stood repeating in monotonous reiteration the plea for peace which she vainly spoke into the ears of Europe on her tour during the war. The speakers' stand was draped in red and behind Miss Hale's solid figure the young statesman recognized the familiar faces of the Socialist leaders of the East Side.

How vain this Socialist symbol of the common red blood that pulses from every human breast! How pitifully tragic their failure in the hour when the war summoned the world to the national colors. The red flag faded from the sky. It was all talk—all wind— all fustian—all bombast—all theory. Men don't die for academic theories. Men die for what they believe. And yet these American Socialists were as busy with their parrot talk as if nothing had happened in the world since that fatal day in July, 1914, when old things passed away and all things became new.

Vassar pressed past the crowd around the Socialist stand and saw beyond the platform from which the woman leader of the new Anti-Enlistment League was haranguing the mob. She too was a suffragette for peace purposes—an aggressive fat female of decisively militant aspect. Her words were pacific in their import.

Her manner and spirit spoke battle in every accent and gesture. She was determined to have peace if she had to kill every man, woman and child opposed to it.

She waved the pledge of the League above her head and recited its form in rasping, challenging, aggravating notes.

"I, being over eighteen years of age, hereby pledge myself against enlistment as a volunteer for any military or naval service in an international war, and against giving my approval to such enlistment on the part of others."

She paused and shouted:

"The Anti-Enlistment League does not stand for puny non-resistance! We appeal to the militancy of the spirit—"

John Vassar looked at his watch.

"We've yet time to hear brother Debs. I like his kind. You always know where to find him."

"No-no—Uncy," Zonia urged, "we must hurry to our stand—"

"*Our* stand, eh?"

"Yes—you mustn't miss a word Miss Holland says. She doesn't speak long—but every word counts—"

"She has one loyal follower anyhow," Vassar smiled.

"I'm going to win her for you, Uncy dear—"

"Oh, that's the scheme?"

"Yes—"

"I don't think it can be done, little sweetheart. I never could like a hen that crows—"

Zonia waved her arm toward the big platform of the Woman's Federated Clubs.

"There they are now!" she cried—"Marya and Grandpa—they're sitting on the steps—"

"So I see—" Vassar laughed.

Old Andrew Vassar was beaming his good-natured approval on the throng that surged about the stand, his arm encircling his little granddaughter with loving touch.

The younger man watched him a moment with a tender smile. His father was supremely happy in the great crowd of strong, healthy, free men and women. He knew nothing of the meaning of the meeting. He never bothered his head about it. The thing was a part of the life of America and it was good. He was seventy years old now—lame from an old wound received in Poland—but had a fine strong face beaming generous thoughts to all men. He had landed on our shores thirty years ago broken, bruised and ruined. He had dared to lift his voice in Poland for one of the simplest rights of his people. A brutal soldier at the order of their imperial master had sacked his home, murdered his wife and daughter before his eyes, robbed

49

him of all and at last left him in the street, bleeding to death with a baby boy of five clinging to his body. His older son had smuggled him aboard a ship bound for New York. He had prospered from the day of his landing. A tailor by trade he had proven his worth from the first. For ten years he had been head cutter for a wholesale clothing house and received an annual salary of ten thousand dollars. Ten years ago the might of kings had gripped the son he left behind. His goods too were forfeited, his life snuffed out and his children orphaned. Big free America had received them now, and the old man's strong arm circled them. The little terror-stricken boy, who had clung to him the day the soldiers left him in the street for dead, was the Honorable John Vassar, the coming man of a mighty nation of freemen.

Old Andrew Vassar made no effort to grasp the current of our social or political life. It was all good. He went to all the political meetings, Democratic, Republican, Socialist, Woman's Suffrage. He liked to test his freedom and laugh to find it true.

He caught John's eye, waved his arm enthusiastically and lifted Marya high above the heads of the crowd that she might throw him a kiss.

Zonia answered with a little cry of love and they

quickly pressed through the throng to a position directly in front of the speaker's stand.

Waldron had just risen to make his opening address. His automobile had brought him quickly from another important engagement with a committee of Western bankers who had met in the stately library of his palatial home on the heights of upper Manhattan.

There was no mistaking the poise of the man, his dignity and conscious reserve power. Vassar studied him for the first time at close range with increasing dislike and suspicion.

He faced the crowd with a look of quiet mastery. A man of medium height, massive bull neck, high forehead, straight intellectual eyebrows and piercing steel gray eyes. There was no mistaking the fact that he was a born leader of men.

A high collar covered the massive neck well up to the ears, concealing the lines of brutality which lay beneath; and a pair of glasses attached to a black silk cord and gracefully adjusted, gave to his strong features a touch of intellectuality on which his vanity evidently fed.

A curious little smile played about the corners of his eyes and thin lips as if he knew a good joke that couldn't be told to a crowd. The smile brought a frown to John Vassar's sensitive face. He instinctively hated a man with that kind of smile. He couldn't tell why. The smile was not a pose. There was something genuine behind it. A crowd would like him for it. But the man who looked beneath the surface for its real meaning felt intuitively that it sprang from a deep, genuine and boundless contempt for humanity.

The sound of his voice confirmed this impression. He spoke with a cold, measured deliberation that provoked and held an audience. His words were clean cut and fell with metallic precision like the click of a telegraph key.

"I have the honor, tonight, ladies and gentlemen," he began slowly, "of introducing to you the real leader of the women of America—"

A cheer swept the crowd and Zonia stood on tiptoe trying to catch a glimpse of her heroine.

"She's hiding behind the others—" she pressed her uncle's arm—"but you'll see her in a minute, Uncy!"

"Doubtless!" Vassar laughed. "She's too wise an actress to stumble on the stage before her cue—"

Waldron's metallic voice was clicking on.

"Before I present her, allow me as a spokesman of this great meeting to give you in a few words my reasons for demanding votes for women. The supreme purpose of my life is to do my part in ushering

52

into the world the reign of universal peace. The greatest issue ever presented to the American people is now demanding an answer. Shall this nation follow the lead of blood-soaked Europe and arm to the teeth? Or shall we remain the one people of this earth who stand for peace and good will to all?

"The militarists tell us that man is a fighting animal; that human nature cannot be changed; that nations have always fought and will continue to fight to the end of time; that war sooner or later will come and that we must prepare for it.

"I say give woman the ballot and she will find a way to prevent war!

"The alarmist tells us that armaments are our only sure guarantee of peace. It's a lie. And that lie is now being shot to pieces in Europe before our eyes. Armaments provoke war. In the fierce light of this hell-lit conflagration even the blind should see that armaments have never yet guaranteed peace.

"Europe in torment calls to us today. O, great Republic of the West, beware! Armaments are not guarantees of peace. They are not insurance. Make your new world different from the old. Beware of guns. Down with the machinery of slaughter. Trust in reason. Have faith in your fellow men. Build your life on love not hate. Proclaim the coming of the Lord—the Prince of Peace—"

Vassar glanced quickly over the sea of uplifted faces and wondered why they did not applaud. Barker's crowd had gone wild over weak platitudes poorly expressing similar ideas. The words of this man were eloquent. The silence was uncanny. Why didn't they applaud?

He turned his head aside and listened intently. It was the metallic click of Waldron's cold penetrating voice that killed applause. There was something in it that froze the blood in the veins of an enthusiast— and yet held every listener in a spell.

"Your alarmists," he went on deliberately, "are busy now with a new scare. When this war is over they tell us we must fight the victors, for they will move to conquer us. Let us nail another lie. This war will leave Europe exhausted and helpless for a generation. We will be the strongest nation in the world—our strength intact, our resources boundless.

"Besides, we have the men and the means for arming them instantly if we are threatened. We have equipped and supplied armies of millions for England, France and Russia. What we have done for them we can surely do for ourselves. Our factories are now producing more military supplies for Europe than we could use for our defense. Our navy is more efficient than ever before in history. Our chief ports are defended by great guns that make them impregnable. Our army is small, but I repeat the Honorable Plato Barker's axiom as a truth unassailable—'We can raise an army of a million men between the suns!' yes and five million more within a week if they are needed—"

John Vassar ground his teeth and set his firm jaw to prevent an outburst of mad protest. As chairman of the House Committee of Military Affairs he knew that every statement in this subtle demagogue's appeal was but half truth, and for that reason the most dangerous lie. The navy *was* more efficient than ever before—so was every navy in the world. Our navy was still utterly inadequate to defend us against any first-class combination of Europe or any single power of the rank of Germany. Our coast guns were good, but a hostile navy triumphant at sea would never come in range of them. They would land at their leisure at any one of a hundred undefended harbors and take our forts from the rear. We could manufacture ammunition—but to no purpose, because we have few guns for field artillery and not enough trained artillerymen to man them if we had the guns. It takes years to train the masters of war machinery. A million men could be raised between the suns, but they would be mowed down by fields of hidden artillery beyond the range of our gunners before we could get in sight.

There was no escape from the deep conviction that the cold-blooded thinker who was smiling into the face of this crowd knew these facts with a knowledge even clearer than his own.

What was the sinister motive back of that frozen smile?

Again and again Vassar asked himself the question. He was still puzzling over the mystery of Waldron's motive when a ringing cheer burst from the crowd and Zonia pressed his arm.

"There she is, Uncy—there she is!"

Waldron was leading to the rail a blushing girl.

"No, no—sweetheart—that's someone else—can't be the Amazon—"

"Of course, you silly—she's not an Amazon—she's my heroine. Isn't she a darling? Now honestly?"

Vassar was too dumfounded to make reply.

Waldron was introducing her, the same cold smile on his thin lips, the same metallic click of his voice.

"Permit me, ladies and gentlemen, to present to you tonight a new force in the world—a real leader of modern women, our Joan of Arc, the President of the Federated Clubs, Miss Virginia Holland!"

Again the crowd burst into applause.

The little head bowed with the slightest inclination and a smile of pure sunlight illumined an exquisite face. The Amazon he had hated stood before him a gentle creature of delicate yet strongly molded features, her high smooth forehead crowned with a tangled mass of auburn blonde hair.

Vassar laughed at the sheer absurdity of it all. Such a woman couldn't be the leader of the brazen mob of clamoring females he had grown to hate. It was too preposterous for words. She was speaking now. He didn't know what she was saying. No matter. It was her personality that held him in a spell. Her voice was the most startling contrast to Waldron's—soft and clear as the round notes of a flute. Its volume was not great and yet the quality was penetrating. It found the ear of the farthest listener in the wide circle of the crowd and at the same time the depths of his inmost being.

There was no resisting her personal appeal.

Before she had spoken two sentences Vassar was ready to agree to any proposition she might make. She seemed so sweet and sane and reasonable. Her appeal was to both the head and the heart of her hearers.

The young statesman mopped his brow in a vague

panic. If this was the leader who had marked him for defeat the situation was serious. If she and her kind should make a personal canvass of the voters of his district, he would have to rise early and go to bed late if he ever expected to see the Capitol at Washington again.

And yet it was not the fear of defeat that really disturbed him. It was the confusion into which her personality had thrown all his preconceived ideas. Great God! If this sort of woman had gotten into the movement where would it end? How could she be denied? He laughed again at his preconceived ideas of the leader of Amazons and the sweet reasonableness of this gentle, brilliant, exquisite girl on whose words the crowd hung breathless.

He was stunned. It was impossible for the moment to adjust his thinking to the situation. He was missing all her speech. For the life of him he couldn't recall a sentence. He pulled himself up with a frown and listened.

"I am not sure, dear friends, that we can prevent war," she was saying, "but I am sure that we will try. And I am absolutely sure that the clothing of women with the sovereign power of the ballot will introduce into the councils that decide peace or war a new element in human history. Man alone has failed to keep the peace. Surely if we help we can do no worse. I have an abiding faith that we can do better—"

She paused and a look of enraptured emotion illumined her face as she slowly continued:

"If a city were besieged and soldiers were defending its strong places, and a breach had been made in the embattlements, the men within would close that breach with the first thing at hand. They would not spare even the priceless marble figure on which an artist had spent years of loving toil—unless the defending soldier were the artist who created the masterpiece! He could not hurl this treasure into the breach to be crushed into a shapeless mass. He would find another way or die in the effort.

"Man is woman's masterpiece. For twenty-five years she broods and watches and works with loving care to fashion this immortal being. Give to her the decisive voice in war and she will find a better way to fill the breach. She will not hurl her masterpiece into this hell. Man has failed to find a better way. May not we who love most and suffer most at least have the chance to try?"

The sweet penetrating voice died softly away and she had taken her seat before the crowd realized that she had stopped.

A moment's dead silence and then cheer after cheer swept the throng.

An excited man lifted high his hand and shouted:

"We'll give you the chance. Yes—yes!"

Zonia's grip tightened suddenly on John Vassar's arm.

"You'll let me introduce you, Uncy?"

Vassar laughed excitedly.

"Will I? Be quick, girl—before she gets away!"

CHAPTER VI

"A REN'T you glad you came?" Zonia asked eagerly.

"Hurry! Don't let her get away with Waldron—"

The girl darted from his side and pushed rapidly to the platform. The crowd had encircled Virginia and a hundred people were trying to grasp her hand at the same time. There was no help for it. He must wait. At least he was glad the jam made it equally impossible for Waldron to reach her. He saw him wave his hand to her over their heads, bow and leave the platform for his waiting car.

Vassar was glad to be rid of his presence. That frozen smile poisoned the air. He could breathe deeply now.

It was fully fifteen minutes before he caught the signal Zonia waved from the steps.

His niece was radiant with joy as she proudly introduced them.

"Uncle John, this is my heroine, Miss Holland, and you've got to shake hands and be good friends now—"

"I trust we shall!" Vassar cried laughingly.

Virginia smiled seriously.

"It depends on you, Mr. Congressman," she responded quietly. "You know I've tried to be friendly for some time, but you have been elusive. I had to threaten you with death even to bring about an introduction—"

He lifted his hand in protest.

"Don't—please! It's unkind now that I know you. I've had such a silly idea of your personality. I repent in sackcloth and ashes—"

"Really?"

"Honestly," he went on eagerly. "You know I had an idea that all suffragettes were ugly, disappointed, soured women whose lives had been beggared by the faults of sinful men—"

"Or Amazons—Uncy!" Zonia broke in with a laugh. "He called you an Amazon, Miss Holland!"

Virginia blushed and broke into a musical laugh.

John Vassar shook his head menacingly at his niece.

"That'll do for you now, Miss!"

"Did you call me an Amazon?" Virginia asked still smiling.

"Before I saw you, yes—"

"And now?"

"Now, I've a new grudge against Waldron for using first an expression on which I could improve—"

"What's that?" she asked, puzzled.

"He called you 'our Joan of Arc'—"

"And you could improve on that?"

"Yes—you're Joan of Arc without the cold touch of sainthood. You're warm and real and human and still the leader—"

She lifted a pair of serious eyes quickly to his and saw that he was in dead earnest. There was no fencing or banter. He meant it. A little smile of triumph played about the corners of her mouth.

She held his gaze in silence and then spoke slowly.

"We're going to be friends?"

"If you'll let me—"

Her eyes still held his steadily.

"There are conditions, of course—"

"All right."

"You wish to know them?"

"At once—"

"My! My! You can come to the point—can't you?" She laughed.

"My political life may depend on it, you know?" he replied lightly.

"Why not walk home with me—"

"With pleasure!" he broke in.

"And we'll have a chat in the library. I'm free to

confess, Mr. Congressman, that we would like very much to come to an understanding with you."

"And I'm going to confess, Miss Holland, that I'm very much ashamed of myself that I haven't made an effort to understand you."

"Well, you know what the old preacher down South always shouted in the revivals?"

"No—what?"

"As long as the lamp holds out to burn the vilest sinner may return!"

"Good. We'll hope that my repentance is not too late—"

"My only fear is, to tell you the truth—that it's a little too sudden—"

"But it's genuine!" he cried. "You'll have to admit that!"

He looked in vain for his father and Marya.

"Zonia may go with us?" he asked.

"Indeed she can! Everybody has tried his hand to draw out our young statesman and she succeeds. She's my little mascot!"

Virginia pressed her arm around the girl and she blushed with pride.

"Come; it's only a short walk to Stuyvesant Square— we spend most of our time now at our country place at Babylon, but we're in for this week's rallies."

Vassar looked for Zonia and discovered her in deep converse with a smiling blond youth of fourteen, the sparkle of whose eyes made no secret of their interest.

"My infant brother Billy—" Virginia explained.

"Indeed!"

"They're old friends."

"Evidently!" he laughed.

"Come," Virginia said in quick business-like tones, "the kids will follow. I want you to meet my father and mother before they're off to bed. In spite of modern progress they are the most pig-headed and persistent pair of fossils with whom I have to contend—"

"I've often seen your father at the soldiers' reunions —the youngest and finest looking man of the Old Guard, I've always thought."

"He is—isn't he?" she said thoughtfully.

"I wonder that the daughter of a soldier should take seriously all this talk about universal peace—"

"Perhaps that's the reason—"

"Nonsense!"

"Seriously. I've listened by the hour to his stories of the war. When I was very young I saw only the glamour and the romance and the glory and then as I grew older I began to think of the blackened chimneys of Southern homes and feel the misery and the desolation of it all. And we began to quarrel about war."

"Your father was in Sherman's army, I believe?"

"Yes—he ran away from his Western home at fourteen and joined the colors. Think of it! At eighteen he was mustered out in Washington a veteran of twenty-six pitched battles. He's only sixty-odd today with every power alert except a slight deafness—and by the way—" she paused and smiled—"I should tell you that his hobby just now is the immigration question. Don't mind anything silly he may say, will you?"

"Certainly not!" Vassar agreed. "I too am fighting against the invasion of this country by a foreign army—"

"Yours a dream—my father's grievance quite real you must admit."

"Seeing that a Pole is his Congressman neighbor—" Vassar admitted good-humoredly. "It must get on the nerves of the old boys who can't see our point of view. The man or woman born in free America inherits it all as a matter of course. He rarely thinks of his priceless birthright. To my old father every day of life is a Fourth of July! To me it is the same. A frail half-starved little orphan clinging to his hand thirty-one years ago, I stood on the deck of a steamer and saw this wonderful Promised Land. You are

American by the accident of birth. You had no choice. We are American because we willed to come. We love this land because it's worth loving. We know why we love it. We lifted up our eyes from a far country— amid tears and ashes and ruins—and saw the light of liberty shining here across the seas. We came and you received us with open arms. You set no hired spies to watch us. You made our homes and our firesides holy ground. We kiss the soil beneath our feet. It is *our* country—our flag, our nation, our people as it can't be yours who do not realize its full meaning— can't you see?"

"Yes," she answered softly. "And I never thought of it in that way before."

She glanced at the tall, straight, intense figure with new interest. They walked in silence for a block and he touched her arm with a movement of instinctive chivalrous protection as they crossed Second Avenue.

She broke into a laugh in spite of an effort at self-control when they had reached the sidewalk.

He blushed and looked puzzled.

"Why do you laugh?" he asked in hurt surprise.

"Oh, nothing—"

"You couldn't have laughed at the little confession I just made to you—"

She laid her hand on his arm in gentle quick protest.

"You know I could not. It was too sincere. It was from the depths of your inmost heart. And I see you and all your people who have come to our shores in the past generation through new eyes after this revelation you have given me—no, I was laughing at something miles removed—"

Again she paused and laughed.

"Tell me"—he pleaded.

"Come in first—we can't stand here on the sidewalk like two spooning children—this is our house—"

CHAPTER VII

WITH light step Virginia mounted the low stone stoop, fumbled for her keys, unlocked the massive door and ushered John Vassar into the dimly lighted hall.

"Come right into the sitting-room in the rear and meet my father and mother," she cried, placing her little turban hat on the rack beside his, man-fashion.

Vassar smiled at the assumption of equal rights the act implied. She caught the smile and answered with a toss of her pretty head as he followed her through the hall.

The older folks were bending over a table deeply absorbed in a game of checkers. The picture caught Vassar's fancy and held him in the doorway, a pleasant smile lighting his dark strong face.

"Mother," Virginia began softly, "it's time for children to quit their games. I want you to meet Mr. John Vassar whom I'm trying to dragoon into our cause—"

The prim aristocratic little woman rose with dignity and extended her hand in a gesture that spoke the ininheritance of gentle breeding. She was a native of

69

Columbia, South Carolina. Her stock joke of self-pity was the fact that she had married a Sherman Bummer who had helped to burn her native city. She excused him always with the apology that he was so young he was really not responsible for the bad company in which she found him. As a matter of fact he had driven a gang of drunken marauders from their house and defended them single handed through a night of terror until order had been restored. It was ten years later before he succeeded in persuading the fair young rebel to surrender.

"Delighted to meet you, I'm sure," Mrs. Holland said quietly. "You must be a Southerner, with that tall dark look of distinction—"

Vassar bowed low over her hand.

"I wish I were, madam—if the fact would win your approval—"

"To look like a Southerner is enough to win Mother on sight," Virginia laughed.

The father extended his hand in a cordial greeting without rising.

"Excuse me, young man, for not getting up," he said. "I'm lame with the gout. You're a suffragette?"

Vassar looked at Virginia, smiled and promptly answered.

"I'll have to confess that I'm not—"

Holland extended his hand again.

"Shake once more! Thank God for the sight of a sane man again. I thought they'd all died. We never see them here any more—"

Virginia lifted her finger and her father took the outstretched arm and drew it around his neck.

"I have to put up with the nincompoops for Virginia's sake. But I'm going to explode some day and say things. I can feel it coming on me—"

He stopped abruptly and leaned forward, releasing Virginia's arm.

"Young man, I can talk to you—you're not a suffragette—you're a real man. Between the women, the Jews and the foreigners this country is not only going to the dogs—it's gone—hell bent and hell bound. It's no use talking any more. I've given up and gone to playing checkers—"

"We may save it yet, sir," Vassar interrupted cheerfully.

"Save it? Great Scott, man, have you been down Broadway lately? Look at the signs—Katzmeyers, Einsteins, Epsteins, Abrahams, Isaacs and Jacobs! It would rest your eyes to find a Fogarty or a Casey. By the eternal, an Irishman now seems like a Son of the American Revolution! The Congressman from this district, sir, is a damned Pole from Posen!"

71

Virginia burst into a fit of laughter.

"What's the matter, Miss Troublemaker?" Holland growled.

"You didn't get the name, father dear—this is Mr. John Vassar, the damned Pole Congressman to whom you have so graciously referred—"

Holland frowned, searched his daughter's face for the joke, and looked at Vassar helplessly.

"It's not so!" he snorted. "I never saw a finer specimen of American manhood in my life, strong-limbed, clean-cut, clear-eyed, every inch a man and not a suffragette. It's not so. You're putting up a job on me, Virginia—"

John Vassar smiled and bowed.

"For the high compliment you pay me, Mr. Holland, I forgive the hard words. I understand how the old boys feel who fought to make this country what it is today. And I love you for it. I don't mind what you *say*—I know where to find your kind when the hour of trial comes—"

"You are Congressman Vassar?" the old man gasped.

"Guilty!"

The mother joined in the laugh at his expense.

Holland extended his hand again and grasped Vassar's.

"I have no friends in this house, sir! We make up.

72

I apologize to Poland for your sake. If they've got any more like you, let 'em come on. But mind you—" he lifted his finger in protest—"I stand by every word I said about the other fellows—every word!"

"I understand!" Vassar responded cheerfully.

"That will do now, Frank," Mrs. Holland softly murmured.

"And you come in to see me again, young man— I want to talk to you some time when there are no women around. You're in Congress. By Geeminy, I want to know why we've got no army while twenty million trained soldiers are fighting for the mastery of the world across the water. Just count me in on the fight, will you? By the eternal, I'd like to meet the traitor who'll try to block your bill—"

"I've important business with Mr. Vassar," Virginia broke in. "Excuse us now, children—"

"That's the way a suffragette talks to her old daddy, Vassar—" Holland cried. "I warn you against their wiles. Don't let her bamboozle you. I'm lame, but I'm going to vote against 'em, if I have to crawl to the polls election day—so help me God!"

Mrs. Holland beamed her good night with a gentle inclination of her silver-crowned head.

"He barks very loudly, Mr. Vassar," she called, "but he never bites—"

73

Virginia led her guest upstairs into the quiet library in the front of the house.

Zonia and Billy were chattering in the parlor.

She pointed to a heavy armchair and sat down opposite, the oak table between them.

"Now, Mr. Congressman, what is it—peace or war?"

There was a ring of subtle defiance in her tones that both angered and charmed her opponent. He had met many beautiful women before. For the first time he had met one who commanded both his intellect and his consciousness of sex. The sensation was painful. He resented it. His ideals of life asked of women submission, tenderness, trust. Here sat before him the most charming, the most fascinatingly feminine woman he had ever met who refused to accept his opinions and had evidently determined to bend his mind and will to hers. To think of yielding was the height of absurdity. And yet he must meet her as his intellectual equal. He could meet her on no other ground. Her whole being said, "Come, let's reason together." He had no desire to reason. He only wished to tell her the truth about the impression she had made on him. He smiled to recall it. He had a perfectly foolish—an almost resistless—impulse to leap on the speaker's stand, take her in his arms, kiss her and whisper:

"Dear little mate, this is silly—come away. I've something worth while to tell you—something big, something wonderful, something as old as eternity but always new—"

He waked from his reverie with a start to find his antagonist holding him with a determined gaze that put sentiment to flight.

"Peace or war?" she firmly repeated.

"If I am to choose," he fenced, "I assure you it will be peace—"

He paused and studied her expression of serious concentration. In spite of every effort to fix his mind in politics he persisted in the silliest old-fashioned admiration of her wistful, appealing beauty. Confound it. She had no right to use such a power for the propaganda of crackbrained theories! He felt the foundations of the moral world tremble at the shock of this resistless, elemental force. The man who desires a woman will sell principle, country, right, God, for his desire. Was he going to be trapped by this ancient snare? Such a woman might play with a victim as a cat a mouse until her purpose was accomplished. Sex attraction is the one force that defies all logic and scoffs at reason. The government of a democracy was a difficult task under present conditions. What would it become when the decision on which the mightiest issues

hung could be decided by the smile of a woman's lips
or the dimple in her cheek?

He felt the pull of this fascination with a sense of
inward panic. What the devil was she laughing at a
while ago as they crossed the street? He had forgotten
it for the moment, and she hadn't explained. He would
fence a little for time before meeting the issue. He
touched the tip of his mustache thoughtfully.

"Anyhow, suppose we shake hands before we begin
the fight. It's one of the rules of the game you know—"

She leaned across the table with a puzzled expression.

"Shake hands?"

"Yes—spiritually, so to speak. I'd like to get on as
friendly footing as possible to appeal to your mercy if
I'm defeated. Would you mind telling me at what you
were laughing when we crossed Second Avenue?"

An exquisite smile illumined her face and a twinkle
of mischief played about the corners of her mouth.

"Shall I be perfectly frank?" she asked.

"Please—"

"I laughed at the silly contradiction of allowing you
to touch my arm in token of your superior strength as
you drew about me the sheltering protection of chivalry.
There were no plunging horses near—not even a push-
cart in sight. The nearest street-car was five blocks

76

away. Why did you think that I needed help in walking ten yards?"

He held her gaze steadily. She was charming—there was no doubt about it. He had to bite his lips to keep back a foolish compliment that might anger her. How should he bear himself toward such a woman? Her whole being breathed tenderness and femininity, yet there was a dangerous challenge of intellect about her that upset him.

"Why did you think I needed help?" she softly repeated.

"To tell you the truth," he answered gravely, "I didn't think at all. The act was instinctive—the inheritance of centuries—"

"Exactly! Centuries of man's patronage, of man's tyranny, of his boasted superiority. As long as woman submits to be treated as a doll, a weakling, an incompetent, the supposed superior being must try to do the proper thing in an emergency—"

"You resented it?" he broke in.

"No. I, too, am suffering from the inheritance of centuries—of dependence and of the hypocrisy inbred by generations of chivalry. It was at my own sneaking joy in your protection that I laughed—"

Vassar moved uneasily, drew his straight brows low and looked at her through their veil for an instant.

77

He was making a desperate effort to keep his brain clear. It would be ridiculous to surrender to such a charming little siren at the first encounter.

"Well, sir," she cried briskly, "now that we've shaken hands the first round is on. Shall I lead?"

Vassar bowed.

"By all means—ladies first!"

"Why do you refuse to give me the ballot?"

"I never knew until tonight that women like *you* wished it. If I had—"

"You would have agreed?"

"My dear Miss Holland, I not only would have agreed but I would have gone out after it and brought it to you. And all against my better judgment. If women are allowed to vote, there must be a law against your kind entering politics—"

"Yes?"

"Decidedly."

"And may I ask why?" she demanded.

He smiled and hesitated.

"If you ever get into Congress—I can see the finish of that aggregation as a deliberative body. You would be a majority from the moment you entered the Chamber—"

"Please, Mr. Vassar—" she protested. "We have no time for chaff—"

He rose abruptly from the depths of the armchair, seized a light one, moved it nearer to the corner of the table, sat down and bent close to his charming opponent.

"I'm not chaffing," he began eagerly. "I'm in earnest. Your personality has upset all my preconceived ideas of the leaders of this woman's movement. I am more than ever alarmed at its sinister significance. You take my judgment by storm because you're charming. You stop the process of reasoning by merely lifting your eyes to mine. Such a power cannot be used to further the ends of justice or perfect the organization of society. The power you wield defies all law—"

Virginia laughed in spite of an effort at self-control.

"Are you making love to me, Mr. Vassar?" she cried.

He blushed and stammered.

"Well—not—deliberately—"

"Unconsciously?"

He mopped the perspiration from his brow in confusion.

"Perhaps."

Virginia rose, and her lips closed firmly.

"I think our interview had better end. We are wasting each other's time—"

"Please, Miss Holland," he begged with deep humility, "forgive me. I was never more sincere in my life. I should have been more careful. But there's something about your frank manner that disarmed me. You seemed so charmingly friendly. I forget that we are enemies—forgive me—"

"There's nothing to forgive. You are the type of man who cannot understand my position—and for that reason cannot meet me as an intellectual equal. I resent it—"

"But I'm not the type of man who cannot understand. I will meet you as an intellectual equal. I'll do more. I concede your superiority. You have baffled and defeated me at every turn tonight—I go puzzled and humiliated. I refuse to accept such a defeat. You cannot dismiss me in this absurd fashion. I'll camp on your doorstep until we have this thing out."

"You'll not call without an appointment, I hope?"

"Oh, yes, I will. I'm going to cultivate your father. I'll accept his invitation. I'll make your house my happy home until we at least come to an intelligent understanding of our differences—"

"Tomorrow then?" she said. "I'm tired tonight. Tomorrow at eleven o'clock—"

Vassar smiled at the business-like hour.

"I've an important engagement at eleven that will keep me an hour. It's Flag Day at my schools—the kiddies expect me—"

"Flag Day?"

"A little device of mine to teach our boys and girls to love their country—won't you join us tomorrow at the old Tenth Armory and inspect my forces?"

Virginia hestitated.

"All right, I will. I'll ask Mr. Waldron to pick me up there at noon."

"I'll expect you at eleven."

He pressed her hand with a new sense of uneasiness, defeat and anger which Waldron's name had aroused.

CHAPTER VIII

JOHN VASSAR'S sleep had been fitful and unsatisfying. Through hours of half-conscious brooding and dreaming he had seen the face of Virginia Holland. He had thus far found no time for social frivolities. The air of America was just the tonic needed to transform the tragic inheritance of the Old World into a passion for work that had practically ruled women out of the scheme of things.

He had dreamed of a home of his own in the dim future—yes—when the work of his career, the work he had planned for his country should have been done. This had been his life, the breath he breathed, his inspiration and religion—to lead an American renaissance of patriotism. America had never had a national spirit. His ambition was to fire the soul of thoughtless millions into a conscious love of country which would insure her glorious destiny.

A woman's smile had upset this dream. Through the night he had tried in vain to throw off the obsession. At daylight he had fallen into a sleep of sheer exhaustion. It was nine o'clock before he was roused by a gentle knock on his door.

Marya's voice was calling somewhere out of space.

"Uncle John—breakfast is waiting—may I come in?"

"All right—dearie—break right in!" he groaned.

"And I've a letter for you—a special letter—"

The sleeper was awake now, alert, eager—

"A special letter?"

"A big black man brought it just now. He's waiting in the hall—says Miss Holland would like an answer."

Vassar seized the letter and read with a broad grin. The handwriting was absurdly delicate. The idea that a suffragette could have written it was ridiculous!

> My dear Mr. Vassar:
>
> I'm heartily ashamed of myself for losing my temper last night. Please call for me at ten o'clock. I wish a little heart-to-heart talk before we go to your Flag Festival. Please answer by the bearer.
>
> Virginia Holland.

Vassar drew Marya into his arms and kissed her rapturously.

"You're an angel—you've brought me a message from the skies. Run now and tell the big black man—Miss Holland's butler—to thank her for me and say that I'll be there promptly at ten. Run, darling! Run!"

The child refused to stir without another kiss which

she repeated on both his cheeks. She stopped at the door and waved another.

"Hurry, Uncle John—please—we're all starved."

"Down in five minutes!" he cried.

The weariness of the night's fitful sleep was gone. The world was suddenly filled with light and music.

"What the devil's come over me!" he muttered, astonished at the persistent grin his mirror reflected. "At this rate I can see my finish—I'll be the secretary of the Suffragette Campaign Committee before the week's over—bah!"

Old Peter, the black butler, ushered him into the parlor with a stately bow.

"Miss Virginia be right down, sah. She say she des finishin' her breakfus'—yassah!"

Vassar seated himself with a sense of triumph. She must have written that note in bed. He flattered himself someone else had not slept well. He hoped not.

Her greeting was gracious, but strictly business-like —he thought a little too business-like to be entirely convincing.

She motioned him to resume his seat and drew one for herself close beside. She sat down in a quiet determined manner that forbade sentimental reflections and began without preliminaries.

"We lost track of our subject last night, Mr. Vassar, in an absurd personal discussion. I've asked you to come back this morning to make a determined effort to win you for our cause—"

She paused, leaned forward and smiled persuasively.

"We need you. Your influence over the foreign-born population in New York would be enormous. I see by this morning's paper an enthusiastic account of your work among the children. You are leading a renaissance of American patriotism. Good! So am I—a renaissance of the principles of the Declaration of Independence. *'We hold these truths to be self-evident*: that all men are created equal! that they are endowed by their creator with certain inalienable rights; that among these are life, liberty and the pursuit of happiness. That to secure those rights, governments are instituted among men, deriving their just powers from the consent of the governed.' Come now, I appeal to your sense of justice. What right have you to govern me without my consent? Am I not created your equal?"

Her eloquence was all but resistless. The word of surrender was on his lips, when the voice of an honest manhood spoke within.

"You're not convinced. The magnetism of a woman's sex is calling. You're a poltroon to surrender your principles to such a force. In her soul a true woman would despise you for it."

She saw his hesitation and leaned closer, holding him with her luminous eyes.

"Come now, in your heart of hearts you know that I am your equal?"

Something in the tones of her voice broke the spell— just a trace of the platform intonation and the faintest suggestion of the politician. The voice within again spoke. There was another reason why he should be true to his sense of right. He owed it to this woman who had moved him so profoundly. He must be true to the noblest and best that was in him.

He met her gaze in silence for a moment and spoke with quiet emphasis.

"If I followed my personal inclinations, Miss Holland, I would agree to anything you ask. You're too downright, too honest and earnest to wish or value such a shallow victory—am I not right?"

The faintest tinge of red colored Virginia's cheeks.

"Of course," she answered slowly, "I wish the help of the best that's in you or nothing—"

"Good! I felt that instinctively. I could fence and hedge and trim with the ordinary politician. With all respect to your pretensions, you're not a politician at all. You're just a charming, beautiful woman entering

86

a field for which God never endowed you either physically, temperamentally or morally—"

Virginia frowned and lifted her head with a little gesture of contempt.

"I must be honest. I must play the game squarely with you! I'm sorely tempted to cheat. But there's too much at stake. You ask if you are not my equal? I answer promptly and honestly. I know that you are more—you are my superior. For this reason I would save you from the ballot. It is not a question of right, it is a question of hard and difficult duty. The ballot is not a right or a privilege. It is a solemn and dangerous duty. The ballot is force—physical force. It is a modern substitute for the bayonet—a device which has been used to prevent much civil strife. And yet man never votes away his right to a revolution. The Declaration of Independence embodies this fact— *'Whenever any form of government becomes destructive of those ends, it is the right of the people to alter or abolish it—'* There you have the principle in full. Back of every ballot is a bayonet and the red blood of the man who wields it—"

"But we will substitute reason for force!"

"How, dear lady? *Government is force*—never was anything else—never can be until man is redeemed and this world is peopled by angels. Man is in the zoological period of his development. Scratch the most cultured man beneath the skin and you find the savage. Scratch the proudest nation of Europe beneath the skin and you find the elemental brute. I do not believe in forcing our mothers, our sisters, our wives and sweethearts into the blood-soaked mud of battle trenches. That work is the dangerous and difficult duty of man. So the ballot, on which peace or war depends, is his duty—not his right or privilege—"

"Give us the ballot and we will make war impossible," Virginia broke in.

"How? If women vote with their men, their voting will mean nothing. We merely multiply the total by two. We do not change results. If women vote against the men on an issue of war or peace, will men submit to such a feminine decision? Certainly not. Force and force alone can decide the issue of force. Back of every ballot is a bayonet or there's nothing back of it. The breath of revolution will drive such meaningless ballots as chaff before a whirlwind—"

"We'll stop your blood-stained revolutions!" Virginia cried.

"All right. Do so and you stop the progress of humanity. The American Revolution was blood-stained. It gave us freedom. The Civil War was blood-stained. It freed this nation of the curse of slavery and sealed the Union for all time. There are good wars and bad wars. True war is the inevitable conflict between two irreconcilable moral principles. One is right—the other wrong. One must live—the other die. Wrong may triumph for a day. Right must win in the end or else the universe is ruled by the Devil, not by God. You cannot abolish war until the Devil is annihilated and God rules in the souls and lives of men and in their governments as well."

For the moment the woman was swept from the moorings of her pet arguments. She quickly recovered.

"We are going to make America the moral and spiritual leader of mankind!" she cried with elation.

"Yes, I know. In the Parliament of Man, the Federation of the World—your poet's dream as far removed from the beastly realities of life today as Heaven is from Hell—"

"We are going to make this dream a living fact in the world—and free America shall lead the way—"

"And how will you begin?"

"By setting the proud example of building our national life on spiritual realities first, not on guns and forts. We will begin the disarmament of the world—"

"And end your movement by surrender to the armed bullies of Europe!"

"At least my dream is a dream," Virginia laughed,

"yours a silly nightmare. But I give you up for the present. I see that Ephraim is joined to his idols. My mission is a failure. At least I thank you for your candor. I shall have to turn you over now to the tender mercies of Mr. Waldron and the Executive Committee. Come, we'll see your flags and the children. The sight will be restful after our battle."

She rose quickly, led the way to the hall, adjusted the little turban on the mass of auburn blond hair and opened the door.

Vassar passed out with a queer sense of defeat. He had vanquished her in the argument. But the trouble was she had not argued. She had merely demanded his submission without argument.

CHAPTER IX

ANOTHER thing that had upset Vassar's equanamity was the baffling quality of Virginia Holland's character. The more honestly he had tried to approach her in friendly compromise the more bristling her mental resistance had become. She held him at arms' length personally.

He was surprised at her final decision to go to the Armory. No doubt only an uncompromising honesty had caused her to fulfil a promise. Clearly she was bored.

As a matter of fact she was anything but bored. She was lashing herself at every step with reproaches at her idiotic inconsistency in accompanying an East Side politician on a fool's errand. No doubt the whole thing was a scheme to pose before enraptured constituents. Why had she consented to come? She asked herself the question a hundred times and finally accepted the weak lie that she was studying his eccentricities to make his defeat the more sure.

With each moment of her association she had become more and more clearly conscious of his charm. Its strength and its antagonism were equally appealing. It would be sweet to demonstrate her own power in his defeat at the polls and then make up to him by confessing her admiration.

She began to receive striking evidence of his popularity. At every street-corner and from almost every door came a friendly nod or wave of a hand.

Schultz, the fat German who kept a delicatessen store on the corner, waved to him from the doorway.

"Mein Frau und der kids—all dere, gov'ner. I vish I could be!"

On the next block Brodski gripped his hand and whispered a word of cheer.

"They all seem to know you down here, Mr. Congressman," Virginia laughed.

"Yes, it's my only hope—if we fight—"

"You'll need help if we do," she answered quietly.

He didn't like the tone of menace in her words. There was no bluster about it. There was a ring of earnestness that meant business.

"Perhaps I'm going to win you to my cause before you know it," he ventured. "I'm going to show you something today that's really worth while—"

"Meaning, of course," she interrupted, "that the cause in which I am at present expending my thought and energy is not worth while—"

"I didn't say that!" he protested. "And I most humbly apologize if I implied as much—"

"All the same you think it, sir—"

She stopped short in amazement at the sight of her brother Billy standing straight and fine beside Zonia at the door of the old Armory, a marshal's sash across his shoulder, arrayed in a captain's uniform of the Boy Scouts of America.

Zonia grasped her outstretched hand in loyal greeting, her eyes sparkling with pride at her uncle's triumphant march beside her heroine.

Virginia's gaze fixed Billy's beaming countenance.

"Well, Mr. Sunny Jim!" she exclaimed, "will you kindly give an account of yourself. How long have you been a marshal of the empire?"

"Oh, ever so long, Virginia—Mr. Vassar didn't know I was your brother, that's all. I'm a captain now. I didn't let you know 'cause I thought you might raise a rumpus. Father and mother know. They don't care. I like it."

He turned abruptly to Vassar and saluted.

"Everything ready, sir!"

Virginia shook her head and smiled at Zonia. She too wore a marshal's sash.

"I want you to meet some of the mothers, Miss Holland," she whispered eagerly. "I made a lot of them go to our meetings."

"With pleasure, dear." She smiled at Vassar. "We'll take occasion to mend some of our fences in this benighted district today!"

The young Congressman turned his guest over to his niece and hurried away with Billy to inspect the assignment of kids for the ceremonies of the Flag.

Virginia was surprised to find the hall packed with women and children, more than a thousand, of all ages and nationalities. They were chattering like magpies —a babel of foreign tongues—German, Italian, Polish, Bohemian, Russian, Greek, Yiddish.

"I must introduce you first," Zonia whispered, "to my favorite mother, an Italian with the cutest little darling boy you ever saw. She heard you speak in the Square—"

She darted into the crowd and led forth a slender, dark-haired young Italian mother with a beautiful boy of five clinging to her skirts.

"Miss Holland, this is my good friend Angela Benda and Mr. Tommaso!"

Angela bowed and blushed.

"Ah, Signorina, I hear you speak so fine—so beautiful! I make my man Tommaso vote for you or breaka his neck! I done tell him so too—"

94

"And did he promise?"

"Si, si, signorina—I mak him—"

Virginia stooped and gathered the child in her arms. Shy at first, he put his hand at last on her shining hair, touched it gracefully, and looked into her face with grave wide eyes.

Virginia pressed him suddenly to her heart and kissed him.

"You glorious little creature!" she cried. The act was resistless. In all her career she had never before done so silly and undignified a thing in public. She blushed at her folly. What crazy spell could she be under today? She asked the question with a new sense of uneasy annoyance as her eyes swept the room in search of the hero of the occasion.

Vassar could scarcely walk for the crowds of joyous women and children who pressed about him and tried to express their love and pride in his leadership.

A fight suddenly broke out between the Benda and Schultz kids close beside Virginia.

Zonia tried in vain to separate them. Vassar saved the situation by picking up Angela's boy by his suspenders, and the German kid by the seat of his pants. He lifted them bodily out of the scene and carried them into a quiet corner.

Virginia laughed heartily.

Vassar demanded mutual apologies.

"He called me 'Sausage,'" complained the Schultz kid.

"He calla me a Dago," answered the Italian.

"Now salute each other with a handshake!" Billy commanded. "And remember that you're good Americans."

"He made them both take off their caps and yell:

"Hurrah for Uncle Sam!"

Virginia looked about the old hall with increasing amazement at the effective way in which the interior had been decorated. Around the walls in graceful festoons the beautiful red, white and blue emblems hung an endless riot of color. From the ceiling they fell in soft, billowing waves stirred by the breezes from the open windows. The eye of every child kindled with delight on entering.

The exercises began with a song.

A band of six pieces led them. Everybody rose and sang one stanza. John Vassar first wrote it in big plain letters on the blackboard where all could read:

MY COUNTRY, 'TIS OF THEE,
SWEET LAND OF LIBERTY,
OF THEE, I SING!

They sang it with a fervor that stirred Virginia's soul.

Vassar took the chair as presiding officer and directed the exercises, Billy acting as his chief lieutenant to Virginia's continuous amusement.

"Now, children, give me the cornerstone of the American nation—let's get that in place first. Now everybody! All together!"

From the crowd came a shout that stirred the big flags in the ceiling:

"ALL MEN ARE CREATED EQUAL!"

Again he wrote it on the blackboard and asked them to repeat it.

They did it with a will.

"Now, children," he said, "I've a distinguished artist here today who gives us this valuable hour of his useful life to draw a picture on the board. Watch him closely and don't forget the message.

With quick, sure stroke the cartoonist drew a wonderful symbolic Stairway of Life for the American child.

On the left of the scene appeared Uncle Sam holding the lamp of knowledge to light the way to success for the crowd of eager boys and girls at the bottom of the hill. In sharp outline he drew the steps upon which they might mount—each step a book they could master. The first step was marked—Primer, the next First

97

Reader and then came Elementary Arithmetic, Second
Reader, Grammar, Geography, History, Physiology,
Rhetoric, Algebra, Physics, Latin, Greek, Geometry,
Political Economy and Trigonometry. The last step
faded out in the blazing light of the Sun of Success
at the top of the hill. He drew the figures of little
boys and girls on the lower rounds, bigger boys and
girls on the middle ones, young men and women mounting the hill crest. At the bottom of the cartoon he
wrote:

"Uncle Sam invites all his children of every race
and kindred and tongue to come up higher!"

"Now, once more, children," Vassar cried, "tell me
on what this country's greatness rests?"

Again the shout came as from a single throat:

"All men are created equal!"

"Good! Now give me the passwords!"

"Liberty!"

"Equality!"

"Fraternity!"

The three shouts came as three salvos from a battery
of artillery.

On another blackboard he wrote the words in huge
capitals and left them standing.

"Now, children, I want you to think for just one
minute every day of your life what it means to be a

citizen of this mighty free Democracy—where men are learning to govern themselves better than any king has ever done it for them. I want you to realize that the inspired founders of this nation made it the hope and refuge of the oppressed of all the world. And I want you to love it with all your heart—"

He lifted his hands and the crowd rose singing "The Star Spangled Banner." They sang it with a swing and lilt Virginia had never heard before. For the first time in her life it had meaning. Her eyes unconsciously filled with tears.

At a wave of Vassar's hand the crowd sank to their seats.

Vassar stooped over the platform and motioned to Angela to hand to him her boy.

The mother proudly passed the child to the leader. Vassar lifted the smiling youngster in his arms and held him high. In ringing tones he cried:

"Don't forget, my friends, that the humblest boy here today may become the president of the United States!"

A ringing cheer swept the crowd.

Vassar passed the child back to the mother and continued his address. The rest of it was lost on Angela. A new light suddenly flashed in her brown eyes.

She sat down, flushed, and rose again. Tommaso

tugged at her dress and begged her to sit down. Her soul was too full. The act of the speaker was a divine omen. She must know if he really meant that her little Tommaso might be the president of a great free nation. The thought was too big. Her heart was bursting. She tried timidly to attract Vassar's attention.

Tommaso, alarmed, drew her back to the seat.

Angela looked across the side aisle and saw Virginia in the front row. Bending low she approached and whispered:

"My own bambino—he may be president—yes?"

Virginia nodded tearfully.

Angela darted back to her seat, snatched the head cloth from her rich brown hair and seized one of her husband's earrings. The fight was brief. The Italian struggled to save his ornaments but the wife won. He also lost a gay sash about his waist. The mother pressed the boy to her heart and whispered passionately to her man:

"We Americano now—our bambino be bigga de boss president!"

Tommaso succeeded finally in quieting her before Vassar noticed the disturbance.

"Now, Captain," Vassar called to Billy, "give us the order of the day for the Boy Scouts of America."

Billy sprang on the little platform, lifted his smiling face, his hands tightly gripped behind his back and spoke in firm, boyish tones:

"My only regret is that I have but one life to give for my country!"

"And what do you say to that, children?" Vassar shouted.

"Three cheers for Uncle Sam!" they answered. Three times three they gave it without the need of a prompter.

Vassar waved a signal to the right and from the dressing-room slowly marched a procession of children of all nations, dressed in their native costume, each child bearing the tiny flag of their old-world allegiance. The line of floating color circled the open space in front of the platform, and, as they passed Vassar surrendered the old flag and received from his hand the Stars and Stripes which each waved in answer to a cheer from the crowd.

When the last nation had surrendered allegiance the procession marched again around the circle to the continuous cheering of the crowd and took their places about Vassar who held aloft the regimental standard of the nation with its golden eagle gleaming from the staff. The little children crowded close and about them gathered a ring of Boy Scouts and beyond them the mothers of the kids.

He lifted high the flag and every Scout and grown up and every child saluted it with uplifted hands and cheered.

"Now, boys and girls!" Vassar cried to the outer circle.

They solemnly responded in chorus:

"I pledge allegiance to my flag and to the Republic for which it stands—one nation, indivisible, with liberty and justice for all."

"Now, kiddies!" he shouted to the little ones.

The answer came in straggling unison:

"I give my hand and my heart to God and my country. One country, one language, one flag—"

"And now!" the leader cried:

"Hurrah for the President of the United States!"

With a shout they gave the cheers and the ceremony ended again in a babel of joyous polyglot chatter.

Vassar found Virginia surrounded by a mob of mothers struggling to shake hands under the guidance of Angela.

"I must say," he laughed, "that your methods are quite up to date."

"I assure you I'm not trying to take advantage of my host to seduce his constituents. I'm only doing my best to make Angela happy by meeting her friends—"

"Si, signor—we will vote for the signorina—and you, too, is it not so?"

"Apparently they need no seduction," Vassar laughed.

Virginia blushed and lifted her hands in protest.

"Well," the young leader asked in conciliatory tones, "how did you like it?"

"I've been charmed beyond measure," was the quick answer. "I've got a new view of my country. I've a new view of the possibilities of political leadership. I'm more determined than ever to wield a ballot—"

"You're not willing to trust me with that duty?"

"No. We can add something you can never give to these people. These mothers know instinctively that I can understand them as you could not."

"And I had hoped," he said regretfully, "that I might win you for a helper in this work. You're determined to be my rival—"

"Not unless you fight—"

"Can't you see," he persisted, "that what America needs today is not the multiplication of her voting population by two—but the breathing of a conscious national soul into the people and giving that soul expression. What we need is not more millions of voters but a deeper sense of responsibility developed in those who already vote. We must show the world that democracy is a success, that democracy means the best in government, the best in commerce, the best in art and literature. I grant you that many of our new foreign voters are ignorant, but, dear Miss Holland, their wives and mothers are far more ignorant. Why add to this sum total of inefficiency? New York is in reality a foreign city set down here in the heart of America. More than one-half of the men of voting age are foreign-born. Only thirty-eight per cent of them are naturalized. More than half a million of these men are in no way identified with our political life. Twenty thousand a year in our city claim their right of citizenship and become voters. We have before us a gigantic task to teach these men the meaning of true Americanism. This work has not been done. It has been left to chance. We must break up these foreign groups. Eighty per cent of our foreign population live in groups and take no interest in any problem which does not directly affect their group life. They neither know nor are known by American-born citizens. Men like your father should get acquainted with these people. They are yet speaking a foreign tongue, living within the narrow ideals of their European origin. In time of supreme trial if this nation should call on them, what could one expect? What have we a right to expect?"

Virginia shook her head in hopeless protest.

"Always your nightmare of an imaginary impossible attack by a foreign foe!"

"I wish it were imaginary," he answered thoughtfully. "Do you think for a moment that there is a foot of soil in the old world of Northern and Central Europe on which I could stand and dare to write the sentences and mottoes on that blackboard? Do the rulers of Europe believe that all men are created equal? Remember, dear lady, that Democracy is a babe not yet out of swaddling clothes. The might of kings is as old as the recorded history of man. The kingly conception of government and its divine right to govern is inbred into the human race through thousands of years until it is accepted without question. The idea becomes as fixed and automatic as the beat of the human heart.

"The American Republic is but a little over a hundred years old. We reckon in years, they reckon by centuries. The founding of this nation was one of the happiest accidents in the history of the world. But it was an accident. The kings were too busy fighting one another in the stirring years of the American Revolution to give their attention to you. Your fathers won on a lucky fluke. And thanks to the barriers of two vast oceans you grew and waxed strong with incredible rapidity. You were safe as long as these oceans protected you and no longer. The genius of man has abolished the ocean barrier. There is no more sea. The ocean is now the world's highway and transport by water is swifter and safer than by land. The oceans no longer protect you. They are a constant menace to your existence—"

"You are assuming that the world is not civilized—that we are still living in the Dark Ages," Virginia interrupted.

"I am assuming only the facts of modern life: that force still rules the world; that government is force; that there are two forms of government and only two, and that they are irreconcilable—government by the people and government of the people by imperial masters. These systems can no more mix than fire and water. The world must yet be conquered by one of them. You assume that we have settled our form of government for all time. We have—provided we are ready to demonstrate to the imperial rulers that we can defend it against all comers—"

Virginia threw up her hands in a gesture of despair.

"You're hopeless!"

"Can you not see this?" he pleaded.

"I refuse to see it. I still have faith in God and my fellow man."

He looked at her flushed exquisite face with deep tenderness—lifted his eyes and saw Zonia and Marya the center of an admiring group of children.

"You like my little Zonia?" he asked in apparently irrevelent tones.

"I love her—"

"Her father, my elder brother, lived in Poland's happiest tomb—in German Poland—"

He stopped abruptly and gave a bitter little laugh.

"His home took fire one night and burned to the ground. By decree of his Imperial master he was not permitted to build a dwelling on his own land. He loved this land, poor fool. His wife and babies loved it. He couldn't be dragged away. He took refuge in a barn. Through the summer they managed to live without a fire inside. They cooked in the open. But when the winter came and the snows fell, he was forced to smuggle a little stove into the barn to boil some eggs and cabbage and make tea for his children. He hid the stove in a deep hole under the floor. Ten days later an officer of the Imperial government, passing, saw the smoke, forced his way in and uncovered the secret. The stove had made the barn a dwelling and he had forfeited his estate and his liberty. He fought—as any man with a soul must fight—for his own! The end was sure. He shot the officer. But there were legions of these Imperial soldiers. They assaulted his frail barricade and riddled his body with bullets. His faithful wife died with him. And little Zonia and Marya were sent to me in free America. And so you see I lack faith in some men——"

He stopped abruptly at the sight of Waldron's heavy face with its arctic smile.

The millionaire lifted his hat, bowed slightly and disappeared from the doorway.

"Come with me to Mr. Waldron's house, we must have a final conference there——"

"Waldron's house?" he asked incredulously.

"Certainly. His library has become our campaign headquarters——"

"You'll have to excuse me——"

"But I won't excuse you. We're going to fight this thing out today."

"I've nothing to say to Waldron."

"But he has something very important to say to you——"

"All right—he knows where I live——"

Virginia laid her hand on his arm in a gesture of appeal that was resistless.

"Won't you come with me?"

The frown slowly faded, and he smiled an answer.

"With you—yes."

CHAPTER X

BILLY volunteered to take the children home, Vassar waved his farewell to the crowd and hurried to the waiting automobile.

Virginia presented him to the banker.

"Our irreconcilable foe, Mr. Waldron!"

The millionaire merely touched his hat with the barest suggestion of a military salute and Vassar bowed. It was not until they were seated in the car that Waldron spoke—the same cold smile about his lips.

"I've wanted to meet you for a long time, Mr. Vassar—"

"I'm surprised to hear that," was the light reply. "Our views could hardly be the same on any subject within my scope of knowledge—"

Waldron smiled patronizingly.

"Anyhow, let us hope that we'll get together to-day—"

"We must," Virginia responded.

The one thing Vassar couldn't endure was patronage. The tone Waldron assumed was offensive beyond endurance. If he tried it again the young leader had

109

made up his mind to find an excuse, stop the car and go back to his office.

To his relief the man of money made no further attempt at conversation, save for an occasional whispered order to his liveried chauffeur. Vassar's eyes rested on the military cut of this chauffeur's clothes with new resentment. The gilded coat of arms on the door of the tonneau had not escaped him as he took his seat beside Virginia. Nor was the lordly manner in which the new master of men condescended to talk with his servant at the wheel lost on the young leader of democracy.

He wondered what Virginia Holland could see in such a man. He refused utterly to believe that she could love him. Elemental brute strength and stark physical courage he undoubtedly possessed. The solid mass of his bull neck and the cold brilliance of his gray eyes left no doubt on that score.

There could be but one explanation of her association with Waldron. He had generously loosed his purse strings and given her cause the unlimited credit needed under modern conditions to conduct a great political movement. No one could blame her for that. It was good politics.

All the same he would give a good deal just now to know whether she cared for the man. He must yield the devil his due. Waldron was the type of domineering brute that appealed to many women. He wondered if Virginia Holland had felt the spell of his commanding character.

For the hundredth time he asked himself the question why should he care. There was the rub. Devil take it, he did care. He had never been so foolishly happy in his life as in the hours he had spent by this girl's side. It infuriated him to think how easy had been his conquest. But yesterday he had scorned her name. They had met and talked a few hours and he had become her lackey. At her bidding he was now on his way to the house of the man he hated.

He caught himself grinning for sheer joy to find himself seated close beside her in the smooth gliding car of his enemy. He could have enjoyed this wonderful ride had they been alone.

The afternoon was one of glorious beauty. The rains of the first days of July had swept the city clean. The sun had broken the clouds into billowing banks of snow-white against the dazzling azure of the skies. A brisk inspiriting breeze swept in from the sea and rippled the waters of the North River into little white lines of foam. The trees along the Drive flashed in splendor.

The temptation was all but resistless to touch her

hand. He started with terror at the crazy thought. She was anything but an Amazon, but he could see her pitching him headforemost into the road for daring the impertinence. He glanced at her furtively, alarmed lest she had read his thoughts.

Well, there was no help for it now. He was in for a fight for his life with this demure, quiet, dangerous little woman, who could sit calmly by his side mistress of her thoughts and no doubt perfectly conscious of her power over his.

Anyhow she was worth a fight. It was worth any man's best to win the heart of such a woman and to make her his own. Could any man really do it? Of course he could! With the next breath he doubted it, and trembled at the happiness he felt bubbling in his soul when he felt the nearness of her exquisite figure.

"Why so grave, Mr. Congressman?" she asked banteringly.

"To tell you the truth, I'm scared," he answered in low tones.

"Of the great man in front?" she whispered.

Vassar's jaw closed with decision.

"Far from it, I assure you!"

"You're not afraid of an automobile?"

"One more guess——"

"You couldn't be afraid of little me?" she asked demurely.

"Yesterday I would have said no with a very loud emphasis. I'm free to confess the more I've seen of you the more I dread your opposition—"

She laughed in his face with a deliberate provoking challenge.

"Now that's unkind of you! I expected a much more gallant answer from a tall handsome apostle of romance and chivalry."

"Perhaps I was afraid you'd laugh at me—"

"No. I hold that the age of true chivalry is only dawning—the age in which man will honor woman by recognizing her as worthy to be his pal and best friend as well as his toy."

There was something so genuine to the appeal of her personality that the man who intellectually disagreed with her philosophy yet found himself in foolish accord with every demand she made.

Vassar was silent a moment, and glanced at her to see if she were chaffing or sparring to uncover his defenses.

He was about to say too much—to confess too much and do it clumsily in the presence of the man he hated when the machine suddenly swung toward the cliff, swept up to a massive iron gate and stopped.

113

The chauffeur sounded his horn and an old man dressed in the peasant costume of the lodge-keeper of a feudal estate of Central Europe emerged from the cottage built into the walls of the cliff and opened the gates without a word. He bowed humbly to the lord of the manor. Waldron nodded carelessly.

The banker's medieval castle, perched on the highest hill on upper Manhattan, was one of the sights of the metropolis. Vassar lifted his eyes and caught the majestic lines of the granite tower thrusting its grim embattlements into the skies. An ocean-going yacht lay at her anchor in the river like a huge swan with folded wings. The Italian boathouse which he had built at the water's edge was connected with his castle by an underground passage bored through the granite cliff into a hall cut out of the stone a hundred feet beneath the foundations of the structure above. A swift elevator connected this hall with the house.

The machine shot gracefully up the steep winding roadway and stopped beneath the vaulted porte-cochère.

Liveried flunkies hurried down the stone landing to greet their master and his guests. There was nothing for them to do but open the door of the tonneau with obsequious bows.

"Will you kindly make our prisoner as comfortable

as possible, Miss Holland," Waldron said in his even metallic voice, "while I give some orders outside. You'll find the library at your disposal."

"Thank you," Virginia answered, mounting the steps without further ceremony.

A feeling of resentment swept John Vassar. How dare this bully assume such familiarity with Virginia Holland! She had met him as a patron of the cause of woman's suffrage. One would think he had the right to her soul and body by the way he asked her to act as the hostess of his establishment. The thought that enraged him was that the banker was so cocksure of himself, his position. No robber baron of the Middle Ages could have felt more irresponsible in the exercise of his power. The consciousness of this power oozed from the fat pores of Waldron's skin. He exuded the idea as he breathed.

Vassar's first impression on entering the great house confirmed his idea of the man's character. The whole conception of the place rested squarely on the royal splendors of the Old World. The lines of the huge building were a combination of two famous castles of medieval France, both the homes of kings. The great hall was an exact copy in form and decoration of the throne room of Napoleon in the palace at Versailles.

His library walls above the bookcases bristled with

arms and armor. Anything more utterly undemocratic could not have been found in the centers of Europe.

The atmosphere of the place was stifling.

Vassar turned to Virginia with a movement of impatience.

"You like this?" he asked.

"I think it very imposing," was the diplomatic answer.

"So do I," he snapped, "and that's why I loathe it. Such ostentation in a democracy whose life is just beginning can mean but one thing. The man who built this castle to crown the highest hill of a city is capable of building a throne in the East Room of the White House if the time ever comes that he dares—"

Virginia shook her head good-humoredly.

"I'm afraid you're prejudiced against our patron saint."

"No," Vassar answered steadily, "I'm not prejudiced. I hate him with the hatred that is uncompromising— that's all. There's not room for the two things for which we stand in this republic. One of us must live, the other die."

"I suppose a woman doesn't look on such a house as this with your eyes," she answered smiling.

"No, that's just it—you don't—and it's one of the reasons why I'm afraid of you—"

116

Vassar turned to examine the collection of chain armor at the end of the room without waiting for her answer. He was in a bad humor. The place had gotten on his nerves.

When he returned again, regretting his curt speech, she was standing at the entrance talking in low tones to Waldron. His footstep had made no sound on the cushion of oriental rugs which covered the inlaid marble floor.

Without so much as a look his way she passed Waldron and left the library.

The banker walked briskly toward Vassar and waved his short, heavy arm toward a chair.

"Won't you sit down, sir?" he asked coldly.

With mechanical precision he opened a jeweled cigarette box and extended it.

"Thanks," Vassar answered carelessly, "I have a cigar."

He struck a match on his heel, lit the cigar and seated himself leisurely.

Waldron sat down opposite and began his attack without delay.

"Miss Holland has just informed me that you are unalterably opposed to woman's suffrage?"

"Until I see it differently, I am," was the tense reply.

"I take it then that it will be a waste of words for us to discuss that question?"

"Yes—and before we waste words on any other question I must ask whom you represent in this conference concerning my career?"

"I'll tell you with pleasure," was the quick answer. "I am perhaps the largest contributor to the cause of woman's suffrage—"

"Do you believe in it?" Vassar interrupted sharply.

Waldron weighed his answer and spoke with metallic emphasis.

"Whether I do or do not is beside the mark for the moment. You have settled that issue between us, and my views are of no importance. I am pressing for a woman's victory for a more important reason than my faith in her ballot or my lack of faith in its ultimate effects. The immediate result of women's vote will be to make war remote. My big purpose is to prevent this nation from sinking into the abyss of militarism in which Europe now flounders—"

"In other words," Vassar broke in, "you mean to prevent this country from preparing to defend herself from the power of Imperial Europe?"

Waldron searched his opponent for a moment of intense silence and slowly answered:

"If you care to put it that way—yes. I represent

the combined forces of peace and sanity in this nation. We have determined that America shall not be cursed by the military caste. We are determined that our country shall not follow in the mad blind race of the Old World in building armaments with which to murder our fellow men. I have made no secret of my purpose and I am going to win. I am going to defeat your bill to place our army and navy on the footing of war-cursed Europe—"

"My bill does not propose to establish a military caste," Vassar protested. "It only demands a trained citizen soldiery for adequate defense, armed and ready to enter the field, an effective wall of patriotic fire if we are assailed. I ask a navy that will be absolutely sure to sink the fleet of any power that may attack us. I do not ask that this fleet shall be in constant commission, only that it shall be built and ready for service."

"Your demand is preposterous," Waldron coldly answered. "You ask for a bond issue of $500,000,000 for naval purposes only—"

"Anything less will be inadequate. We are behind the world in guns, behind the world in aircraft, behind the world in submarines. We invented the aeroplane. We invented the machine gun. We invented the iron-clad. We invented the submarine. We must lead the world in these arms of defense—not follow, the last lame duck in the march! An *inadequate* navy no matter how great its size is worse than none. It will merely lead us into trouble and murder our defenders. War is now a merciless science. Skill, not physical courage, wins. The machine has become the master of the world—"

"Please!" Waldron cried with hand uplifted in a gesture of impatience. "I know your speech by heart. It's old. It doesn't interest me. Come to the point. If you'll agree as chairman of the Committee on Military Affairs to modify your bill to train and arm a million citizen soldiers, and reduce your naval programme to two battleships, four cruisers, twenty-four submarines and twenty-four aeroplanes, we can come to terms—"

Vassar rose, fixed his opponent with a searching look and said:

"I'll see you in hell first—"

"All right," Waldron snapped. "I'm going to wipe you off the map. There'll be a new chairman of your Committee when Congress meets in December—"

Vassar held his enemy with a steady gaze.

"You haven't enough dirty money to buy my district, Waldron," he answered. "We're a humble people on the East Side, but I'll show you that there are some things in this town that are not for sale—"

A smile of contempt played about the banker's cold lips as he rose.

"I'll be there when you make the demonstration," he responded with careful emphasis.

"You'll excuse me now?" Vassar said politely.

"Certainly. My car will drop you at any address you name."

"Thank you, I prefer the subway."

"As you like," the metallic voice clicked.

CHAPTER XI

VASSAR turned with a quick movement, passed into the hall and ran squarely into Virginia who was about to enter the library.

"Your interview at an end so soon? I took a turn in the garden for only five minutes. I was to join your conference. You have quarreled?"

"No—just agreed to fight, that's all—"

"A compromise is impossible?"

"Utterly—"

"I am sorry," she answered gravely.

The iron doors of the elevator softly opened with a low click and two slender young men of decidedly foreign features stepped briskly out, accompanied by the tall, straight figure of Villard. They crossed the hall and ascended the broad stairway as if at home. The clothes of the younger men were fitted with extreme care. The waist line was gracefully modeled. It was evident that they both wore corsets. They walked with the quick, measured tread of the trained soldier. From their yachting caps it was evident they had just entered the house through the tunnel from the river landing.

Their slight waxed mustaches particularly caught Vassar's attention and brought a smile of contempt. Undoubtedly they were the pampered darlings of a foreign court, friends of Waldron's whom he was cultivating for some purpose. The Congressman wondered what the devil they could be doing in America when all the Old World was at war? He also wondered who Villard was—Villard with his fierce upturned mustache after the style of von Hindenberg. They might be South Americans or from the Balkan states of course. Waldron's banking house was one of the international group and his agents came from every corner of the globe.

When they had passed Virginia quietly asked:

"May I go downtown with you?"

In the tumult of anger that still raged within over Waldron's challenge the incongruity of the proposal struck him with new force. The offer seemed almost brazen. Under conditions of a normal environment it would have meant nothing more than a pretty attempt to console him in an hour of disappointment. Coming at the moment of his departure from the sinister establishment of the man he hated, it struck him as suggestive of a secret understanding between the two.

His one desire now was to be alone and breathe clean air.

"You'll not like the long rough walk to the subway I'm afraid," he protested.

"You will not return in the car?" she asked in surprise.

"I prefer to walk—"

"You'll do nothing of the kind," she answered firmly. "You'll go with me—and I'm not going to walk."

"You must excuse me"—he persisted.

"I will not. And I'll never speak to you again unless you obey my orders for this one afternoon at least."

He searched her face to see if she meant it, caught the look of determination and answered in quick tones of apology.

"Of course, if you really wish it, you know that it will give me pleasure—"

Virginia returned to the library, spoke to Waldron and in a few minutes they were again seated by each other's side swiftly gliding down the Drive.

"Stop at the Claremont," she called to the chauffeur. "I'm starved. We would have had lunch served in the library if your lordship had not been so proud and particular—"

"I couldn't eat at Waldron's table. I'd choke," he answered in low tones.

"I'm afraid you're not a good politician after all,"

she observed. "You are too emotional. You allow your temperament to betray you into errors of diplomacy. You should have cultivated Waldron, flattered his vanity and studied his character—"

"I know it already—"

"I thought so at first myself," she answered thoughtfully. "The more I see of him the less I know him. He's a puzzle—"

"He's merely an ape of foreign snobs—that's all."

"You utterly misjudge him," Virginia protested. "He has too much strength for that. His ambitions are too great."

"Then he's more dangerous than I have thought."

"What do you mean?" she asked in surprise.

"Nothing that I could put into words without making myself ridiculous in your eyes perhaps, yet the idea grows on me—"

Virginia laughed.

"You can't do an opponent justice, can you?"

"No—can you?"

The car swept gracefully up the roadway to the rose-embowered white cottage on the hill. They leaped out and found a table in the corner overlooking the majestic sweep of the river and Jersey hills beyond.

Vassar was moody in spite of the inspiring view and the radiant face opposite. Again and again he tried to pull himself out of the dumps and enjoy this wonderful hour with the most fascinating woman he had ever met. It was no use. Waldron's frozen smile, his royal establishment, his corseted pets, his big friend with the fierce mustache, his white yacht and the soft click of the doors of that elevator filled his mind with sinister suggestions.

"I'm so disappointed in you," Virginia said at last.

"Why?"

"I'd planned to relax a little this afternoon. It's Saturday you know. I thought you might be human enough just to play for a few hours. I wanted to find the real man side of you—not the statesman or the politician—"

"To study me under the microscope as another specimen of the species and plan my extermination?"

"No—to get acquainted in the simplest kind of old-fashioned way. But I see it's no use today. You're a greater enigma to me than Waldron. But I'm not going to be beaten so easily. I'm going to find you out now that I've made up my mind. I've a proposal to make before we begin the scrap in your district—"

"A proposal?" he asked mischievously.

"Yes! It's hardly decent I know. Anyhow, I'm not wholly responsible for it. You've made a wonderful hit with my old soldier Dad. He has talked

126

nothing else but your bill for an adequate national defense. He has positively ordered me to make you our guest for a couple of weeks at our country place on Long Island—"

Vassar blushed like a schoolboy.

"I should be only too happy—"

"I warn you that the Old Guard will talk you into a spell of sickness about war and the certainty of this country being captured by the Germans or Japs—"

"He can't say too much to me on that subject," Vassar declared.

"And if you'll bring your father and the children I'm sure we could keep you until I've wormed the last secret out of you—"

"It wouldn't be imposing on you?"

"You would do us a favor. Zonia would keep Billy at home. Marya and your father would be an endless source of joy to my mother. We've a big old house and a lot of vacant rooms. You'll bring them all?"

"My dear Miss Holland," he answered gratefully, "you overwhelm me with your kindness. My father and the kids have never been so honored. You will make them supremely happy—"

"You see," Virginia interrupted, "I've a scheme back of this invitation. I've not only determined to find you out, but I'm a politician whether you like it or not.

127

I'm going to make it just as difficult as I possibly can for you to fight me. You'll walk into the trap with your eyes wide open—"

"I absolve you from all responsibility for my ruin," he laughed.

"You'll join us at Babylon on Sunday?"

"Tomorrow?"

"The sooner the better. We go down this evening—"

The clouds suddenly lifted. Vassar couldn't keep his face straight. He was so happy it was absurd. An hour ago he was in the depths of despair. The foundations of the nation's life were sinking. The sky had cleared. The sun was sparkling on the waters of the river in dazzling splendor. The world was beautiful and the country safe.

His mind was planning absurd programs for each day. He wondered for just a moment if she could be capable of plotting with Waldron to remove him from the district for two weeks, to lay the foundations of a movement to wreck his career—

He looked into the depths of her brown eyes and threw the ugly thought to the winds.

CHAPTER XII

VASSAR determined that every day of the two weeks at Babylon should be red lettered in his life. He had never taken a vacation; nor had his father. It was time to adopt this good custom of the country. It was mid-July. The campaign would not really be under way until October. There was nothing to worry about. Neither the suffragettes with their organization nor Waldron with his money could break his hold on the hearts of his people.

He gave himself up to the sheer joy of living for the first time in life. Through the long glorious early days he drove with Virginia in her little dogcart about the beautiful country roads of Long Island. He had never dreamed the panoramas of ravishing landscape that stretched away in endless beauty. He found gentle hills and valleys, babbling brooks and shady woods and always seaward the solemn white sand dunes of the beach and the changing mirror of the bay reflecting their shining forms. On days when the wind was right the far-away roar of the surf could be distinctly heard.

Each day alone with the charming and brilliant

woman by his side had led him deeper and deeper into the mazes of a fascination that had become resistless. They talked with deep earnestness of the great things of life and eternity. She made no effort to conceal her keen personal interest in the man she was studying.

With deliberate purpose she had abandoned herself to the romantic situation of being sought and courted by a handsome, fascinating man. He wondered vaguely if she were experimenting with her own character, and merely using him for the moment for the purpose of chemical reaction? He shivered at the uncanny idea. It was disconcerting. She might be capable of such a gruesome process. For the life of him he couldn't make out as yet whether such a woman was capable of real passion.

There was no longer any doubt about his own situation. He had faced the fact squarely. He was in love—madly, passionately, hopelessly—the one grand passion of mature manhood. Its violence frightened him. He was afraid to put it to the test with a declaration. He must wait and be sure of a response on her part. There was too much at stake to bungle such an issue. If he could win her by surrender on the suffrage question, he would give her two ballots if she wanted them. He knew her character too well to believe that such ignoble surrender of principle merely to please could succeed. She would accept his help in her cause and despise him for a weakling in her heart.

As the time drew near that he must go he knew with increasing fear the supreme hour of life had struck. He must put his fate to the test. He took his seat in a rowboat facing her and drifted into the silver sea of moon, fully determined. An hour passed and he had only spoken commonplace nothings. With each effort his courage grew weaker.

If she were like other girls he would have dared it. "Faint heart ne'er won fair lady," he kept repeating as he tried in vain to screw his mind up to the point of speech. It was no use. She was not the fair lady of song and story. She had a disconcerting way of demanding the reason for things.

He gave it up at last and spent an evening of supreme happiness drifting and listening to the soft round flute-like notes of her voice. He would speak tomorrow. They had two days more. Tomorrow they were to take a long ride down the smooth road to Southampton in her little runabout. She was an expert at the wheel of an automobile and they had explored the whole south side of Long Island in the past five days.

He had grown to love the peace and charm of this wonderful isle—homes—homes—homes—everywhere! laughing children played beside the roadways. Smiling boys and girls made hill and valley ring with joy.

He had promised Zonia and Marya to take the cottage across the turnpike in front of the spacious lawn of the Holland homestead and let them spend the summer there. His father had joined in their clamor and he had consented. The cottage was furnished and a power launch went with it for a reasonable rent. They were to move down next week. There would be but two days' break in the new life they had begun in this fairyland of sun and sky, trees and flowers, laughing waters and shining seas.

Why should he press his suit? He would wait and see more of her. And then the crisis came that hurled him headlong into a decision.

CHAPTER XIII

THE idea that her child might attain the highest honor within the reach of any man on earth had stirred Angela to the depths and given new meaning and dignity to life. She lifted her head. She had borne a child whose word might bend a million wills to his. The world was a bigger, nobler place in which to live.

She was stirred with sudden purpose to leave no stone unturned to bring this dream to pass. She bought books of the lives of the presidents. Twice she read the life of Abraham Lincoln, the humble backwoodsman rail-splitter who became president.

But her vivid Italian imagination loved the stories of George Washington, the first president, best. He was nearest in history to Columbus, the Italian who discovered America. She read the legends of little George Washington's adventures and began to play the mighty drama of her own son's career by guiding his feet in the same path.

She had laughed immoderately over George cutting his father's cherry-tree. She was sure her bambino

133

was capable of that! If George cut cherry-trees, of course his father had cherries to eat. She got at once a lot of cherries and fed them to the boy, laughing and nursing her dream.

She found a picture of Washington in his Colonial dress. The style pleased her fancy. She went forthwith, bought the material and made her boy a suit with cockade hat exactly like it.

Tommaso was amazed on entering the living-room from the fruit store to find the kid arrayed in the strange garb. Angela was stuffing some cotton under the cockade hat to make it fit, studying the picture to be sure of the effect.

When she explained, Tommaso joined in the play with equal zest.

When the boy had exhausted the admiration of his father and mother he sallied forth into the street to meet his little friends and show his clothes.

He had scarcely cleared the door when "Sausage" emerged from the Schultz delicatessen store and the two met halfway. No hard feelings had lingered from their fight in the old Armory. Sausage's admiration was boundless. He had just persuaded little Tommaso to go home and show them to his own mother when they turned and saw Meyer unloading a truck filled with curious looking long boxes.

They ran up to investigate just as a case fell and a gun dropped to the pavement.

The kids rushed to Benda's to tell Angela and Tommaso.

"I told you that man was no good!" Angela exclaimed. "Go—and see quick and we tell Vasa'—"

Tommaso hurried across the street and found Meyer standing over the broken case. Meyer faced the Italian without ceremony:

"Cost your life to open your yap about these guns—see?"

Tommaso snapped his finger in the other's face:

"Go t'ell!"

He turned on his heel to go, saw his wife and the children near, rushed back and snapped his finger again in Meyer's face:

"Go t'ell two times—see—two times!"

Meyer merely held his gaze in a moment of angry silence and turned to his work.

Tommaso rushed back into his flat, pushed things from the table, seized a pen and wrote a hurried note to his leader.

CONGRESSMAN VASA:

Men unload guns in our street. He say killa me if I tell. I tell him go t'ell. I tell him go

135

t'ell two times. I Americano. My kid he be
president—maybe—

Tommaso Benda.

He hurried Angela into her best new American cut
dress and sent her with the boy to Long Island to tell
Vassar.

The visit all but ended in a tragedy for poor Angela.
While searching the spacious Holland grounds for her
leader, the boy suddenly spied a hatchet with which
the master had been mending a box in which he was
cultivating a precious orange-tree that had been
carefully guarded in a hothouse during the winter
months.

The kid saw his chance to emulate the example of
George Washington. He lost no time. The tree was
well hacked before Holland pounced upon him.

The old man had him by the ear when Angela dashed
to the rescue. She saw the scarred tree with horror
and her apologies were profuse.

"Ah, pardon, signor! You see his little suit—he
play George Wash—and cutta the cherry-tree—"

She paused and shook the boy fiercely.

"Ah—you maka me seek!"

Holland began to smile at the roguish beauty of the
boy glancing up from the corners of his dark, beautiful eyes.

136

Vassar, Virginia, Zonia and Marya hearing the commotion, rushed up.

Angela extended her apologies to all.

"You see, he really think he's leetle George Wash—I mak him speak his piece—you like to hear it?"

Her offer was greeted by a chorus of approval.

Angela fixed the child with a stern look.

"Speeka your piece!"

The boy shook his head.

"Speeka-your-piece!" The order was a threat this time and little Tommaso yielded.

Bowing gracefully, he faced the group and recited with brave accent:

> My Country, 'tis of thee
> I cutta the cherry-tree,
> Sweet land of libertee
> My name is George Wash!

He bowed again as all laughed and applauded. Virginia took him in her arms and kissed him. While she was yet complimenting the boy on his fine speech Angela whispered to Vassar:

"My man Tommaso—he want to see you, signor! He send this—"

She slipped the note into Vassar's hand, repeated her apologies and hurried from the lawn, shaking Tommaso:

"Ah, you leetle mik! You maka me seek—! I tella you play George Wash and cutta the cherry-tree—and oh, my Mother of God! You play hell and cutta the *orange*-tree!"

Little Tommaso took the scolding philosophically. Orange or cherry-trees were all the same to him. He merely answered his mother's dramatic rage with a twinkle of his eye until she stooped at last and kissed him.

CHAPTER XIV

VASSAR looked at the scrawled note and saw that he must return to the city. The incident probably meant nothing and yet it brought to his mind a vague uneasiness.

He instinctively turned to Virginia who was looking at him with curious interest. She spoke with genuine admiration:

"I had no idea that any politician in America could win the hearts of his people in the way you hold yours—"

"It's worth while, isn't it?"

"Decidedly. It makes my regret all the more keen that you will not accompany me on my tour of the state—"

"You go soon?" he asked.

"I leave Monday morning for a month. It has been one of my dreams since we met that I'd win you—and we'd make a sort of triumphal tour together—"

"You're joking," he answered lightly.

"I know now that it is not to be, of course," she said seriously.

139

He hadn't thought of her being on such a fool trip. Waldron no doubt as her campaign financier would meet her at many points. The thought set the blood pounding from his heart.

"Shall we sit down a moment?" he suggested.

"By all means if I can persuade you," she consented.

Behind a rich fir on the lawn stood a massive marble seat. They strolled to the spot and sat down. Hours of debate they had held here and neither had yielded an inch. A circular trellis of roses hid the house from view and sheltered the seat from the gaze of people who might be crossing the open space. The hedge along the turnpike completely hid them from the highway.

By a subtle instinct she felt the wave of emotion from his tense mind.

A long silence fell between them. Her last speech had given him the cue for his question. He had brooded over its possible meaning from the moment she had expressed the idea. He picked a pebble from the ground, shot it from his fingers as he had done with marbles when a boy.

Lifting his head with a serious look straight into her brown eyes he said:

"Did you believe for a moment that I could go with you on such a campaign tour?"

She met his gaze squarely.

"I thought it too good to be true, of course, and yet your unexpected sympathy and your—your—shall I say, frankly expressed admiration, led me into all sorts of silly hopes."

"And yet you knew on a moment's reflection that such a surrender of principle by a man of my character was out of the question."

"It has turned out to be so," she answered slowly.

"Could you have respected me had I cut a complete intellectual and moral somersault merely at the wave of your beautiful hand?"

"I could respect any man who yields to reason," she fenced.

He smiled.

"I didn't ask you that—"

"No?"

"You're fencing. And I must come to the real issue between us. I do it with fear and trembling and with uncovered head. I had to be true to the best that's in me with you for the biggest reason that can sway an honest man's soul. I have loved you from the moment we met—"

He stopped short and breathed deeply, afraid to face her. His declaration had called for no answer. She

141

remained silent. From the corner of his eye he noted the tightening of her firm lips.

"I've tried to tell you so a dozen times this week and failed. I was afraid, it meant so much to me. I had hoped to be with you another month at least in this beautiful world of sunlight and flowers, of moon and sea. I hoped to win you with a little more time and patience. But I couldn't wait and see you go on this trip. I had to speak. I love you with the love a strong man can give but once in life. It's strange that of all the women in the world I should have loved the one whose work I must oppose! You'll believe me when I tell you that the fiercest battle I have ever fought was with the Devil when he whispered that I might win by hedging and trimming and lying diplomatically as men have done before and many men will do again. At least you respect me for the honesty with which I have met this issue?"

He had asked her a direct question at last. Her silence had become unendurable. Her answer was scarcely audible. She only breathed it.

"Yes, I understand and respect you for it—"

His heart gave a throb of hope.

"I don't ask you if you love me now. I just want to know if I've a chance to win you?"

The impulse to seize her hand was resistless. She

made no effort to withdraw it and he pressed it tenderly.

A wistful smile played about the sensitive mouth and she was slow to answer.

"Tell me—have I a chance?" he pleaded.

Her voice was far away but clear-toned music. He heard his doom in its perfect rhythm before the words were complete.

"I can't see," she began slowly, "how two people could enter the sweet intimacy of marriage with a vital difference of opinion dividing them. I couldn't. Your honesty and intellectual strength I admire. This honesty and strength will keep us opponents. Such an union is unthinkable—"

"Not if we love one another," he protested eagerly. "There is but one issue in human life between man and woman and that is love. If you love me, nothing else matters—"

She shook her head.

"It isn't true. You love me—but other things matter. Otherwise you would give them up to win your love. I claim to be your equal in brain and heart if not in muscle. You say that if I love nothing else matters and yet you say in the same breath that you risk your love to save your principles. In your heart you know that other things do matter, and with me they matter deeply.

I believe with every beat of my heart that the progress of the world waits on the advent of women in the organization of its industries, its politics and its thinking. This consciousness of her mission in the modern woman is the biggest fact of our century—"

She paused and faced him with a look of iron purpose.

"No matter if I did love you—I'd tear that love out of my heart if it held me back from the fulfilment of the highest ideal of duty to my sex—"

"What higher ideal can any woman hold than her home?"

"For the woman whose horizon is no larger there can be none. She can only see the world in which she moves. To some of us God has given the wider view. What is one life if it is sacrificed to this higher ideal? You are leading the renaissance of America. So am I. Our beautiful country with her teeming millions must rise in her glory and live forever when you and I have passed on. The soldier sees this vision when he dies in battle. So I see it today."

He stooped again and gathered a handful of pebbles, rolling them thoughtfully in his hand. His eyes were on the ground.

"It isn't Waldron?" he asked.

She smiled with a touch of mischief.

144

"No. But I confess such a man might tempt me—"

He threw the pebbles on the ground with a gesture of impatience.

"It's not true!" he cried, facing her suddenly. With a fierce resolution he seized her hand.

"I won't take any such answer," he breathed desperately. "You're not playing this game fairly with me. I've torn my heart open to you. You're hedging and trimming. I won't have it. You haven't dared to deny your love. You can't deny it. You love me and you know it and I know it—"

She lifted her free hand in a gesture of protest.

"You love me! I feel it! I know it!" he repeated fiercely.

With quick resolution he swept her into his arms and kissed her lips again and again. For just an instant he felt her body relax.

The next minute she had freed herself and faced him, her eyes blazing with anger. Her anger was not a pose. He saw to his horror that he had staked all on a mad chance and lost.

He stammered something incoherent and mopped his brow lamely.

"I suppose it's useless for me to say I'm sorry—"

"Quite," she said with cold emphasis.

"All right I won't. Because I'm not sorry I did it.

145

I'm only sorry you resent it. I love you. True love is half madness. I won't apologize. If I must die for that one moment, it's worth it."

"There can be nothing more between us after this," she said evenly.

He bowed in silence.

"Please play the little farce of polite society before my father and mother as you leave tonight. It's the only favor I ask of you."

"I understand," he answered.

CHAPTER XV

THE perfection with which Virginia played her part in the little drama of deception at their parting was a new source of surprise and anger to Vassar. Her acting was consummate. Neither the children nor her parents could suspect for a moment that there had been the slightest break in their relations.

Self-respect compelled him to act the part with equal care in detail.

The old soldier had grown very fond of Marya. He held her in his arms chattering like a magpie.

"Now don't you go back on me when you get to town and fail to take that cottage!" he protested.

"Oh, we're coming on Tuesday—aren't we, Uncle John?" she cried.

Virginia watched his face. He caught the look and answered its challenge by an instant reply.

"Certainly, dear. Everything's fixed. I can't be with you much but grandpa'll be here every day."

The child clapped her hands.

"You see"—

"All right," Holland answered. "I'll meet you at

147

the station! The fact is—" his voice dropped to confidential tones—"between you and me—I haven't any little girl. My girl's grown clean up and out of my world. She's going on a wild goose chase over the country and leave her old daddy here to die alone. But you'll be my little girl, won't you, honey?"

Marya slipped her arms around his neck and whispered:

"I'd like two granddaddies. I never had but one you know—"

Virginia wondered at Vassar's audacity in persisting in the plan of thrusting himself and his people under her nose. She had thought he would have the decency to change his plans now that any further association between them had become impossible. She listened in vain for any protest on his part against the plans of happiness between her father and his little niece. His face was a mask of polite indifference.

She had worked herself into a rage when he extended his hand in parting. The others were looking or he would have omitted the formality. He made up his mind to part without a word.

The children and his father turned to enter the coach. Billy was saying good-bye to Zonia assuring her for the tenth time that he would drive with his father to the train for them on Tuesday.

With the touch of her hand Vassar's angry resolution melted. Soul and body was fused suddenly into a resistless rush of tenderness. If she felt this she was complete mistress of her emotions. There was no sign.

In a voice of studied coldness she merely said:

"Good-bye."

His hand closed desperately on hers in spite of her purpose to withdraw it instantly.

"I won't say it," he answered fiercely. "I won't give you up. You haven't treated me fairly. I won't submit. I'm coming again—do you hear?"

She stared at him a moment with firmly set lips and answered:

"There is nothing in common between us, Mr. Caveman. We live in different worlds. We were born in different ages—"

He dropped her hand and sprang to the platform of the moving train without looking back.

CHAPTER XVI

ARRIVING at Stuyvesant Square, Vassar decided to go at once and see Angela's husband. The door of his tiny apartment opened on the little crooked street before the old Armory. He caught the gay colors of Angela's dress at the window. She was leaning far out over the flower boxes, and gesticulating to her man in the street below.

Benda, the center of a group of children, was playing the hand organ which Pasquale had given the boy. The kids were dancing.

He stopped short his music at the sight of his leader, waved the children aside and hurried to meet him.

"Ah, you come so soon, signor!" he exclaimed. "I am glad. Angela—she tell you?"

"Yes. What's the trouble?"

"You see the house over dere?"

He pointed to the low apartment across the way.

"Yes."

"Well, signor, men unload and swing boxes—beeg—long boxes inside. One of them fell and brak—"

He stopped and looked about.

"It was guns, signor!—all bright, new. I ask them what for they put so many guns in the old house. The boss say I must join his Black Hand Alliance—" Benda laughed. "I tell him go t'ell—

"He say it's war and I die unless I do—I tell him go t'ell two times. And I send word to you, signor. What you tink?"

"I don't know. I'll find the owner of the building and tell you. Thanks, Tommaso," he added cordially. "I appreciate your confidence. I'll see about it."

"Si, si, signor!"

With another wave of his hand to the children Benda resumed his concert.

Vassar walked to the door and glanced at the building. There was nothing to mark it from a number of dingy structures along the East River. A speculator was probably buying old guns from our government for their transfer in secret to the agent of a faction in Mexico or South America. Naturally the trader must use the utmost caution or a Secret Service man would nip his plans in the bud. He was so sure of the explanation that he took it for granted, and dismissed the incident from his mind.

He was destined to recall it under conditions that would not be forgotten.

CHAPTER XVII

VASSAR plunged next day into his fight. Waldron had moved rapidly. His opponents had already nominated an Independent Democrat of foreign birth, a Bohemian of ability, whom he knew to be a man of ambition and good address.

The women had begun a house to house canvass of voters and the number of fairy-tales they had started for the purpose of undermining his position and influence was a startling revelation of their skill in the art of lying.

Virginia Holland was booked for a canvass of each election district the last week in October. He knew what that meant. Waldron had held his trump card for the supreme moment.

The depths of vituperation, mendacity and open corruption to which the campaign descended on the part of his opponents was another revelation to Vassar of woman's adaptability to practical methods. Never since the days of Tweed's régime had the East Side seen anything that approached it.

152

He steadfastly refused to lower his standard to their level. That Virginia Holland knew the methods which Waldron had adopted was inconceivable. Vassar watched the approach of her canvass with indifference. If his people were weak enough to fall for Waldron and his crowd of hirelings, he had no desire longer to represent the district.

He ceased to worry about results. He foresaw that his majority would be reduced. He decided to let it go at that.

The gulf which separated him now from the woman he loved was apparently too deep to be bridged. On the last night of the canvass he slipped into the meeting at which she spoke just to hear her voice again. He half hoped that she might say something so false and provoking about his record that he might hate her for it. Her address was one of lofty and pure appeal for the redemption of humanity through the trained spiritual power of womanhood. She even expressed her regret at the necessity of opposing a man of the type of John Vassar.

A hundred of Vassar's partisans were present and burst into a fierce round of applause at the mention of his name. He watched the effect with breathless interest. The cheers were utterly unexpected on the part of the speaker, and threw her for the moment off her balance. She blushed and smiled and hesitated, fumbling for words.

Vassar's heart was pounding like a trip hammer. He could have taken the boys in his arms and carried them through the streets for that cheer. No one knew of his presence. He had slipped into a back seat in the gallery unrecognized in the dim light.

Why had she blushed when they cheered his name? The crowd, of course, could not know of the secret between them. Would she have blushed from the mere confusion of mind which the hostile sentiment of her hearers had provoked? It was possible. And yet the faintest hope thrilled his heart that she cared for him. He had played the fool to lose his head that day. He realized it now. Such a woman could not be taken by storm. Every instinct of pride and intellectual dignity had resented it.

He went home happy over the incident with the memory of her scarlet cheeks and the sweet seriousness of her voice filling his soul. His managers brought glowing reports of the situation in his district. It didn't matter if he had a chance to win Virginia.

The results proved that his guess of a reduced majority was correct. He barely pulled through by the skin of his teeth. His margin was a paltry seven hundred and fifty. At the election two years before it had been more than six thousand.

When Congress met in December he was confronted with a situation unique in the history of the Republic. A lobby had gathered in Washington so distinguished in personnel, so great in numbers, so aggressive in its purpose to control legislation, that the national representatives were afraid of their shadows.

The avowed aim of this vast gathering was the defeat of his bill for the adequate defense of the nation. The outlines of his measures had been published and had the unanimous backing of the Army and Navy Boards, the National Security League and all the leaders of the great political parties.

Both of our ex-Presidents, Roosevelt and Taft, had endorsed it and asked for its adoption. It was known that the President and his Cabinet approved its main features. And yet its chances of adoption were considered extremely doubtful.

The lobby, which had swarmed into Washington, overran its hotels, and camped in the corridors of the Capitol, was composed of a class of men and women who had never before ventured on such a mission. What they lacked of experience they made up in aggressive insolence—an insolence so cocksure of itself that a

Congressman rarely ventured from the floor of the Chamber if he could avoid it.

The leaders of the movement were apparently acting under the orders of the Reverend A. Cuthbert Pike, President of the Peace Union. Vassar was amazed to find that this Union was composed of more than six hundred chartered peace societies. He had supposed that there might be half a dozen such associations in the country. To be suddenly confronted by five thousand delegates representing six hundred organizations was the shock of his political life. But one society alone, the National Security League, was there to preach the necessity of insurance against war by an adequate defense.

Against this lone organization were arrayed in a single group the five thousand delegates from the six hundred peace societies. They demanded the defeat of any bill to increase our armaments in any way, shape or form. Their aim was the ultimate complete disarmament of every fort and the destruction of our navy.

In co-operation with this host of five thousand fanatics stood the Honorable Plato Barker with a personal following in the membership of Congress as amazing as it was dangerous to the future of the Republic. The admirers of the silver-tongued orator labored under the conviction that their leader had been inspired of God to guide the destinies of America. They believed this with the faith of children. For sixteen years they had accepted his leadership without question and his word was the law of their life.

Barker was opposed to the launching of another ship of war, or the mounting of another gun for defense. He was the uncompromising champion of moral suasion as the solution of all international troubles. He believed that an eruption of Mount Vesuvius could be soothed by a poultice and cured permanently by an agreement for arbitration. He preached this doctrine in season and out of season. The more seriously out of season the occasion, the louder he preached it.

That he would have a following in Congress was early developed in the session. Barker was not only on the ground daily; his headquarters had been supplied with unlimited money for an active propaganda and his office was thronged by delegates from his mass meetings called in every state of the Union.

The Socialists had once more swamped the American labor unions with their missionaries and the labor federations were arrayed solidly against an increase of our army or navy.

But by far the most serious group of opponents by whom Vassar was confronted were the United Women Voters of America, marshalled under the leadership of the brilliant young Joan of Arc of the Federated Clubs. In the peculiar alignment of factions produced by the crisis of the world war the women voters held the balance of power. They practically controlled the Western states while the fear of their influence dominated the Middle West and seriously shaped public opinion in the East. Pennsylvania, New Jersey and New York had defeated the amendments for woman's suffrage, yet the vote polled by their advocates had been so large the defeat was practically a triumph of their principles.

A convention of five hundred delegates, representatives of the women voters, had been called to decide on the casting of the votes of their senators and representatives. That their orders would be obeyed was a foregone conclusion. To refuse meant political suicide.

The thing which puzzled Vassar beyond measure was the mysterious unifying power somewhere in the shadows. The hand of this unseen master of ceremonies had brought these strangely incongruous forces together in a harmony so perfect that they spoke and wrote and campaigned as one man. Behind this master hand there was a single master mind tremendous in grip, baffling, inscrutable, always alert, always there. That Waldron was this mysterious force he suspected from the first. On the day he was booked to make the final address in closing the debate on his bill, the banker boldly appeared in the open as the responsible leader of the movement for the defeat of national defense.

Vassar, with a sense of sickening rage, saw him in conference with Virginia Holland and her executive committee. They held their little preliminary caucus at the door of the House of Representatives, as if to insult him with a notice of coming defeat. The young leader knew that if there were yet a man in the House who could be reached by money, Waldron would find him. And he knew that there were some who had their price.

The influence of such a man in a free democracy was to Vassar a cause of constant grief and wonder. That he despised the principles of a democratic government he scarcely took the trouble to conceal. His pose was for higher ends than party gains or even the selfish glory of nation. He was large, his vision world-wide. He pleaded always for the advancement of humanity. His following was numerous and eminently respectable. Vassar had never for one moment believed in Waldron's adherence to the principles of American democracy. That he would form a monarchy if given the chance was a certainty. One of his hobbies was the criminal extravagance and inefficiency of our state and municipal

159

governments as compared to the imperial kingdoms of the Old World. In season and out of season he proclaimed the superiority of centralized power over the ignorant, slipshod ways of the Republic. The Emperor of Germany and the German ways of ruling were his models.

To accuse Waldron of a conspiracy with the crowned heads of the Old World would be received with scornful incredulity. And yet there were moments in his brooding and thinking when Vassar felt that that was the only rational solution of the man's life and character. That he was the personal friend of three crowned heads was well known. That he was in constant consultation with the ambassadors of a dozen European nations was also well known. The explanation of this fact, however, was so simple and plausible that no suspicion of treachery would find credence in America. His bank had branch establishments in London, Paris, Berlin, Petrograd, Vienna, Constantinople and Rome.

And yet, why in God's name, Vassar kept asking himself, should all these peace societies and all these labor organizations and all these women's clubs move heaven and earth in unison to kill this one measure of defense, and leave our nation at the mercy of any first-class European power? Their sentimental leanings were against arms and armaments—of course. But who set them all barking at the same moment? Who had kept them at it in chorus continuously from the first throb of the patriotic impulse to put ourselves in readiness to defend our life? Who had held them together in this fierce and determined assault on the Capitol to arouse and threaten Congress? No such movement could be caused by spontaneous combustion. Such an agitation against patriotic defense could not happen by accident. The world war could not have caused it. The great war should have been the one influence to have had precisely the opposite effect. The world war should have spoken to us in thunder tones:

"Remember Belgium! Eternal vigilance is the price of liberty!"

Instead of this, the advocates of peace suddenly rose as a swarm of locusts to tell us that, as umbrellas cause rain so guns cause war, and the only way to save ourselves in a world of snarling, maddened wild beasts is to lay down our arms and appeal to their reason! This strange crusade to make the richest nation of the world defenseless was no accident. The movement was sinister. Vassar felt this on the last day of his struggle in the House with increased foreboding.

He rose to deliver his final appeal with quivering heart. His eye rested on Waldron's stolid, sneering face in the gallery. On his right sat Barker, on his left Virginia Holland.

Every seat on the floor and in the galleries was packed. Every foot of standing room above and below was crowded. A solemn hush fell on the throng as the young leader of the House rose.

He began his address in low tones of intense emotion:

"Mr. Speaker, I rise to give to this House my solemn warning that on the fate of this bill for the defense of the nation hangs our destiny. I've done my work. I've fought a good fight. The decision is in your hands. A few things I would repeat until they ring their alarm in every soul within the sound of my voice to-day.

"I tell you with the certainty of positive knowledge that while we are the richest nation of the known world we are the least prepared to defend ourselves under the conditions of modern war. Our navy is good —what there is of it. But if it is inadequate, it is of no value whatever. I tell you that it *is* inadequate and my statement is backed by every expert in the service. If we were attacked tomorrow by any nation of Germany's sea power our ships would sink to their graves, our men to certain death.

"No braver men walk this earth than ours. They
162

are ready to die for their country. We have no right to murder them for this reason. If they die, it should be to some purpose. We should give them the best weapons on earth and the best training. They have the right to a fair chance with any foe they face. We have a mobile army of thirty thousand men with which to defend a hemisphere! We assert our guardianship of all America. It is known to all men that a modern army of one hundred and fifty thousand landed on our shores could complete the conquest of the Atlantic seaboard in twelve days.

"Our friends who clamor for peace in a world at war tell us that an attack on our nation is a possibility too remote for discussion. The same men in June, 1914, declared that war in Europe was a physical and psychological impossibility. Now they tell us with equal solemnity that this war, which they declared could never be, is so appalling that it will be the last. They tell us that the world will now disarm and *we must lead the way!*

"If the world disarms, Europe must lead the way. We are already practically disarmed.

"Who in Europe will dare to lead in such a movement!

"Will Germany disarm?

"Will she at this late hour surrender her ambitions

to expand? Will she sign the death warrant to the aspirations of the men who created her mighty Empire? Will she expose her eastern frontier to the raids of Cossack hordes?

"Could Russia disarm?

"Would she consent to risk the dismemberment of her vast domain?

"Could England with her empire on which the sun does not set—could England disarm and lay her centers of civilization open to the attack of black and yellow millions?

"To ask the question is to answer it.

"The disarmament of the modern world is the dream of an unbalanced mind.

"Take any group of nations. If the Allies win, would Germany and Austria-Hungary agree to disarm? If they should ever tear the German Empire into pieces could they stamp out the fighting soul of the Germanic race?

"If Germany and Austria-Hungary win, can England, France, Italy, and Russia disarm before the menace of world dominion?

"Do you believe that out of the vast horror of this war a compact of international peace may be signed by all nations?

"Let us remind you that the heart of Europe is aristocratic and imperial. Their rulers hate democracy as the devil hates holy water. The lion and the lamb cannot yet lie down together—except the lamb be inside the lion.

"This nation is the butt of ridicule, jibes, caricatures and coarse jests of the aristocrats of the Old World. Our government and our people are cordially loathed.

"International peace can rest only on international democracy. The great war has brought us face to face with grim realities. We must see the thing that is— not the thing our fancy says ought to be.

"Belgium has taught us that the only scrap of paper we can be sure of is one backed by millions of stout hearts with guns in their hands, aeroplanes above their heads, ships under the seas and afloat and big black steel eyes high on their shores bent seaward.

"Men of America! I call you from your sleep of fancied safety! The might of kings is knocking at your doors demanding that you give a reason for your existence! If you are worthy to live you will prove it by defending your homes and your flag. If you are not worth saving, your masters will make your children their servants.

"The fate of a nation is in your hands. The sea is no more. The world has become a whispering gallery. And such a world cannot remain half slave and half free. It is for you to decide whether your half shall sink again into the abyss of centuries of human martyrdom and human tyranny.

"I warn you that the fight between autocracy and democracy has just begun. Poland attempted to establish a free commonwealth in Central Europe. She was ground to powder between imperial powers. The one big issue in this world today is the might of kings against the liberties of the people. Never before in human history has imperial power been so firmly entrenched. And the rulers of Europe know that sooner or later they must crush Amercan democracy or be crushed by its reflex influence."

Vassar ceased to speak and resumed his seat amid a silence that was painful. His eloquence had swept the House with tremendous force. So intense was the spell that a demonstration of any kind was impossible. A murmur of relief rippled the crowd and the hum of whispered comment at last broke the tension.

Waldron's keen cold eye had seen the effect of the young leader's appeal. He lost no time in taking measures to neutralize its influence.

CHAPTER XVIII

THE caucus of the delegates of the Women's Convention was booked to meet at six o'clock. The House would hold a night session and the vote on the Defense Bill would be called between ten and eleven.

To prevent the possibility of any influence from Vassar's speech reaching the caucus, Waldron succeeded in changing the hour to three o'clock. He would prolong the discussion until six and deliver their orders to the members of Congress in ample time.

Vassar saw him whispering in earnest conference with Barker and Virginia, guessed instinctively a change of program and in ten minutes his secretary had confirmed his suspicions.

There was no time to be lost. He made up his mind instantly to throw pride to the winds and make a personal appeal to the one woman whose influence in the crisis could dominate the councils of the opposition.

He called a cab and reached the Willard at the moment Barker was handing Virginia from Waldron's car.

An instant of hesitating doubt swept him as he thought of the possibility of a public refusal to meet or confer. He couldn't believe she would be so ungracious. He must risk it. The situation was too critical to stand on ceremony.

He raised his hat and bowed with awkward excitement.

"May I have a few minutes of your time, Miss Holland?" he asked.

She blushed, hesitated and answered nervously.

"Certainly, Mr. Congressman. Your speech was eloquent but unconvincing. I congratulate you on your style if I can't agree with your conclusions."

Barker laughed heartily and Waldron's face remained a stolid mask.

"You will excuse me, gentlemen," she said to her associates. "I'll see you in ten minutes—"

She paused and smiled politely to Vassar:

"The ladies' parlor?"

"Yes," he answered, leading the way to the elevator, and in two minutes faced her with his hands tightly gripped behind his back, his eyes lighted by the fires of tense emotion.

Her control was perfect, if she felt any unusual stir of feeling. He marvelled at her composure. He had vaguely hoped this first meeting after their break

168

might lead to a reconciliation. But her bearing was as coldly impersonal as if he were a book agent trying to sell her a set of ancient histories.

He throttled a mad impulse to tell her again that he had loved her with every beat of his heart every moment since they had parted.

"You know, of course," he began, "that in this crisis you hold the balance of power in a struggle that may decide the destiny of America?"

"I have been told so—"

"It is so," he rushed on, "and I've come to you for a last appeal to save the nation from the appalling danger her defenseless condition will present at the close of this war. My bill will place us beyond the danger line. If we are reasonably ready for defense no great power will dare to attack us—"

"Preparation did not prevent the war of the twelve nations—" she interrupted sharply.

"Certainly not. Fire engines do not prevent fires, but our organized fire department can and does prevent the burning of the whole city. Preparation in Europe did not prevent war. But it did save France from annihilation. It did save Germany from invasion. It did save England from death. The lack of it snuffed out the life of Belgium. I only ask that a million of our boys shall be taught to hold a rifle on a mark and shoot straight—"

"And that mark a human body over whose cradle a mother bent in love. I do not believe in murder—"

"Neither do I! I'm trying to prevent it. Can't you see this? Our fathers shot straight or this Republic had never been born. Your father shot straight or the Union could never have been preserved. Conflict is the law of progress. I didn't make this so, but it's true, and we must face the truth. You are the daughter of a soldier. I beg of you for the love of God and country to save our boys from butchery, our daughters from outrage and our cities from devastation!"

"I'm going to do exactly that by doing my level best to prevent all war—"

Vassar lifted his hand and she saw that it was trembling violently.

"Your decision is final?" he asked.

"Absolutely—"

"Then all I can say is," he responded, "may God save you from ever seeing the vision my soul has dreamed today!"

She smiled graciously in response to his evident suffering.

"I shall not see it," was the firm answer. "Your fears are groundless. I will be a delegate to the first

Parliament of Man, the Federation of the World which this war will create."

He turned to go, paused, and slowly asked:

"And I may not hope to see you occasionally? You know that I love you always, right or wrong—"

She shook her head and gazed out of the window for a moment on the majestic shaft of the Washington Monument white and luminous against the azure skies of Virginia. Her voice was tender, dreamlike, impersonal.

"Our lives were never quite so far apart as now—"

He turned abruptly and left her, the sense of tragic failure crushing his heart.

CHAPTER XIX

WOMAN'S political power was hurled solidly against an increase of armaments, and Vassar's Bill for National Defense was defeated.

Waldron's triumph was complete. His lawyers drew the compromise measure which Congress was permitted to pass a few weeks later. It made provision for a modest increase of the Army, Navy and the National Guard.

The banker's newspapers led the chorus of approval of this absurd program and the nation was congratulated on its happy deliverance from the threatened curse of militarism.

Waldron chartered two trains and took the entire delegation of five hundred women members of the Convention as his guests. He entertained them for a week at the best hotels and closed the celebration with a banquet at his palatial home in honor of Virginia Holland.

At the close of the dinner when the last speaker had finished a brilliant panegyric of praise for the modern

Joan of Arc, the master of the feast whispered in her ear:

"Will you remain a few minutes when the others have gone? I've something to tell you."

She nodded her consent and Waldron hurried their departure.

She wondered vaguely what new scheme his fertile brain had hatched, and followed him into the dimly lighted conservatory without a suspicion of the sensation he was about to spring. In his manner there was not the slightest trace of excitement. He found a seat overlooking an entrancing view of the cold, moonlit river below, and began the conversation in the most matter of fact way.

"I have a big announcement to make to you, Miss Holland," be began evenly.

"Indeed?"

"My life work is rapidly reaching its consummation. You like this place?"

He adjusted his glasses and waved his hand comprehensively. The gesture took in the house, the grounds, the yacht, the river and possibly the city.

Virginia started to the apparently irrelevant question. In her surprise she forgot to answer.

"You like it?" he repeated.

"Your place," she stammered, "why, yes, or course,

it's beautiful, and I think the banquet a triumph of generosity. Our leaders will never cease sounding your praises. I must say that you're a master politician. I wonder that you became a banker—"

Waldron's cold smile thawed into something like geniality.

"I had good reasons for that choice, you may rest assured. The man who does things, Miss Holland, leaves nothing to chance which his will may determine. It was not by accident that I became a multimillionaire. It was necessary—"

He stopped abruptly and fixed her with his steel-gray eyes.

"The triumph of my life work is in sight. I may breathe freely for the first time. I have chosen you to be the queen of this house. I offer you my hand in marriage—"

Virginia caught her breath in genuine amazement. Never before had he even hinted that the thought of marriage had entered his imagination. He had made his proposal with a cocksure insolence which assumed that the honor was so high the girl had not been born who could refuse it.

A little angry laugh all but escaped before she repressed it. The situation was dramatic. She would play with him a moment—and test his sense of humor.

"You honor me beyond my deserts, Mr. Waldron," she answered naively.

"I must differ with you," he answered briskly. "On the other hand I am sure there is not a woman in America who could grace these halls with your poise, your brilliance, your beauty. The home I have built is worthy of you—yes. That you will fill the high position to which I have called you with dignity and grace I am sure—"

She lifted her hand with a movement of impatience—a mischievous smile playing about her mouth.

"But you haven't told me that you love me—" she protested.

"You are a modern woman. You have outgrown the forms of the past—is it necessary to repeat the formula? Can't you take that much for granted in the offer of my hand?"

Virginia shook her head.

"I've traveled pretty far from the old ways, I know," she admitted. "I can't give up all the past. I've an idea that a man and woman should love before marriage—"

"If the centuries have taught Europe anything," he argued, "it is that reason, not passion, should determine marriage. I hold to the wisdom of the ages on the point. I ask you to be my wife. Don't joke. You cannot refuse me."

Virginia rose with decision.

"But I do refuse you."

The banker was too surprised to speak for a moment. It was incredible. That a girl with a paltry dowry of a hundred thousand should refuse his offer of millions, his palace in New York, his estates in Europe—a feeling of blind rage choked him.

"You cannot mean it?" his cold voice clicked.

"Such high honor is not for me," she firmly replied. "I do not intend to marry—"

He studied her with keen eyes, rubbed his glasses and readjusted them again.

"You will accept the position I offer without marriage?" he asked eagerly.

Her face went white and her body stiffened.

"If you will call the car please—I will go—"

Waldron's heels came together with a sharp military click, his big neck bent in the slightest bow, and he led the way into the hall without a word.

He made no pretense at politeness or apology. He left her to his servants and mounted the grand stairway in a tumult of blind rage.

CHAPTER XX

FOR two years the nation drifted without a rational policy of defense, while the world war continued to drench the earth in blood. The combination of forces represented by Waldron had succeeded in lulling the people into a sense of perfect security. We had always been lucky. A faith that God watched over children and our Republic had become one of the first articles of our creed.

John Vassar became an officer in the National Security League and attempted to extend its organization into every election district of the Union. For two years he had given himself body and soul to the task. At every turn he found an organized and militant opposition. They had money to spend and they had leaders who knew how to fight.

In spite of his hatred of Waldron he was compelled to acknowledge his genius for leadership, and the inflexible quality of his will. Within a week of the date his Security League was organized in a district, a fighting "peace" organization appeared overnight to destroy his work.

The optimism of the American people was the solid rock against which his hopes were constantly dashed.

He ignored the fact that Virginia Holland was the most eloquent and dangerous opponent of his propaganda. It was the irony of fate that he should feel it his solemn duty to devote every energy of his life to combating the cause for which she stood. It was the will of God. He accepted it now in dumb submission.

In the midst of his campaign for Congressmen pledged to national defense, the great war suddenly collapsed and the professional peace advocates filled the world with the tumult of their rejoicing.

It was useless to argue. The danger had passed. Men refused to listen. Vassar was regarded with a mild sort of pity.

The first rush of events were all with his enemies and critics. The war had been fought to an impassable deadlock.

Germany entrenched had proven invincible against the offensive assaults of the Allies. The Allies were equally impotent to achieve an aggressive victory. When the conviction grew into practical certainty that the struggle might last for ten years, the German Emperor gave the hint to the Pope. The Pope sounded the warring nations and an armistice was arranged.

Embodied in this agreement to suspend hostilities for thirty days was the startling announcement that the nations at war, desiring to provide against the recurrence of so terrible and costly an experiment as the struggle just ending, had further agreed to meet at The Hague in the first Parliament of Man and establish the Federation of the World!

Waldron proclaimed this achievement the greatest step in human progress since the dawn of history. He claimed also that his newspapers and his associates in their fight against armaments had won this victory. He announced the dawn of the new era of universal peace and good will among men.

John Vassar was the most thoroughly discredited statesman in the American Congress. His hobby was the butt of ridicule. Woman's suffrage swept the northern section of the eastern seaboard in every state which held an election in November.

The Parliament of Man met at The Hague. The preliminary session was composed of the rulers of the leading states, nations and empires of the world.

Through the influence of Japan, the four hundred millions of China were excluded.

It was well known in the inner councils of the great powers of Europe that the real reason for her exclusion was the avowed purpose of the rulers of

Europe and Japan to divide the vast domain of the Orient into crown dependencies and reserve them for future exploitation.

Their scholars had winked gravely at the charge of a lack of civilization. What they meant was a lack of the weapons of offense and defense. China was the center of art and learning when America was an untrodden wilderness and the fathers of the kings of Europe were cracking cocoanuts and hickory nuts in the woods with monkeys. China had lost the art of shooting straight—that was all. India had lost it too and her three hundred millions were not even permitted the courtesy of representation in the person of an alien viceroy. A handful of Englishmen had ruled her millions for a century. India had ceased to exist as a nation.

One-half the human race were thus excluded at the first session of the Committee.

When the roll was finally called, each nation answered in alphabetical order, its ruler advanced and took the seat assigned amid the cheers of the gallery. The President of Argentina, the Emperor of Austra-Hungary, the King of Belgium, the President of Brazil, the King of Bulgaria, the President of Chile, the King of Denmark, the President of France, the Emperor of Germany, and King of Prussia,—and with him the King of

Bavaria, the King of Saxony, the King of Wurtemburg, the Duke of Anhalt, the Grand Duke of Baden, the Duke of Brunswick, the Grand Duke of Hesse, the Grand Duke of Mecklenburg-Strelitz, the Grand Duke of Oldenburg, the Duke of Saxe-Altenberg, the Duke of Saxe-Coburg and Gotha, the Duke of Saxe-Meiningen, the Grand Duke of Saxe-Weimar, the Prince of Weldeck,—the King of Great Britain and Emperor of India, the King of Greece, the King of Italy, the Mikado of Japan, the Grand Duchess of Luxembourg, the President of Mexico, the Queen of the Netherlands, the King of Norway, the President of Portugal, the King of Roumania, the Tzar of Russia, the King of Servia, the King of Spain, the King of Sweden, the President of Switzerland, the Sultan of Turkey and the President of the United States of America.

Virginia Holland saw the Chief Magistrate of the foremost republic of the world answer to the last name called on the roll and take his seat beside the Sultan of Turkey.

The minor republics of South and Central America had all been excluded by the Committee on Credentials as unfitted either in the age of their governments, or their wealth, population and power for seats in this august assembly. Only Argentina, Brazil and Chile from South America, and Mexico from Central America were allowed seats.

The principle of monarchy was represented by thirty-four reigning emperors, kings, princes and dukes; the principle of democracy by eight presidents. The first article on which the organization agreed was the reservation by each of the full rights of sovereignty with the right to withdraw at any moment if conditions arose which were deemed intolerable.

To find a working basis of development, therefore, it was not merely necessary to obtain a majority vote, it was absolutely necessary that the vote should be unanimous, otherwise each decision would cause the loss of one or more members of the Federation.

Queen Wilhelmina, of the Netherlands, the only full-fledged woman sovereign was unanimously elected the presiding officer of the assembly.

The women representatives of the suffrage states of the American Union were admitted to the gallery as spectators. They rose en masse and cheered when the gracious Queen ascended the dais and rapped for order.

They kept up the demonstration until the Emperor of Germany became so enraged that on consultation with the Emperors of Austria-Hungary and the Tzar of Russia, the sergeant-at-arms was ordered to clear the women's gallery. The American women continued their cheers in the streets until dispersed by the police.

For the first time in her career Virginia Holland lost patience with her associates. She was in no mood to shout for royalty, either in trousers, knickerbockers or skirts. Her keen intelligence had caught the first breath of a deep and fierce hostility to the land of her birth. She had watched the growing isolation of the President of the United States with slowly rising wrath. But a single member of the august body had agreed with him on everything. The President of Switzerland alone appeared to have anything in common with our Chief Magistrate. Even the French President appeared to have been reared in the school of monarchy in spite of the form of his government. The President of little Portugal was too timid to express an opinion. And the four presidents of South and Central America were the social lions of royalty from the day the assembly had gathered in an informal greeting in the Palace of Peace. The South Americans had been wined and dined, fêted and petted until they had lost their heads. They treated the President of the United States not only with indifference, but in the joy over their triumphant reception had begun to openly voice their contempt.

The President of the United States accepted the situation in dignified silence. The Parliament of Man was less than one day old before he realized that he was a single good-natured St. Bernard dog in a cage of Royal Bengal tigers. How long his position would remain tolerable he could not as yet judge. As a Southern-born white man he rejoiced that the full right of secession had been firmly established in this Union!

He composed his soul in patience.

The first three days were consumed in congratulations and harmless flights of oratory. The kings had never had such a chance before to indulge in declamation. They were like a crowd of high-school boys on a picnic. They all wished to talk at one time and each apparently had a desire to consume the whole time. The smaller the kingdom, the louder the voice of the king.

On the fourth day the Parliament got down to business. The treaty of peace which closed the great war had fixed the boundaries of the belligerent nations. They were practically identical with the status preceding the struggle.

The Parliament unanimously reaffirmed the decision of this treaty and fixed the boundaries for all time.

The partition of China was immediately raised by Japan and again the United States of America and

Switzerland alone stood out for the rights of 400,000,-
000 men of the yellow race.

France and Portugal, Brazil, Chile, Argentina and
Mexico sided with the royalist spoilers against our protest.

China was divided into spheres of influence by a vote
of forty against two. Both the United States and
Switzerland registered their protest in writing and recorded their possible secession.

The continent of Africa was next divided by the same
recorded vote forty against two.

The President of the United States rose from his
uncomfortable seat beside the Sultan of Turkey and
was recognized by the presiding Queen in a silence that
was deathlike.

"With the permission of your Majesty," he began
gravely, "I wish to introduce at once the following
resolutions." He calmly adjusted his glasses and read:

"Resolved: That the Parliament of Man recognize
the principle that a people shall have the right to maintain the form of government which they may choose
consistent with the laws of civilization. That the Western Hemisphere, comprising the Americas, have chosen
the form of free democracy. That the Monroe Doctrine shall therefore be affirmed as the second basic
principle on which the Federation of the World shall

be established, and that the royal rulers unanimously agree that their standards shall never be lifted on the continents of North or South America."

The sensation could not have been greater had an anarchist's bomb exploded beneath the presiding Queen.

A babel of angry protests broke forth from the thirty-three royal and imperial rulers. France and Portugal remained silent and distressed. Brazil, alone, of the South American republics, raised a voice in support of the proposition. Even Switzerland smiled skeptically. Argentina, Chile and Mexico joined the pandemonium of abuse with which the crowned rulers of the world received the first American tender of principle.

The session ended in confusion bordering on riot. In vain the gracious Queen attempted to restore order. The President of the United States stood with folded arms and watched the indignant sovereigns sweep their robes about their trembling figures and stalk from the Palace.

A caucus of imperial rulers was held at which the Emperor of Germany presided. It was unanimously resolved that the proposition of the United States was an insult to every monarch of the world and in the interests of peace and progress he was asked to withdraw it.

Our President stood his ground, refused to retreat an inch and demanded a hearing. His demand was refused by a strict division of monarchy against democracy, thirty-three imperial rulers casting their votes solidly against the eight presidents.

The moment this vote was announced, the President of the United States seized his hat and started to leave the chamber. The South Americans crowded around him and begged him to stay. The little President of Chile, the fighting cock of the South Pacific, led the chorus of appeal.

"Stay with us," he cried, "and I promise to pour oil on the troubled waters. I have a compromise which will be unanimously accepted. I have conferred with the three great emperors and they have assured me of their support."

Our President smiled incredulously but resumed his seat.

Chile declared that South America had always scorned the assumptions of the Monroe Doctrine. The monarchs cheered. He declared that the nations of the South no longer needed or desired the protection of the United States. They sought the good will of all men. They feared invasion by none. He proposed an adjournment of six months in order that a Pan-American Congress representing all interests might meet in Washington and decide this issue for themselves. Their decision could then be reported to the Parliament of Man.

His suggestion was unanimously adopted and the Parliament successfully weathered its first storm by adjourning for six months.

Again the world rang with the shouts of the orators of peace. A beginning had actually been made in the new science of war prevention. The Appeal to Reason had triumphed.

Waldron remained a day to congratulate his friends among the crowned heads and hurried home to organize a great Jubilee to celebrate this meeting of the Pan-American Congress and hail its outcome as the first fruits of the reign of universal peace.

Virginia Holland returned to her home with a great fear slowly shaping itself in her heart.

CHAPTER XXI

THE outcome of the First Parliament of Man was hailed by the professional peace-makers as the sublimest achievement of the ages. A way had been found at last to banish war. The dream of the poet had been fulfilled. They called on all men to beat their guns into plowshares, their swords into pruning-hooks. They proclaimed the end of force, the dawn of the Age of Reason.

Our nation once more demonstrated its love for the orator who preaches smooth things. The Honorable Plato Barker praised the President for his brave stand for the rights and dignity of the Republic in his heroic defense of the Monroe Doctrine.

In the same breath he acclaimed the President of Chile who led the way to the court of reason as a new prophet of humanity. He would not yield one inch in the maintenance of the Monroe Doctrine—no! But it had been demonstrated that such issues could be settled by moral suasion! The next session of the august Parliament of Man, he declared, would ratify the decision of the Pan-American Congress without a dissenting voice.

The long pent energies of our nation drove us forward now at lightning speed. During the last year of the great war our commerce had practically come to dominate the world. Anticipating conditions at its close, Congress passed a new high tariff which closed our ports to the flood of cheap goods Europe was ready to dump on our shores. Every wheel in America was turning, every man at work, wages leaped upward with profits mounting to unheard-of figures. The distress in Europe from the glut of an overstocked market sent us millions of laborers and still our industries clamored for more.

A hundred million Americans went mad with prosperity. Our wealth had already mounted steadily during the war. We were not only the richest nation on earth, there was no rival in sight.

New York ascended her throne as the money center of the world, and wealth beyond the dreams of avarice poured into the coffers of her captains of industry.

The one thing on which we had failed to make relative progress was the development of our national defenses. We had more ships, more guns, more forts, more aircraft and more submarines than ever before, but our relative position in power of defense had dropped to the lowest record in history.

At the beginning of the great war in 1914 our navy

stood third on the list in power and efficiency. Only Great Britain and Germany outranked us and Germany's balance of power was so slight that our advantageous position was deemed sufficient to overcome it.

At the end of the great war we had sunk to sixth place among the nations in power and efficiency of defense.

Great Britain, Germany, France, Russia and Japan outranked us so far that we could not consider ourselves in their class. The armies of each of these powers were so tremendous in their aggregate the mind could not grasp the import of such figures.

In spite of all the losses, Germany's mobile forces, ready at a moment's notice, numbered 5,000,000 trained veterans with muscles of steel and equipment unparalleled in the history of warfare. Russia had 9,000,000 men armed and hardened by war, France had 3,000,000, Great Britain 3,000,000, Austria-Hungary 3,000,000, Japan 4,000,000.

The navies of the world had also grown by leaps and bounds in spite of the few ships that had been sunk in the conflict. Great Britain still stood first, Germany next and then France, Russia and Japan. The navies of each of these nations not only outranked us in the number of ships, submarines, hydroplanes and the range of their guns, but the complete and perfect organization of their governing and directing powers more than doubled their fighting efficiency as compared to ours, gun for gun and man for man.

We were still trusting to blind luck. We had no general staff whose business it is to study conditions and create plans of defense. We had no plans for conducting a war of defense at all either on land or sea. Our admirals had warned the Government and the people, under solemn oath before Congress, that it would require five years of superhuman effort properly to equip, man and train to battle efficiency a navy which could meet the ships of either of the five great nations with any hope of success.

And nothing had been done about it.

The energies of a hundred million people were now absorbed, under the guidance of Waldron and his associated groups of propagandists, preparing to celebrate the great Peace Jubilee the week preceding the meeting of the Pan-American Congress called to settle the problem of the Monroe Doctrine.

This celebration was planned on a scale of lavish expenditure, in pageantry, oratory, illuminations, processions, and revelry unheard of in our history. The programmes were identical in New York, Boston, Philadelphia, Pittsburg, Washington, Baltimore, Norfolk,

New Orleans, Cleveland, Detroit, St. Louis, Denver, San Francisco, and Los Angeles and a score of smaller cities.

John Vassar refused to accept the invitation of the Mayor of New York to address the mass meeting of naturalized Americans in the Madison Square Garden.

Virginia Holland not only refused to lead the grand Pageant of Peace in its march up Fifth Avenue to the speakers' stand, but she resigned as president of the Woman's Federation of Clubs of America, shut herself in her room at their country place on Long Island and refused to be interviewed.

John Vassar read the announcement with joy. The leaven of his ideas had begun to stir the depths of her brilliant mind and pure heart! The defeats of the past were as nothing if they brought her again into his life.

He wrote her a long, tender, passionate appeal that he might see her again.

He posted it at midnight on the opening day of the Jubilee. He had read of her resignation only in the afternoon papers. The managers of the ceremonies had taken for granted her approval and announced that she would lead the pageant of symbolic floats on a snow-white horse as grand marshal.

Vassar waited with impatience for her answer the

next day. If the mails were properly handled his letter should have reached her by noon. An immediate answer posted in Babylon at one o'clock might be delivered at Stuyvesant Square by six. He started at every call of the postman's whistle in vain. He was sure an answer would come in the morning. Nothing came. He put his hand on the telephone once to call her and decided against the possibility of a second bungling of his cause.

Instead he called the post-office and learned that a congestion of mail, owing to the disorganization of the service by the Jubilee, had caused a delay of twenty-four hours in the delivery to points on Long Island.

He waited in vain another day. He walked alone through the crowded streets that night studying the curious contagion of hysteria which had swept the entire city from its moorings of an orderly sane life.

The din of horns and the shouts of boys and girls, crowding and jostling on the densely packed pavements, surpassed the orgies of any New Year's riot he had ever witnessed. Every dance hall in Greater New York was thronged with merrymakers. The committee in charge of the Jubilee, supplied with unlimited money, had hired every foot of floor space that could be used for dancing and placed it at the disposal of the social organizations of the city. Wine was flowing like water. The police winked at folly. A world's holiday was on for a week.

Vassar visited Jack's, Maxim's, Bustanoby's, Rector's, and Churchill's to watch the orgie at its height. Every seat was filled and surging crowds were waiting their turn at the tables. Hundreds of pretty girls, flushed with wine, were throwing confetti and thrusting feathers into the faces of passing men. The bolder of them were seated on the laps of their sweethearts, shouting the joys of peaceful conquest.

Professional dancers led the revelry with excesses of suggestive step and pose that brought wild rounds of approval from the more reckless observers.

Vassar left the last place at 12:30 with a sense of sickening anger. The fun had only begun. It would not reach the climax before two o'clock. At three the girls who were throwing confetti would be too drunk to sit in their chairs.

He drew a deep breath of fresh air and started up Broadway for a turn in the park.

He paused in front of a vacant cab. The chauffeur tipped his cap.

"Cab, sir? Free for two hours. Take you anywhere you want to go for a song. All mine on the side. Engaged here for the night. They won't be out till morning. They've just set down."

A sudden impulse seized him to drive past Waldron's castle and see its illumination. No doubt the place would be a blaze of dazzling electric lights.

He called his order mechanically and stepped into the cab. His mind was not on the glowing lights or pleasure mad crowds. He was dreaming of the woman who had taken him to that house a little more than two years before. Every detail of that ride and interview with Waldron stood out now in his imagination with startling vividness. His mind persisted in picturing the two corseted young men who stepped from the elevator so suddenly. He wondered again what the devil they had been doing there and where they came from—and above all why they were accompanied by Villard.

Before he realized that he had started the river flashed in view from the heights south of Waldron's castle. He had told the chauffeur to keep off the Drive, stick to Broadway and turn up Fort Washington Avenue which ran through the center of Waldron's estate.

To his amazement the banker's house was dark save the light from a single window in the tower that gleamed like the eye of a demon crouching in the shadows of the skies. The tall steel flag staff on the tower had been lengthened to a hundred and fifty feet. Its white line could be distinctly seen against the stars. And from the top of this staff now hung the arm of a wireless station. Waldron had no doubt gone in for wireless experiments as another one of his fads.

Far up in the sky he caught the hum of an aeroplane motor. He leaped from the cab and listened. The sound was unmistakable. He had been on the Congressional committees and witnessed a hundred experiments by the Army Aviation Corps.

"What the devil can that mean at one o'clock at night?" he muttered.

He leaped into the cab, calling to his driver:

"Go back to Times Square and drop me at the Times Building—quick."

He made up his mind to report this extraordinary discovery to the night editor and try by his wireless plant to get in touch with Waldron's tower.

The cab was just sweeping down Broadway between two famous restaurants and the orgies inside were at their height. The shouts and songs and drunken calls, the clash of dishes, the pop of champagne corks and twang of music poured through the open windows.

The cab suddenly lurched, and rose into the air, lifted on a floor of asphalt. An explosion shook the earth and ripped the sky with a sword of flame.

The cab crashed downward and lit squarely on the flat roof of a low-pitched building right side up.

Vassar leaped out in time to hear the dull roar of the second explosion.

The first had blown up and blocked the subway and elevated systems. The second had destroyed the power plants of the surface lines.

It had come—the war he had vainly fought to prevent! And he knew with unerring certainty the hand and brain directing the first treacherous assault.

CHAPTER XXII

VASSAR smashed the skylight of the low roof on which he had been hurled, reached the ground floor and kicked his way through a window.

The half-drunken crowd of revelers were pouring out of restaurants close by. The electric lights on the four blocks about the gaping hole had been extinguished and only the gas lamps on the side streets threw their dim rays over the smoking cavern.

The merrymakers were still in a jovial mood. What was one explosion more or less? A gas main had merely blown up—that was all. They took advantage of the darkness to kiss their girls and indulge in coarse jests.

A fat Johnny emerging from a restaurant shouted:

"Where was Moses when the light went out?"

A wag who was still able to carry his liquor to the street wailed in maudlin falsetto:

"The question 'fore the house is, 'Who struck Billy Patterson?' "

A series of terrific explosions shook the earth in rapid succession, and the crowd began to scramble back into

199

the banquet halls, or run in mad panic without a plan or purpose.

A company of soldiers in dull brown uniforms with helmets of the pattern of the ancient Romans swung suddenly into Broadway from a vacant building on a darkened side street and rushed northward at double quick.

"In God's name, what regiment's that?" Vassar asked half to himself.

A gilded youth with battered hat slouched over his flushed face replied:

"Search me, brother—and what's more I don't give a damn—just so they turn on the lights and send me a cab—I've just gotter have a cab—I can't travel without a cab— What t'ell's the matter anyhow?"

Vassar left him muttering and followed the troops at a brisk trot.

They turned into Sixty-second Street, into Columbus Avenue, and poured through the smashed doors at the Twelfth Regiment Armory—they had been blown open with dynamite.

A sentinel on the corner stopped him.

"Will you tell me what company just entered the Armory?"

The soldier answered in good English with a touch of foreign accent.

"'In God's name, what regiment's that?'"

"Certainly, mein Herr—Company C, Twelfth Regiment of the Imperial Confederation, at present on garrison duty in the city of New York—"

"How the devil did you land?"

"We've been here for months awaiting orders—"

He saw the terrible truth in a flash. The secret agent of Imperial Europe had organized a royal army and armed them at his leisure, Villard acting under Waldron's guidance. The six months' delay in the meeting of the Pan-American Congress was made for this purpose. They were all trained soldiers. Their officers had landed during the past three months. The Peace Jubilee was the mask for their movements in every great center of population.

At a given signal they had blown in the doors of every armory in Greater New York, disarmed the National Guard and mounted machine guns on their parapets.

In ten minutes machine guns were bristling from the corners of every street leading to the captured armories.

It was a master stroke! There were at least a million aliens, trained soldiers of Northern and Central Europe, living in the United States.

A single master mind could direct this army as one man.

He thanked God that his father and the girls were

at Babylon. He had sent them there to avoid the scenes of the Peace Jubilee. He was too cautious now to play into the hands of the enemy.

He made his way to a telephone booth and attempted to call the Mayor's house.

There was no answer from Central. The telephone system was out of commission.

He hurried to a Western Union office to wire Washington. Every key was silent and the operators were standing in terror-stricken groups discussing the meaning of it all.

He hurried to the Times Building to try and reach the President by wireless and found the plant a wreck.

It was ten o'clock next day before the extent of the night's horror was known to little groups of leading men who had been lucky enough to escape arrest by the Imperial garrison.

Vassar stood among his friends in the dim back room of Schultz's store pale and determined, speaking in subdued tone.

Scrap by scrap the appalling situation had been revealed.

A federation of crowned heads of Northern and Central Europe had decided in caucus that the United States of America was the one fly in the ointment of world harmony. They determined to remove it at once, and extend the system of government by divine right not only into South America but North America as well. The great war had impoverished their treasuries. The money had flowed into the vaults of the despised common herd of the United States. They would first indemnify themselves for the losses of the world war out of this exhaustless hoard and then organize the social and industrial chaos of the West into the imperial efficiency of a real civilization.

The result would make them the masters of the Western World for all time. Their system once organized would be invincible. The slaves they had rescued from anarchy would kiss the hand of their conquerors at last.

This was the whispered message a trusted leader had received from an officer half drunk with wine and crazed by the victory they had already achieved for the approaching imperial fleet.

Their business was to arrest and hold as hostages every man of wealth in New York, guard the vaults and banks to prevent the removal of money, garrison and control the cities until the fleet had landed the imperial army.

The completeness with which the uprising of royalist subjects had been executed was appalling. They had taken the trunk lines of every railroad in America. Not a train had arrived in New York from any point south of Newark, New Jersey, and no train from the north had reached the city beyond Tarrytown on the Hudson or South Norwalk on the New York, New Haven and Hartford.

A motor-cycle reached New York from Philadelphia bearing to the Mayor the startling information that the Navy Yard had been captured, the Quaker City's transportation system paralyzed and that the Mayor had surrendered to the commanding general of a full army corps of twenty thousand foreign soldiers.

An automobile arrived from Boston with the same startling information from the capital of New England. Not only had the Navy Yard at Boston fallen into the hands of the enemy but the Yard at Portsmouth, New Hampshire, as well.

Not a wheel was turning in the great terminal stations of New York. The telephone and telegraph and cable systems were in the hands of the enemy. To make the wreck of the means of communication complete every wireless plant which had not been blown up was in the hands of an officer of the imperial garrison.

It was impossible to communicate by wire, wireless or by mail with Baltimore or Washington, to say nothing of the cities further inland.

Hour by hour the startling items of news crept into the stricken metropolis by automobile and motor-cycle messengers. The motor-cycle had proven the only reliable means of communication. Pickets were now commandeering or destroying every automobile that attempted to pass the main highways. But one had gotten through from Boston. The motor-cycles had taken narrow paths and side-stepped the pickets.

Not only had the great cities and navy yards been betrayed into the hands of a foreign foe mobilized in a night, but every manufactory of arms and ammunition, and every arsenal had been captured with trifling loss of life. The big gun factory at Troy, the stores of ammunition at Dover, New Jersey, the Bethlehem Iron Works, the great factories at Springfield, Bridgeport, Hartford, Ilion, Utica and Syracuse were defenseless and had fallen. In short, with the remorseless movement of fate every instrument for the manufacture of arms and ammunition was in the hands of our foes, locked and barred with bristling machine guns thrusting their noses from every window and every street corner leading to their enclosures.

The thing had been done with a thoroughness and lightning rapidity that stunned the imagination of the men who had dared to think of resistance.

The only problem which confronted their commander was to hold what he had captured until the arrival of the fleet and transports bearing the first division of the regular army with its mighty guns, aeroplanes and submarines.

Unless this fleet and army should arrive and land within a reasonable time, the overwhelming numbers of the populated centers, the scattered forces of the regular army of the United States and the National Guard, with the volunteers who possessed rifles would present a dangerous problem. The amount of dynamite and other high explosives yet in the hands of the people could not be estimated.

They had yet to reckon with the regular army. The traitors had already found foemen worthy of their steel in the police force of New York. Our little army of ten thousand policemen had given a good account of themselves before the sun had risen on the fatal morning.

A force of five thousand reserves fought for six bloody hours to recapture the Armory of the Seventy-first Regiment at Park Avenue and Thirty-fourth Street. They used their own machine guns with terrible effect on a regiment that had been rushed to assist the garrison inside. This regiment had been annihilated as they emerged from the tunnel of the Fourth Avenue Street car system at Thirty-third Street. The police had received word that they were in the tunnel, placed their machine guns to rake its mouth and when the gray helmets emerged, they were met with a storm of death. Their bodies were piled in a ghastly heap that blocked the way of retreat. But the men inside were invisible. Their machine guns and sharpshooters piled our blue coats in dark heaps over Thirty-fourth Street, Fourth Avenue, Thirty-third Street and Lexington Avenue. At ten o'clock their commander determined to smash the barricade of the main entrance where the doors had been dynamited and take the armory or wipe out his force in the attempt.

In this armory had been stored enough guns for the new National Guard to equip an army large enough to dispute possession of the city with their foes. Behind the cases containing these rifles were piled five hundred machine guns whose value now was beyond estimate.

The Colonel of the regiment quartered inside knew their value even better than his assailant. The fight at the barricades of the door was to the death.

When the firing ceased, there was no bluecoat left to give the order to retreat. Their bodies were piled in a compact mass five feet high.

The police force of the metropolis were not defeated. They were simply annihilated. In pools of blood they had wiped out the jibes and slurs of an unhappy past. Not one who wore the blue surrendered. They had died to a man.

The Brooklyn Navy Yard escaped the fate of the yards at Boston and Portsmouth by a miracle.

The superdreadnought *Pennsylvania* had not been assigned to the fleet which had just been dispatched through the Panama Canal to the Pacific. She had entered the basin to receive slight repairs. By a curious piece of luck her Captain had refused shore leave to his men to attend the festivities of the Jubilee.

A premonition of disaster through some subtle sixth sense had caused him at the last moment to issue the order for every man to remain on the ship. The sailors had pleaded in vain. They had turned in cursing their superior for a fool and a tyrant.

The explosions which wrecked the doors of the armories and paralyzed the traffic of the city found the Captain of the *Pennsylvania* awake, pacing her decks, unable to sleep.

When the division of the Imperial Guard assigned to storm the yard rushed it they ran squarely into the guns of the big gray monster, whose searchlights suddenly swept every nook and corner of the inclosure.

In ten minutes from the time they dynamited the gates and rushed the grounds the shells from the *Pennsylvania* were tearing them to pieces and incidentally reducing the Navy Yard to a junk heap.

When the Yard had been cleared, the Captain landed

his marines, searched the ruins and picked up a wounded officer who in sheer bravado, cocksure of ultimate victory, gave him the information he demanded.

"Who the hell are you anyhow?" the Captain asked.

"Lieutenant Colonel Harden of the Sixty-ninth Imperial Guard of the American Colonies—"

"Colonies, eh?"

The young officer smiled.

"From tonight, the United States of America disappears from the map of the world. It will be divided between the kingdoms comprising the Imperial Federation of Northern Europe. England and France are yet poisoned with your democratic ideas. They have remained neutral, following your illustrious example in the world war. We don't need them. Our task is so easy it's a joke. You have my sympathy, Captain. You're a brave and capable man. You would do honor to the Imperial Navy. You surprised me tonight. I was informed—reliably informed—that you and your men were celebrating the reign of universal peace—"

"Who is your leader?"

"A great man, sir, known in New York as Charles Waldron. The Emperor in command of the forces of United Europe has been informed already by wireless that America is in his hands. Tomorrow morning this leader's name will be Prince Karl von Waldron, Governor-General of the Imperial Provinces of North America."

"So?"

"I advise you, Captain, to make the best terms you can with your new master."

"Thank you," was the dry reply.

The Captain dispatched a launch to Governor's Island reporting to General Hood the remarkable information he had received. His guns had already roused the garrison. The launch met General Hood's at the mouth of the basin.

The two men clasped hands in silence on the deck of the *Pennsylvania*.

"The first blow, a thunderbolt from the blue, General—without a declaration—"

"A blow below the belt too—a slave insurrection is honorable war compared to the treachery that would thus abuse our hospitality!"

They tried the telephones and telegraph stations in vain. A council of war was called and through the grim hours from two A. M. until dawn they sat in solemn session.

CHAPTER XXIII

VASSAR'S Committee of Public Safety in the rear room of Schultz' store grew rapidly into a recruiting stand for volunteers.

Before twelve o'clock the old Armory across the way was packed with hundreds of excited followers eager to fight. A bare hundred of them had permits to carry revolvers. A few had secured sticks of dynamite from builders. A hundred old muskets Vassar's East Side Guard had used were there—but not a shell.

While they talked and raged in stunned amazement over the situation, a newsboy's hoarse cry of extra startled the meeting. The morning papers had all gone to press before the blow had been struck.

"Get a paper—quick!" Vassar cried to Brodski, his district leader.

The familiar call of the two newsboys yelling from each side of the street could now be heard. This time their words were clearly heard above the din.

"Wuxtra! Wuxtra!"

"New York City captured!"

"Proclamation of Prince Karl von Waldron!"

"Wuxtra! Wuxtra! Wuxtra!"

Brodski returned with copies of the *Herald*, *Tribune*, *Times*, *World*, *Sun*, and *Press*.

Each had issued a morning extra.

On the front page, in double-leaded black-faced type, surmounted by an imperial coat-of-arms supporting a crown, the proclamation of the new Governor-General was printed:

TO THE PEOPLE OF THE UNITED STATES

Your Republic no longer exists, The invincible fleet of the Imperial Federation of Northern and Central Europe is now rapidly approaching New York. The transports which it guards bear the first division of the Imperial Army of Occupation, one hundred and fifty thousand strong.

The chief cities of the country have already surrendered to my garrisons of 200,000 veteran soldiers. Under my immediate command in Greater New York are 50,000 soldiers—25,000 infantry and cavalry and 25,000 men equipped with 8000 machine guns.

We are here to preserve order, guard your property and deliver the first city of America intact to the Commander-in-Chief of the approaching Imperial Army.

All saloons are ordered closed until opened by

license of the new government. All assemblies in schools, churches, theaters, public halls or on the streets or parks are forbidden under penalty of death.

All persons found with firearms, explosives or weapons of any kind which might be used in war or for the purpose of rioting will be given until noon tomorrow to deposit the same in the Seventy-first Regiment Armory, Park Avenue and Thirty-fourth Street.

After that hour the penalty for any citizen, male or female, caught bearing arms, will be instant death and the confiscation of property.

All automobiles, motor-cars, bicycles and horses are hereby proclaimed the property of the Imperial Government and it is forbidden under penalty of death for any person save a soldier in royal uniform to use them.

The railroads will be opened for traffic under Imperial control within forty-eight hours. No uneasiness need be felt, therefore, that your food supply will fail. The subways and surface lines will be ready for use within twenty-four hours.

All persons are ordered to resume their usual occupations tomorrow morning at daylight when the means of transportation have been restored.

Resistance of any kind will be absolutely futile. The President of the United States and his entire Cabinet are prisoners of war, and your Capitol, duly guarded, is in my hands. Your fleet is in

213

the Pacific, and I have destroyed the locks of the Panama Canal.

The Imperial Government earnestly desires that all bloodshed be avoided. We have the best interests of the people at heart. We will establish for the first time in your history a government worthy of this nation. My Imperial Master will treat all loyal subjects as his beloved children. His foes will be ground to dust beneath his feet. For these no quarter will be asked, none given.

I have already caused the arrest and imprisonment of two hundred well-known citizens to be held as hostages for your good behavior.

Your great churches, your municipal buildings and your big commercial houses have all been mined. At the first outbreak of rebellion, your hostages will be shot and your city reduced to ashes.

In the name of my Imperial Master I command the peace.

> PRINCE KARL VON WALDRON,
> Governor-General of the
> Provinces of North America.

Vassar read this remarkable proclamation aloud amid a silence that was strangling.

He opened the papers and glanced at the editorial columns. It was as he feared.

A free press in America no longer existed.

Waldron was dictating every utterance from his tower on the heights of Manhattan.

Each paper earnestly appealed to all citizens to refrain from violence and make the best of their situation until intelligent advice could be given after a sufficient time had passed for reflection and conference with all parts of the nation.

Vassar mopped his brow and groaned.

"Well, boys," he began, "we must give them credit for doing a good job. They don't bungle, they don't muddle, they don't leave anything to chance. They've got us for the moment. There's but one thing to do, submit—"

"No!—No!" came the angry growl.

Vassar smiled.

"Submit for the present, I was trying to tell you, until we can find the nucleus of an army to support. He didn't mention our forts or our little army. They failed to get those forts from the rear and they're intact. There are half a dozen battleships somewhere on the Atlantic side. The main fleet cannot reach us within a month. The Panama Canal has been blown up of course. But the ships that are here with two dozen efficient submarines and aeroplanes will be heard from before the army lands—"

"That's the talk!" Benda cried. "We're all Americans, signor!"

"Ya, gov'nor!" Schultz whispered. "This is *my* country now—I fight—if you'll give me a gun."

A boy of eighteen, smeared with dirt and mud, pushed his way into the crowd and thrust a note into Vassar's hand.

"In God's name, Billy!" the young leader cried. "What are you doing here?"

The boy saluted.

"My duty, sir. When I heard what was happening I reported to General Hood. I'm on secret dispatch work."

Vassar gripped the boy's hand, dropped it, tore the letter open, read it hastily, and turned to the crowd:

"Now men, listen! The forts are intact. General Wood appoints me on his staff, with the rank of colonel. He is establishing his headquarters at Southampton, Long Island. The *Pennsylvania* has slipped to sea and is gathering our fleet. She has picked up wireless messages which leads her to believe that the landing will be made at that point. Our little fleet is getting ready for the fight. I want every man that can find a gun to hustle over to Jamaica. The army holds the Long Island Railroad from Jamaica. Trains are now waiting for you there.

"They can't begin to enforce that proclamation until their army lands. The garrisons here will stick to the armories and their machine guns until reinforced—"

A suppressed cheer swept the crowd.

Vassar lifted his hand for silence.

"Now I want volunteers to take this order to every election district in New York—"

"Si—si, signor," Benda cried. "Angela and my bambino—they go too. I play and shout for the Emperor. Angela she beat the tambourine and play for the soldiers. We get the word in the danger places, quick!"

"Good boy!" Vassar exclaimed. "I'll send you where the others might fail—"

In rapid succession he sent his five hundred followers through the city bearing the whispered word to every district.

When the last man had hurried away he turned to Billy.

"Your sister and the children?"

"Virgina's gone to a mountaineer's cabin in the Adirondacks—left the night the Jubilee began—"

"No wonder she didn't reply—" Vassar muttered.

"She'll be back here in double quick time, though, when she hears of this. You know Virginia's got no commonsense—"

"And the kids?"

"I took Zonia and Marya over to our house. The old man and your father's with them. They've a couple of shotguns and two revolvers. They're all right."

Vassar smiled grimly at the boy's faith.

"Report to General Hood that I will reach Jamaica within six to eight hours and that he may expect twenty thousand men to be there before nine o'clock tonight. How'd you get here?"

"Hid my bicycle in Brooklyn and walked across the bridge."

"I'll follow suit. I know where I can put my hand on a good bicycle or two at the Athletic Club—"

Billy saluted and hurried on his mission.

At nine o'clock, the Jamaica terminal was jammed with forty thousand volunteers armed with every weapon conceivable, from a crowbar to a yacht cannon. A sailor had actually smuggled an old brass saluting piece into a ramshackled automobile and gotten into the station with it. These relics from the ark were left in the basement of the terminal.

General Hood had succeeded in getting sixty thousand rifles from the Brooklyn Navy Yard, Governor's Island, the Forts and one uncaptured armory in Brooklyn which the guns of the *Pennsylvania* had torn open and held until occupied by his troops.

All night the Volunteers from Brooklyn and New York streamed into Jamaica. Before daylight a hundred thousand men were struggling to board the trains for Southampton.

But fifty thousand were allowed to leave. There were no more guns. The remaining fifty thousand were held as reserves with such rude weapons as they possessed. Guards were placed defending the approaches to Brooklyn and New York and a camp established for drilling and training the new recruits into the semblance of an army.

CHAPTER XXIV

THE sun rose on a day never to be forgotten by the people of Long Island. Refugees were pouring along every road from the city. A wild rumor of the bombardment of New York had spread and they were determined to get behind General Hood's thin line of half-armed defenders. They were still imbued with a blind faith that somewhere our mighty nation had an army of adequate defense.

Virginia Holland had reached home by automobile to find her father's house turned into a recruiting camp. Old soldiers of the Grand Army of the Republic and the Confederate veterans of New York and Brooklyn, were out in their faded uniforms demanding guns with which to defend the flag.

Holland received them in his house and began to drill on the lawn. Virginia with sinking heart hurried to serve refreshments to the mob of excited men. Marya and Zonia joined with enthusiasm.

Benda was there awaiting Vassar's arrival with a squad of his friends for whom he had procured uniforms and a few guns. He was drilling them in his earnest, awkward way when Angela suddenly appeared in the line of refugees from New York.

He rushed to stop her:

"Ah, my Angela, you here! And I told you stay home!"

Angela tossed her head with contempt for his fears.

"I come with you—"

"Go back—back—I say!"

Angela merely laughed and resumed her march with the refugees. If they could live she could.

Tommaso threw up his hands in despair and returned to his drill.

At noon Vassar approached at the head of a division of raw troops. The road was lined with cheering people. He halted his men at the gate, dismounted and entered the Holland lawn, hoping against hope for a word with Virginia. He watched for a moment old Holland at the pathetic task of drilling his blue and gray veterans.

"It won't do, Mr. Holland," he said with a smile. "Your fighting is done—"

"Nonsense!" Holland protested. "I'll show you—"

He put his line of veterans through the manual of arms and one of them fainted.

Vassar slipped his arm about him tenderly.

"It's no use. I need your guns. Give them to me—"

Tommaso marched in and took the half-dozen guns against the bitter protests of the old men.

They gathered at the gate and cheered and cried as the boys answered the assembly call.

Vassar met Virginia and extended his hand in silence. She turned away fighting for self-control. Her heart was too sore in its consciousness of tragedy for surrender yet. His tall figure straightened, he turned and hurried to his men.

It was not until she saw him riding bravely toward the enemy to the certain doom that awaited our men that she lifted her hands in a vain effort to recall him and sob her repentance in his arms.

CHAPTER XXV

IN vain officers tried to stem the torrent of humanity that poured out in the wake of the volunteers.

The wildest rumors had deprived them of all reason. They had heard that the city would be shelled by the foreign fleet within six hours and reduced to ashes. It was reported that the enemy's giant submarines had already passed the forts at Sandy Hook and the Narrows and were now taking their places around the city in the North and East Rivers. The guns of these dreadnaught submarines threw five-inch shells and New York was already at their mercy.

It was useless to argue with these terror-stricken people. They merely stared in dumb misery and trudged on, mothers leading children, dirty, bedraggled, footsore and hungry—little boys and girls carrying their toys and pets—the old, the young, scrambling, crowding, hurrying they knew not where for safety.

Vassar arrived at General Hood's headquarters in time to witness the clash of our squadron with the advance fleet of the enemy.

The battle was not more than five miles at sea in plain view of the shore.

223

He watched the struggle in dumb misery.

It was magnificent. But it was not war. He felt this from the moment he saw our five ships with their little flotilla of torpedo boats and submarines head for the giant armada that moved toward them with the swift, unerring sweep of Fate.

Our great red, white and blue battle flags suddenly fluttered in the azure skies as the *Pennsylvania's* forward turret spit a white cloud of smoke. A long silence, ominous and tense followed and the sand dunes shivered with the roar of her mighty guns.

The big cruiser leading the van of the advancing foe answered with two white balls of smoke and Vassar saw the geysers rise from their exploding shells five hundred yards short of our ship.

From out of the distant sky above the armada emerged a flock of gray gulls—tiny specks at first, they gradually spread until their steel wings swept a space five miles in width. The hydroplanes of the enemy had risen from the sea and were coming to meet our brave airmen with their pitiful little fleet of biplanes.

Higher and higher our boys climbed till but tiny specks in the sky. The great gray fleet of the hostile gulls began to circle after them.

The guns of our battleship were roaring their defiance now in salvos that shook the earth. The imperial armada, with twenty magnificent dreadnaughts, advanced to meet them with every gun thundering.

"O my God!" Vassar groaned. "To think our people closed their eyes and refused to see this day!"

Had his bill for national defense become a law our navy would have ranked second, if not first, in the world. It would not have been necessary to shift it from the Atlantic to the Pacific. We could have commanded both oceans. It would be too late when our main fleet returned by the Straits of Magellan.

Our ships were putting up a magnificent fight. One of them had been struck and was evidently crippled, but her big guns were still roaring, her huge battle flags streaming in the wind.

Vassar lowered his glasses and turned to General Hood.

"They're going to die game!"

The General answered with his binoculars gripped tight, gazing seaward. "They're gamecocks all right—but I'm just holding my breath now. You notice the enemy does not advance?"

"Yes, by George, they're afraid! There's not a dreadnaught among them that can match the guns of our flagship!"

"Nonsense," Hood answered evenly, "they've slowed

down for another reason. Unless I'm mistaken they've led our squadron into a school of submarines—"

The words were scarcely out of his mouth before a hugh column of water and smoke leaped into the heavens beside the flagship, her big hull heeled on her beam's end and she hung in the air a helpless, quivering mass of twisted steel slowly sinking.

"They've got her!" Vassar groaned.

Before the *Pennsylvania* had disappeared her three sister ships had been torpedoed. They were slowly sinking, the calm waters black with our drowning men.

The sea was literally alive with submarines. The conning towers of dozens could be seen circling the doomed ships.

The *Oklahoma* had been disabled by shell fire before the submarines appeared. She was running full steam now for the beach, with a dozen submarines closing in on her. The white streak of foam left by their upper decks could be distinctly seen from the shore. Utterly reckless of any danger from the after guns of the dying dreadnaught they were racing for the honor of launching the torpedo that would send her to the bottom.

Her after guns roared and two submarines were smashed. Their white line of foam ended in a widening mirror of oil on the dark surface of the sea.

At almost the same moment a torpedo found her bow and sent the huge prow into the air. She dropped and her stern lifted, the propellers still spinning. Two swift submarines making twenty-two knots an hour had circled her on both sides and brought their torpedoes to bear on her bow at the same moment. Her battle flag was flying as she sank headforemost to her grave.

The wind suddenly shifted and the men who watched with beating hearts heard the stirring strains of "The Star Spangled Banner" floating across the waters from her slippery decks. Weird and thrilling were its notes mingling with the soft wash of the surf at low tide. The music was unearthly. Its strains came from the deep places of eternity.

Instinctively both men lowered their glasses and stood with uncovered heads until the music died away and only the dark blue bodies of our boys were seen where a mighty ship had gone down.

"We've but one life to give!" Hood exclaimed. "It's a pity we haven't the tools now to make that life count for more!"

The little torpedo boat flotilla closed in and dashed headlong for the submarines. To the surprise of the watchers not one of the undersea craft dived or yielded an inch. Their five-inch disappearing guns leaped from the level of the water and answered our destroyers gun for gun. Their decks were awash with the sea and armored so heavily that little danger could be done by our shells.

The battle of the sharks was over in thirty minutes. Not a single destroyer escaped. They had dashed head-long into a field of more than a hundred dreadnaught submarines. One by one our destroyers broke in pieces and sank to rise no more.

A few dark blue blots on the smooth waters could be seen—all we had left afloat—and they were sinking one by one without a hand being lifted to their rescue.

The imperial armada was mistress of the seas. The great ships moved majestically in and prepared to shell the shores to clear the way for their landing.

CHAPTER XXVI

So intense and spectacular had been the battle of the fleets that neither Vassar nor his superior officer had lifted their eyes to the dim struggle of the skies. The birdmen had climbed to such heights they were no larger to the eye than a flock of circling pigeons. The tragedies of this battle were no less grim and desperate. Two of these daring defenders of our shores had been ordered to stay out of the fight and report to General Hood if the fleet should be sunk.

They saw one of these couriers descending in swift, graceful circles. He landed on the sand dunes, sprang from his seat and saluted the General.

"Well, sir?" General Hood cried.

The birdman was a smiling young giant with blond hair and fine blue eyes. They were sparkling with pride.

"It was some fight, General—believe me! Our fellows covered themselves with glory—that's all! I nearly died of heart failure because I couldn't go in with 'em."

"How many escaped?"

"I didn't see any of the boys try to get away, sir—"

"They all fell?"

"Oh, yes sir, of course, they all fell—but, take it from me, they gave those fellows merry hell before they did—"

He paused and mopped his brow.

"My, but it's hot down here!" he complained. "They looked like fierce eagles up there and every time they made a dash at an enemy their claws brought blood. Honest to God, General, I saw one of our big biplanes smash six taubes and send them swirling into the sea before they got him. They were as thick after him as bees too. He'd climb up and then dip for them with a devilish swoop—his machine gun playing a devil's tattoo on the fellow below. Six times he got his man, and then I saw them close in on him—not two to one or ten to one—it was twenty to one! He didn't have a chance. It was a crime. If our fellows had just had half as many machines, they'd have won hands down. There were only nine of them in the fight against fifty of the enemy—"

"How many of the enemy all told did they account for?" Hood asked sharply.

"God knows—I couldn't take it all in. But I saw fifteen of them go down. There wasn't one of our men that failed to score. They fought like devils. I never saw such skill. I never saw such daring. I'm proud I'm a citizen of this Republic. We gave the world the aeroplane and we're going to show them how to use it before we get through!"

The General scribbled an order and handed it to the birdman.

"Take that to the commander at Fort Hamilton, and report to me at Patchogue, my new headquarters."

The birdman touched his goggled cap, his assistant started the engines and in a minute the great bird was swinging into the sky. With two graceful circles mounting steadily she straightened her course for the Narrows and Vassar turned to the General.

"You will retreat to Patchogue?"

"There's no other course possible. We can't fight the guns of those ships. They can land at their leisure. My hope is that they will be delayed by the weather. God may help us a little if Congress wouldn't."

"You want time to intrench?"

"Yes and get our artillery in position. If we can't get some big guns in place to meet theirs—it's no use. I've asked the forts to send me two battalions of coast artillery organized for the field. We'll get a battalion of artillery from Virginia by boat tomorrow. Our men are coming as fast as they can get here over hundreds and thousands of miles, with our railroads blocked. If the weather delays this landing until we can mass two hundred guns against their four hundred we may make a stand by digging in. I'll have my mob underground by tomorrow night in some sort of fashion. If they give me a week—it may take some time to smoke me out—"

"It's breezing up!" Vassar interrupted excitedly.

"And it's from the right point too, thank God," the General responded. "I could have shouted when I heard the first strains of that band floating in from sea."

Already the sea was roaring with a new angry note. The barometers on the armada had given the signal too. The mighty fleet was standing far out to sea now awaiting a more favorable moment to spring on the land that lay at the mercy of their great guns.

CHAPTER XXVII

THE General hastened to give orders for the retirement. By noon the next day his battle-line stretched from Patchogue through Holtsville to Port Jefferson and a hundred thousand men were wielding pick and shovel with savage determination. There was one thing these men didn't lack whatever was missing in their equipment. They hadn't enough guns. They had no uniforms—save on the handful of regulars sprinkled among them. They hadn't much ammunition. They did have courage. They were there to do and die.

For three days the wind blew a steady gale from the southwest and piled the white foaming breakers high on the sand dunes.

Through the pounding surf the sea lifted our bloated dead until they lay in grim blue heaps on the white sands at low tide. General Hood despatched Vassar to see that they were buried. He piled them in big trenches one on top of the other.

The wind died to a gentle caress as Vassar stood and watched them dumped into unmarked trenches—brave boys whose lives we could have saved with a few paltry millions spent in preparation.

His thoughts were bitter.

Had we been prepared no nation on earth had dared attack us. Our fighting force in men would fill an army of 16,000,000. Our strength in money was greater than Continental Europe combined. We had the men. We had the money. We were just not ready—that was all. We could have whipped combined Europe had we been prepared, and combined Europe, knowing this, would have courted our favor with bows and smiles.

The thin line of the new moon broke through the soft fleece of clouds and the stars came out in countless thousands. The lights were playing far out at sea too, the big searchlights of the scouts and battle cruisers. They flashed on the grave diggers now, held steady for a moment and swung in search of guns. They were not interested in the dead.

Vassar's heart went out in a throb of pity as he watched the scene—pity for the men whom a mighty nation had murdered for nothing—pity for the well-meaning but foolish men and women whose childish theories of peace had made this stupendous crime possible.

He thought too with the keenest pang of the anguish that would come to the heart of the woman he loved when the magnitude of this betrayal of a nation crushed her soul. Men like Barker and Pike would continue their parrot talk perhaps until Death called them. The heart of Virginia Holland would be crushed by this appalling tragedy. If he could only take her in his arms and whisper his love!

At dawn next morning Vassar stayed to watch from the hills the landing of the armada. They had scorned to waste a shot from their big guns to cover the landing. It was unnecessary. Their airmen had reconnoitered and reported the defending army miles away hastily digging their trenches.

"Good!" the imperial commander replied on receiving this report. "The bigger and longer their trenches, the bigger the battle. What we want is one fight and that settles it."

Through four days the landing proceeded with marvelous precision, each man at his post. The whole great movement went forward without a hitch with scarcely an accident to mar its almost festive character.

Twenty-five huge transports lay in the offing discharging their thousands of troops from barges and lighters. The men swarmed on the sands like locusts. Nothing had been left to chance. Nothing had been forgotten. They had cavalry in thousands—huge artillery that covered acres. Fifty magnificent horses were hitched to a single gun of the largest type. Their food supplies were apparently exhaustless. Each regiment had its moving kitchens, its laundry wagons, its bakery.

The signal corps were already stringing their wires. A wireless plant had been in communication with the commander on the flagship since the work of landing began.

When the last ship had discharged her cargo, it was known that four full army corps, each with complete equipment of cavalry, artillery and machine guns, had been landed and that this first division of the invading host consisted of not less than one hundred and sixty thousand officers and men—every one of whom spoke good English as well as his native tongue.

The news spread with lightning rapidity through the army of defense and on past their lines into the terror-stricken city. The thousands of half-mad refugees who had fled to the country began now to turn again toward New York. They had slept in the fields and woods for more than a week. Their condition was pitiful and their suffering a source of constant worry to the officers.

On the day that the invaders began their march from the beach to form on the turnpike for their final sweep against the trenches, Hood had massed from all sources two hundred pieces of artillery to defend his trenches against more than five hundred of the enemy. What the range and caliber of these hostile guns might be he could only guess. He knew one thing with painful certainty—whatever their range and caliber might be they were manned by veteran artillerymen who had fought them for years under the hideous conditions of modern war. Not a man in his army had ever been under the fire of modern artillery. That his gunners would give a good account of themselves, however, he had not the slightest doubt.

The rub would come when they began to fall. Trained men to take their places were not to be had. If it should come to cold steel, he could trust the raw volunteers in his trenches to defend their homes against a horde of devils. The trouble was but a handful of his men were equipped with bayonets.

He had just inspected his lines and given his final instructions to his brigade commanders when an extraordinary procession marched into his lines from Brooklyn, headed by the Honorable Plato Barker and the Reverend Dr. A. Cuthbert Pike, still president of the Peace Union.

The General refused to see or speak to them. Pike sought Vassar and begged him as an old political associate of Barker's to secure ten minutes' interview.

"I assure you, Congressman," Pike insisted in his nervous fidgety way, "that Barker may be able to open negotiations with the invaders if you will let us through the lines!"

Vassar sought for ten minutes to dissuade Pike from his purpose. His faith was unshaken—in sheer asinine fatuity it was sublime. It was so ridiculous that the young leader decided that the best thing that could happen to the country was to get both Barker and Pike inside the enemy's lines.

Barker had not been able to reach New York for the Peace Jubilee. He had regarded this great work of his career complete—crowned with glorious success. He had passed on to greater things. So remarkable had been his triumph in the Parliament of Man, so complete the vindication of his theories of arbitration and moral suasion as a substitute for war, that he had been able to raise the price of his Chautauqua lecture fees to five hundred dollars guarantee and one-third the gate receipts.

When the tragic crash came which threatened at one stroke to dislocate his process of reasoning and destroy his lecture bookings at the same moment, he was at the little town of Winona, Indiana, lecturing to five thousand enraptured Chautauqua peace enthusiasts. He had just finished counting the gate receipts, twenty-five hundred dollars on the day. His share was five hundred dollars and the half of the remaining thousand, making fifteen hundred dollars—the largest fee ever received by a lecturer in the history of the country.

With a regretful look at their pile, he was congratulating the management on having so much left over after he had been paid, when the astounding message was read announcing the insurrection of two hundred thousand armed foreigners, their capture of the President, his Cabinet, the Capitol and the fall of the cities.

The great man laughed.

"It's a huge hoax, my friends!" he shouted in soothing tones. "A wag is putting up a joke on me—that's all. I'm an old timer. I take these things as they come—don't worry."

His soothing words quieted the crowd for an hour until the second message arrived announcing the surrender of Chicago, and St. Louis to the same mysterious power and announcing that the landing from a great armada of the hostile army was hourly expected at New York.

The silver-tongued orator at once took up his burden and hastened East to meet the coming foe.

He lifted his hand in solemn invocation over the vast throng of panic-stricken hearers as he took his departure.

"Be of good cheer, my friends!" he cried. "I have always held the high faith that if we appeal to the heart of the misguided foe who invades our soil we can make him a good American. I, for one, will set my life on the issue. I will go as your ambassador to this foe. He is a man of the same hopes and faith even as you and I. Touched by the same divine influences that have lifted us from the barbarism of war we can save him also!

"Have no fear—this is all senseless panic. Personally I do not believe this wild canard of a foreign invasion. Our cities may be the victims of a wide conspiracy of dissatisfied Socialists and Anarchists—but a foreign foe—bah! I go to meet him with faith serene!"

Pike related the story of this scene with a hush of awe in his voice as if he had seen a vision of the living God and the sight had stricken him partly dumb.

Vassar appealed finally to the General to give them a pass through the lines.

"Tell those two windbags to go through my lines if they wish—I don't give a damn where they go," Hood snapped. "I only hope and pray that a friendly bayonet lets the air out of them so that we shall never hear them again. I won't see them. I won't speak to them. I won't give them a scrap of paper. If they

240

dare to pass with any fool proposition of their disordered brains, it's their affair—not mine. Tell them to get out of this camp quick—I don't care whch way they go."

At Pike's solicitation Vassar escorted Barker through the lines and watched the pair disappear arm in arm down the turnpike toward Southampton.

They walked five miles before they found a conveyance. They tried to hire a rig from a farmer. He refused to move at any price—even after Barker explained who he was and the tremendous import of his mission.

Through much dickering they succeeded in buying of him an old horse that had been turned out to graze. The Long Islander drove a hard bargain. After loud protests, and finally denunciation for his lack of patriotism, Barker counted out two hundred and fifty dollars of his last lecture fee. He still carried the fifteen hundred dollars in cash in his inside pocket.

They tried in vain to find another horse. For this one they had no saddle. As Barker was getting stout, and puffed painfully at the hills, little Pike insisted that he ride.

"You first, Brother Pike—" the orator maintained.

"No—no—Brother Barker, you ride, I can walk!" Pike protested.

They finally compromised on the principles of the peace propaganda and both of them mounted the old steed—the silver-tongued orator in front and his faithful henchman behind holding to his ample waist.

The compromise worked until the horse got tired of it. At the end of an hour's journey he refused to move another inch, bucked and threw them both in a heap. In vain they tried to move him. He not only refused to carry double, he bucked and threw Barker, who ventured to mount alone. To Pike's horror the great orator lost his temper, swore a mighty oath and smote the beast with a gold-headed cane which he had received as a token of his supremacy as an advocate of peace.

They now had the horse on their hands as an encumbrance. Barker refused to let him loose. He was of a thrifty turn of mind even in a crisis. He determined to ship that horse West and make him earn the two fifty. So leading the steed, with stout hearts still undaunted, the two apostles passed on toward the coming foe.

CHAPTER XXVIII

WHEN the unique voluntary peace delegation finally reached the headquarters of the imperial army, the commander was conducting a prayer meeting. They must wait.

They waited with joy.

Pike's little wizened face beamed with good will to men. From the moment he heard that the army was at prayers he had no doubt of the final outcome of their mission.

He turned once more to the soldier who had arrested and brought them in.

"Your General always leads the service?" he asked genially.

"Always—before a battle—"

"Of—yes, yes, I see—I see—" Pike fluttered.

"If it's going to be a real battle," the man continued, "he prays all night in his tent sometimes. For this little skirmish we're going into, I don't think the service will last more than ten minutes."

Pike didn't like this soldier's conversation. He had a rude way of smiling while he talked. The President

243

of the Peace Union decided to withhold further conversation with him.

To the amazement of Barker and Pike the divine services suddenly ended in a shout. The sinister brownish-gray hosts that knelt in prayer leaped to their feet with a fierce cry that rent the heavens:

"For God and Emperor!"

The Peace delegates were slightly distressed by this strange ending of a prayer meeting. It had an uncanny sound. There was something about the leap and shout too that suggested the rush of hosts into battle.

However, they were nothing daunted. God was with them. At least Pike knew that the Almighty was with him. Since Barker's fall and oath and blows on that horse's head he had moments of doubts about the orator's perfect purity of faith. Still for one righteous man the Lord would spare a city!

Pike brushed the dust from his black broadcloth suit, adjusted his limp, dirt-smeared white bow tie and made ready to meet the foe with a plea that could not be shaken.

Barker was so absorbed in thought preparing his noble address that he remained oblivious to his dishevelled condition. His silk hat had been crushed in the second fall, and refused to be straightened. It was this fact that had caused him to lose his temper and smite the horse.

His broken tile drooped on one side in a painfully funny way that worried Pike. He gently removed the great man's hat and tried to straighten it.

"Permit me, Brother Barker," he said nervously. "Your hat's a little out of plumb."

Barker's moon-like face was beaming now with inspiration. He made no objection. He was used to being fussed over by women and preachers. Barker turned his horse over to an obliging army hostler and took Pike's arm from his habit of being escorted through crowds to the platform.

The soldier led them without further ceremony to the tent of the commander of the advancing army.

From the pomp and ceremony, salutes and clicking heels, the peace pioneers knew that they were being ushered into the presence of the Commander-in-chief.

General Villard, who had dashed from Waldron's side to assume first command, came out laughing to meet them—a tall, stately figure, booted and spurred—his entire staff following. He carried a silver-mounted riding-whip in his hand and looked as if he had been born in the saddle.

"You bear a message under a flag of truce from the enemy?" he asked sharply.

Barker bowed graciously, removing his lame tile, and stood holding it on a level with his shoulder after the fashion of committees at the laying of cornerstones. His bald head and smiling open face beamed. He plunged at once into his eloquent address.

"We have come, General," he began suavely, "in the name of a hundred million happy, peaceful citizens of this great Republic to bid you welcome to our shores. Our vast and glorious domain, washed by two oceans, stretching from the frozen peaks of Alaska to the eternal sunshine and flowers of the tropics, is large enough for all who bless us with their coming.

"We welcome you as brothers! We want you to stay with us. We offer you the blessings of peace and freedom. We do not meet you with guns. We come with smiles and flowers, extend our hands and say: 'God bless you!'"

The orator was swept away with the melodious sound of his own voice. He replaced his crushed hat and extended his hand in a smile of glowing enthusiasm.

With a sudden crash the silver-mounted riding-whip whistled through the air and tore through the orator's tile. The battered hat fell into pieces and dropped to the ground revealing an ugly red lane across the great man's shining bald pate.

Barker was too dumfounded to dodge or protest. The thing happened with such swiftness, it had stunned him into silence.

Pike danced nervously on first one foot and then the other, lifting his hands in little attempts at apologies.

"Hats off in the presence of your superiors!" the General thundered.

Pike's hat was already off. He hadn't ventured to put it on. Still he ducked his head instinctively and then rushed into the breach.

"My dear General," he pleaded. "You do not understand, I am sure. No possible offense could have been intended by my distinguished colleague. It is the custom of our country often to speak with hats on in the open air. The Honorable Plato Barker is a veteran outdoor speaker, your Excellency. He is one of the most distinguished men in America—"

"That is nothing to me," the General curtly interrupted. "He stands in the presence of an officer of his Imperial Majesty's Army. Your greatest civilian is my inferior. Keep that in mind when in the presence of your superiors—proceed!"

Barker was too astonished and hurt to say more. For the first time in his illustrious career as a peddler of words, he had failed to move his audience to accept his wares at any price. His world had collapsed. He could only rub the swelling red line on his head and glance uneasily about his unpromising surroundings.

The preacher's hour had struck. He rose grandly to the occasion. His manner was the quintessence of courtly deference, nervously anxious deference.

"My name is Pike," be began tremblingly—" the Reverend A. Cuthbert Pike, D.D., president of the American Peace Union—"

"Proceed, Cuthbert!" was the short answer.

"We have come, your Excellency—" he paused and bowed low—"to initiate here today for all the world a constructive policy that will eliminate the necessity for war. Our plan is the appeal to reason.

"We marvel at the amazing delusion that has led Europe into this unprovoked and unnecessary assault. Nobody wants war—least of all I'm sure the great General who knows its full horrors.

"The only question, therefore, is how best to prevent it. This nation has always been too strong, too great in the consciousness of her strength, to desire war. We have sixteen million men ready to die at our call! Why should we sacrifice their precious lives? To what end if we can by any means save them?

"The prime cause, your Excellency—" again he bowed low—"of war is excessive armament—"

The General laughed heartily, and adjusted his glasses for a better look at Pike. The little man was slightly flustered at this act of uncertain import, but went on bravely in spite of Barker's look of dejection.

"We proclaim it to all nations that we are not ready to fight, and that we are glad of it because it is not possible in this condition for us to threaten or bully anyone! An unarmed man has ten chances to one over the armed man in keeping out of trouble!"

Again the General laughed and looked the preacher over from head to foot.

"Boundaries," Pike proceeded, "when armed constantly provoke clashes of the forces on either side. Boundaries unarmed, as the long line between us and Canada, promote fellowship and good will.

"We say to your Excellency, come let us reason together. We are determined not to be dragged into war. We have negotiated thirty treaties with the nations of the world, some of whom your army represents, providing for a year's delay before hostilities can begin.

"We claim our rights under these solemn treaties and ask of you an armistice for twelve months for the discussion of our differences.

"Name your demands and we will lay them before our Congress. Tell us your real mission and we will help you to accomplish it. Make us your friends and fellow workers. Why have you come?"

"I'll tell you," snapped the General. "For two hundred years you have been keeping a great pigsty on this continent, in which swine have rooted and fattened on the abundance of nature which you haven't had the brains to conserve.

"Well—it's time to clean up and make sausage! We have come for that work. We have come to teach a race of slatterns the first principles of law, order and human efficiency. We have come to clean this pigpen, put swine-herders into aprons and give them the honor of serving their superiors—and therefore for the first time in life doing something worth while.

"You are sick with overeating and much prosperity. Our Emperor sends you a tonic of blood and iron warranted to cure all ills. Our benign sovereign is the world's physician. He takes his crown and divine commission from God alone. On him the Divine Spirit has descended. In his luminous mind is the wisdom of the ages. He who dares to oppose his royal will shall be ground to powder beneath the iron heel of his soldiers. You speak of a hundred million people as if their opinion was of the slightest value. Public opinion is the source of public ills. You speak of treaties.

Treaties are the thin disguises by which divinely chosen leaders *conceal* their ultimate aims!

"Might is right and the right can only be decided by the sword. War in itself is the fiery furnace that tries man's character. The dross perishes. The pure gold shines with greater splendor. Efforts to abolish war are foolish and immoral. Peace is not our aim or desire. The sight of suffering does one good. The infliction of suffering does one more good. This war will be conducted as ruthlessly as science and human genius can make possible—"

He paused and turned to an orderly.

"The bald-headed one to the bakery! He has forfeited his life by daring to purchase a horse that belongs to his Majesty. I graciously spare his life. Tell my head cook to make him a scullion. If he's any good report to me at the end of the month and I'll promote him to the honor of acting as my valet. He has a beautiful voice. He could be trained to yodel—"

Barker lifted his hand to protest and the orderly kicked him into a trot. When he turned to protest, the bayonet changed his mind.

Pike watched his chief disappear with a groan of amazement.

The General and his staff gathered around the Reverend President of the Peace Union with jovial

251

faces. They were inclined to like him. He had contributed something new to the hilarity of nations. They put on their glasses, adjusted and removed them, adjusted them again, looked him up and down, turned him around and wagged their heads gravely.

"Well, gentlemen," the Commander laughed, "we're all agreed that it's a rare specimen—the real question is—what is it?"

Each answer brought a roar of laughter.

"It looks like a man—"

"Can't be!"

"It might have been once!"

"But not now!"

"A new microbe?"

"Sure—that's it—the microbe Pacificus americanus!"

The preacher fidgeted in a sorry effort to smile with his tormentors.

"I suppose, of course, gentlemen," Pike fluttered, "as I'm a tenderfoot you will have your little jokes— it's all in the day's work—so to speak—as it were!"

The Commander turned to a sergeant.

"Put an apron on this little man and make him a dishwasher—tin dishes—he might ruin my silver—"

The officers roared.

"If he's any good I'll make a butler out of him. I like his whiskers. They're distinctly English—"

With a loud guffaw the staff dispersed and the General turned to his tent.

Pike danced a little jig in his effort to recall the judge and correct the error of his sentence.

The sergeant gave him a resounding smack on the side of his head that spun him round like a top.

Pike was livid with rage. He bristled like a bantam rooster for a minute to the amazement of his guard.

"Don't do that! Don't do it—don't do it again! Upon my soul, this surpasses human belief, sir! I shall denounce the whole proceeding in a series of resolutions that will resound over this nation—mark my word!"

The soldier waited until Pike's breath ran short and then kicked him three feet, lifting him clear of the ground. When the preacher struck he fell flat on his face.

The blow took out of him what wind there was left. He scrambled to his feet and edged out of reach.

"I—I—return—good for evil, sir—" he stammered at last. "I bless them that despitefully use me—God bless you!"

The soldier snorted with rage and gave him another kick, crying: "The same to you! And many of 'em!"

When Pike scrambled to his feet again and wiped the dust out of his lips he shook his head in despair:

"God bless my soul! God bless my soul!"

The Sergeant grinned in his face.

"Cheer up, Cuthbert, you'll soon be dead!"

Ten minutes later he thrust poor Pike into the kitchen inclosure and shouted to the cook:

"The sooner you kill him the better—go as far as you like!"

CHAPTER XXIX

TO Vassar sleep had been impossible for the past two nights. He dozed for an hour during the day from sheer exhaustion, but the nearer the hour came for the test of strength between the opposing armies on which hung the fate of a hundred million people, the deeper became his excitement.

All life seemed to mirror itself in a vast luminous crystal before his eyes—the past, the present, the future.

He nodded in the saddle as he watched the construction of the second line of entrenchments five miles in the rear of the first. He wondered at the long reach of that first possible retreat. It was an ominous sign. It revealed the fear in the heart of the American commander.

He fell into a fevered dream. Far up in the sky he saw the sneering face of the Devil bending low over our shores and from his right hand shaking dice. The dice were the skulls of men. They rattled over the wide plain of our coming battlefield. The hideous face twisted with demoniac laughter as he shook the skulls and threw again.

He watched the game with bated breath. The count was made at last and we had lost!

And yet somehow it was well with the dreamer's soul. An angel took him by the hand and led him from the field on which the skulls lay.

He looked at the angel and it was the face of his beloved. With a cry of joy he woke to find a courier by his side with a message from General Hood.

He rubbed his eyes and smiled for the joy of the dream that still lingered in his heart and quickly read the order.

To COLONEL VASSAR:

Please report immediately to the officer in command at Babylon and tell him to entrench his men at once. We shall make our third and last stand there.

(Signed) HOOD.

Vassar scribbled a reply and turned his horse's head to the staff headquarters.

Babylon was home! He would see his little girls on the eve of battle—but more than all he hoped to see Virginia.

He was still hoping and fearing as he delivered his horse to the hostler and ordered an automobile.

He was just leaping into the machine when Billy

appeared on his motorcycle and handed him a crumpled sealed note.

The boy saluted, smiled and turned back.

It was too good to be true—and yet there it was in his hand—a letter from Virginia!

He waved to the chauffeur:

"To Babylon—headquarters—third reserves—"

The machine swept down the white smooth turnpike and he settled into his seat still holding the precious message unopened.

He broke the seal at last and read through dimmed eyes:

"Come to me at the earliest possible moment. I have much to tell you. I can't write—"

There was no formal address. There was no name signed. He kissed the delicately lined words and placed the note in his inside pocket.

What did the foolish happiness in his soul mean? Could fate mock him with an hour's joy and send him to his death tomorrow? He would ride where men were falling like leaves before the sun should set—there could be no doubt of that. He shut his eyes and could see only the face of the woman he loved. He wondered what she would say? He wondered if she would make him ask her forgiveness for the wrong she herself had done, woman-like?

257

He would be afraid to kiss her again— Nonsense! She couldn't refuse her lips if she loved. He'd risk it again if he died for it.

He delivered his orders and turned without delay for the Holland homestead. The flowers were in glorious bloom again.

The sun was sinking behind the trees in scarlet and purple glory. His father strolled thoughtfully across the lawn with one arm around Zonia and Marya's hand clasped in his.

As the car turned into the drive and swept toward the house, the girls saw him and rushed with cries of joy to smother him with kisses.

"Our men are ready?" his father asked gravely.

"To die—yes—they are as ready as they can be without drill or quipment—or artillery to defend them."

The old man shook his head.

"And the enemy—they are many?"

"A hundred and sixty thousand hardened veterans and the most magnificent equipment of the modern world—"

Old Andrew Vassar lifted his hands in a gesture of pain.

"God help us!"

"Only He can now. We've done our best—that's all—"

"'It's all love's victory, dearest'"

He paused and turned to Zonia whispering softly:
"Where is she?"

The girl nodded toward the rose-embowered oak.

"Waiting for you. Billy telephoned us. She's been there ever since."

Vassar hurried across the lawn. The twilight was deepening and the new moon hung a half crescent in the evening sky.

She rose as he passed the trellis and stood smiling tenderly until he came close. Her hands were clasped tightly. Neither was extended to greet him.

She lifted her eyes to his in a long, tender gaze, deliberately slipped both arms around his neck and kissed his lips.

He held her close in a moment of strangling joy. She lifted her lips to his again, and spoke in tones so low that only the heart of love could hear:

"My darling—my own—my hero—my mate! I've loved you always from the first. I was too proud to surrender my will and mind, my body and soul to any man. I went away into the mountains to fight it out and love conquered, dear! I surrendered before I knew that your prophetic soul was right in sensing this black hour in life. I'm glad I gave up before I knew. It's all love's victory, dearest. I love you. I love you

259

—I love you—and now Death is going to throw his shadow between us—"

A sob caught her voice.

"But I shall love you through all eternity and I thank God for this holy hour in which we meet and know, face to face—"

For two glorious hours they sat and held each other's hands in the soft light of the half-fledged moon.

And then he rose, kissed her again and swiftly rode into the night toward the red dawn of Death.

CHAPTER XXX

THE grim gray wave of destruction from the sand dunes had rolled into battleline and spread out over the green clothed hills and valleys of the Island—swiftly, remorselessly, with an uncanny precision that was marvelous.

The scouts were soaring in the clear blue skies with keen eyes searching for the position of our guns.

As they found them, a puff of black smoke streamed downward and the distant officer, perched high on his movable observation tower, took the range and called it mechanically to the gunners of his battery.

Our rifles cracked in vain. The birdmen laughed and paid no attention. We had no high-powered, high-angle guns that could touch them. Over every section of our lines the huge vultures hung in the air and circled.

The giant guns miles away beyond the distant hills toward Southampton began to roar. Their first shells fell short from five to six hundred yards.

Our boys gazed over their earthworks and watched the geysers of earth and stone and smoke leap into the heavens and sink back in dull crashes. The wind brought in the acid fumes of the poisonous gases.

They stood in silence, clutching their rifles and waiting for the word to fire.

The vultures circled again and dropped more smoke balls. The invisible gunners at their places caught the singsong call from the tower, touched a wheel and raised the noses of their gray monsters the slightest bit.

Again the earth trembled. The air vibrated with the rush of projectiles like the singing of telegraph wires far above the heads of the listening men.

They struck within a hundred yards of where Vassar sat with the field telephone at his ear awaiting General Hood's orders—a giant shell landed squarely in our trenches, tore a cavern in the earth sixteen feet deep, hurling our mangled men in every direction. Within a radius of a hundred feet no living thing could be seen when the smoke and dust had cleared. Those who had not been killed by stone and flying fragments of iron had been smothered to death where they stood by the deadly fumes.

Our guns answered now in deep thunder peals that shook the trenches.

For two hours without a pause the artillery of both armies sent their mighty chorus crashing into the heavens, their missiles of death whistling through the skies.

The fire of the enemy was incredibly accurate. Their shells struck our trenches with unerring certainty—and where one struck there was nothing left but an ugly crater in the ground. They simply annihilated every object in their track and left a mass of blackened dust and pulp.

Gun after gun of our batteries were silenced.

The vultures were still soaring aloft calling the range of each concealed battery as the fight revealed its place.

The battle had opened at dawn. By ten o'clock fifty pieces of our artillery had been reduced to junk and one-third of our trenches pulverized into shapeless masses of dust, broken stone and gaping caverns.

Apparently our heavy gun fire had made no impression on the enemy. Their long range pieces were hurling death with a steady clock-like regularity that was appalling. Our army was being ground to dust without a chance to strike their hidden foe. We had never possessed an aviation corps of any serviceable strength. The year before the nucleus of one had been authorized by Congress. This little group of efficient men had followed the fleet into the Pacific and the remaining dozen had been left to die in our tragic meeting with the armada.

General Hood possessed but two aeroplanes. It was madness to send them up against two hundred of the enemy. By an accident to his machinery a taube had fallen within our lines. The men had been captured, their uniforms taken, and delivered to General Hood. The machinery of the hostile aeroplane was promptly repaired, our blond sky pilot forced himself into the greenish-gray suit and stood by waiting for the chance to rise in a cloud of smoke and take his chance among the enemy as a spy.

At noon a wave of fog slowly crept in from sea and the guns had died away. As the mist rolled over the battlefield Hood stood beside the courier of the skies.

"Up with you now, boy, in this fog bank. Mix with the enemy and take your chances. Stay until the firing is resumed and give me the position of their guns. I must know whether we have reached them with our shells."

The birdman saluted and swung the taube into the clouds. He circled toward the sea and disappeared in the mists.

It was three o'clock in the afternoon before he landed far in the rear of our lines and made his way by automobile to headquarters.

Hood sprang from his desk and rushed to meet him.

"Well?"

"Got over their lines all right, sir," the scout answered. "Watched our shells for an hour. Not one of them fell closer than half a mile short of their batteries."

The General pressed his hand in silence.

"All right. It's as I thought. You're a brave boy, my son. You're marked for promotion for this day's work."

There was nothing to be done but move his lines five miles back to the second trenches. They were being pounded into pulp without a chance to strike back.

We had exhausted half our stock of shells without scoring a hit. Our losses in men and guns had been frightful. The tragic feature of the day was the loss of trained artillerymen whose places could not be filled. It takes three years to train the man behind the gun.

By daylight the retreat of five miles had been effected. The ground in front was more favorable here for long range work. From captive balloons the position of the batteries could be located. We hoped that some of them could be reached and put out of action. If so, we would give them a taste of cold steel.

All night the great guns growled in the distance

while our shattered lines retreated and reformed in the second intrenchments.

At dawn the vultures signalled the retreat and the green-gray wave of Death rolled forward with incredible swiftness.

By noon their greatest guns, each drawn by fifty magnificent horses, had been brought up and were sweeping into position along the low hills that would form their new battleline.

Our commander made up his mind to pot at least one of those guns. He planted a battery of heavy artillery to sweep the road that curved gracefully over these hills. A clump of trees concealed its presence from the circling scouts.

The moment the huge siege gun swept into view— its fifty horses plunging forward with steady leaps, their sides a lather of white foam—our battery roared a salvo and four shells sang in chorus. The gunners lifted their glasses and watched. Every shell struck within dead range of the long line of plunging horses. A cloud of smoke and dust rose high on the crest of the hill and when it lifted the tangled mass of torn and mangled horses and men blocked the way. A second salvo landed squarely in the wreck and blew the tangled mass into fragments—the glasses could no longer find a moving object.

266

The vultures circled above the hidden battery, their signals flashed and then from five different points behind the hills the shells began to shriek. In thirty minutes they were silenced and torn to bits. But two men were left alive to reach headquarters with the brave story.

The second battle began in earnest at three o'clock in the afternoon. The pitiful story was repeated. With remorseless accuracy their guns tore our men to pieces. They held their own just half a mile beyond the range of our artillery.

All night our men clung blindly to their position and at the dawn of the third day the enemy's infantry in solid formation, their bayonets flashing, moved swiftly and silently into line for their first charge.

A hundred machine guns were concentrated to relieve them. They formed at their leisure in plain view of our ragged trenches. Our field artillery got their range and began to pour a storm of shrapnel on their ranks. They closed up the gaps with clock-like precision and moved forward at double quick. Round after round of our artillery failed to stop them. The ranks closed automatically. They were cheering now—the breeze wafted their cries across the little valley that separated them from our trenches:

"For God and Emperor!"

When the ranks in front fell, the mass behind rushed over their bodies and shouted again:

"For God and Emperor!"

Our machine guns were mowing them down as wheat falls beneath the teeth of a hundred singing harvest machines on the prairies of Minnesota.

When the first division had been wiped out the second came rushing over their bodies as if they had been denied their just honors in losing the privilege of dying. The second wave of green reached the earth of our trenches before the last man fell and still a third wave was moving across the valley. Their shouts rang a mighty chorus now in the ears of our crouching men:

"For God and Emperor!"

Our fire was held until the third wave was within a hundred yards. The low words of quick command from charging officers could be distinctly heard as their waving swords flashed in the sunlight.

Vassar watched the thrilling scene with a smile of admiration. He saw their flag now for the first time— a huge scarlet field of silk, in its center an imperial crown wrought in threads of gold.

The Federated Monarchs of Europe had taken the red emblem of the Socialists to proclaim the common cause of royal blood against the mob, and on it set the seal of imperial power.

The cheering, rushing wave rolled within fifty yards and then from every trench poured a sheet of blinding flame. So terrific was the shock, the whole division seemed to drop to their knees at the same moment. Those who had not fallen staggered as if drunk and turned in blind circles as if groping their way in the darkness. In five minutes the last man of the third host had fallen and the slopes of the hill below were piled with the dead, the wounded and dying.

The charges ceased.

The big guns in the distance beyond the hills broke forth again in a savage chorus, continuous and infernal in its incredible power.

Vassar listened with new interest. There was a deep bass voice now in this artillery oratorio that had not been heard before. The monster guns were booming for the first time. The effects of their explosions were appalling. They spoke between the roar of the smaller guns as if the basso were answering the cry of a chorus of superhuman singers. A single shot from one of these guns rang with the volume of a salvo of ordinary artillery. Their shells weighed two thousand pounds—two thousand pounds of dynamite.

Vassar heard one of them coming toward the crest of the hill that was red with heroic blood. It came through the air with the uncanny roar of an express train. The sound rose until the heavens quivered with the howl of a cyclone.

And then came the crash squarely in the center of our trenches! An explosion followed that rocked the earth and sent a great billowing cloud of smoke and dust high over the treetops into the skies. Fragments of the débris were hurled half a mile in every direction. No living thing was left to tell the story within a hundred yards of the spot. A breach had been made in the trenches through which a regiment might have charged as over an open field. For eighteen hours this terrific hail of huge projectiles continued without pause. The dull thunder was incessant and its vibration shook the world in tremors as from an earthquake.

With grim persistence our men still clung to what was left of their trenches until the night of the second day.

Hood sullenly ordered the retreat to his last line of entrenchments resting on Babylon. The discovery of the movement lead to a fierce rear guard action with the pursuing cavalry of the enemy. Their great field searchlights now swept the heavens and flooded every open space with deadly glare.

The attacking cavalry fell into ambush carefully prepared and were annihilated. They didn't repeat the attack. But our guns had no sooner limbered up and withdrawn from their position when a squadron of the new steel cavalry, guided by the searchlights, charged at full speed seventy miles an hour down the turnpike straight into our retreating infantry. An armored automobile, spitting a storm of lead from its machine guns, plunged headlong into a regiment of volunteers, worn and half-starved and ready to fall for the lack of sleep. The huge wheels rolled over prostrate men like a great juggernaut, hurling others into the fields and dashing them among the limbs of trees.

The monster stopped at last choked by the mangled bodies caught in its machinery. A hundred desperate men swarmed over its sides and in a fierce hand to hand fight captured the car and killed its crew.

Again and again through the night of this terrible retreat these tactics were repeated. Not one of the six machines that charged our lines ever returned to tell the story. Not one that charged failed to pile the dead in heaps along the white shining turnpike.

The Holland house was inside the third line. Vassar hurried forward to beg Virginia to return with the girls and the older people to New York.

They refused to stir.

"What's the use, sir?" Holland snapped. "We're as safe here as anywhere. If Hood can't hold this railroad junction—it's all over. The wildest reports come

271

in hourly from New York. The looting and outrages surpass belief—"

"Your house has been raided?" Vassar asked.

"I've just heard that every house on both Stuyvesant Square and Gramercy Park has been smashed and wrecked. The soldiers have been looting private dwellings at their leisure—while mobs of thieves and cutthroats join in the sport."

There was no help for it then.

He whispered a hurried good-bye to Virginia, kissed Zonia and Marya and rushed for his horse.

The first gray streaks of dawn were already tinging the eastern sky. The invading army had followed with amazing rapidity. Whole regiments armed with machine guns had been hurled forward by automobile transports. Hood had destroyed the railroad as he retreated. The advancing hosts didn't need it. The hardened veterans who marched, with quick swinging gait, smoking their pipes and singing, could make thirty miles a day and be ready for a fight at the end of their march. They meant to rush our trenches today and make quick work of it. They were not going to waste any more big shells which might be needed elsewhere.

The wind was blowing directly in the faces of our men for the first time since the landing had been made.

They wondered if the wild stories we had heard of the use of poisonous gases and liquid fire in the great war were true. We had begun to scout these tales as press work of the various governments. The day was destined to bring a rude awakening.

CHAPTER XXXI

THE first day's battle brought to many a raw recruit the sharp need of military training. Many a man who had never consciously known the meaning of fear waked to find his knees trembling and hung his head in shame at the revelation.

Tommaso had led his squad into the trenches before his bitter hour of self-revelation came. He had caught a glimpse of his wife and boy in a group of panic-stricken refugees and the sight had taken the last ounce of courage out of him. He was going to be killed. He knew it now with awful certainty. What would become of his loved ones? All night in the trenches he brooded over it. When the sun rose he was only waiting for a chance to run in the excitement of battle. He swore he would not leave his wife and child to starve!

Angela carrying the poor little fear-stricken monkey, with the boy tightly gripping his dog Sausage, trying to save his kitten and his mother lugging a huge bundle had penetrated the American lines and found Vassar the day of the opening fight.

The leader had hustled them from the field and they had taken refuge in a cabin behind the trenches. With the first gray dawn, the aeroplanes began to drop shells from the sky. An aerial bomb exploded within twenty feet of the cabin.

Angela leaped to the door, gathered her boy and pets and shouted to her terror-stricken neighbor.

"Come—quick! we will be torn to pieces—we must run—"

In dumb panic, Mrs. Schultz gathered her own boy convulsively in her arms and refused to stir.

Angela sprang through the door and hurried across the hills. The others crouched in the corner of the cabin and waited.

A black ball again shot downward, crashed through the roof of the cabin, exploded and sent the frail structure leaping into the heavens.

The airmen far up in the sky saw the column of flame and smoke and débris:

"Good—we got 'em that crack!" the driver shouted above the whirr of his motor.

By one of the strange miracles of war Sausage crawled over the dead body of his mother still clinging to the kitten and found his way into the woods without a scratch.

Angela was just staggering to the crest of the ridge

275

when the shell exploded and hurled the cabin into space. A sickening wave of horror swept her soul and she suddenly sank in a heap. In vain poor Sam the monk tried to rouse her. His deep curious monkey eyes swept the smoke-wreathed heavens in terror as again and again he stroked the white still face of his fallen mistress.

For the first time since they had left home on the wild journey the childish smile left the boy's face. His war picnic had ended in grim tragedy after all. He couldn't believe it at first and the tears came in spite of his struggle to hold them back. In vain he shook his mother. She lay flat on her back now, her chalk-white face upturned in the sun.

The boy was still crying when he felt the nudge of another arm against his. He lifted his tear-stained face and saw Sausage's smoke-begrimmed cheeks and the look of dumb anguish in his eyes.

"What's the matter?" the boy sobbed.

"My mamma's killed"—was the low answer.

The swarthy face of the little Italian pressed close to the fair German, and their arms stole round each other's neck.

Angela waking from her faint found them thus and gathered them into her arms.

She was still soothing their fears when Tommaso

"Tommaso staggered to the breastworks and stood one man against an army"

"Palmer stepped to the footlights and stood one man against the town."

crawling on hands and knees in mortal terror from the battlefield, suddenly came upon them.

In her surprise and joy over his protection Angela failed to note at first the meaning of his sudden appearance.

"O my Tommaso!" she cried, throwing herself into his arms.

He held her close for a moment and whispered excitedly:

"I come to take you home, my Angela. You will be killed—you must not be here—"

It was not until he had spoken that the wife caught the note of cowardly terror in his voice. Her arms slipped slowly from his neck.

He hurried to repeat his warning:

"You must go quick, my Angela!"

The wife searched his soul and he turned away. She put her hand on his shoulder and her own eyes filled with tears.

"Come—we must hurry"—Tommaso urged, seizing his gun and starting to rise.

Angela held his hand firmly and pointed to the smoke-covered field below.

"No—no—my man. Your place is there to fight for our bambino and his country—you just forgot for a little while. I know—I understand. I felt my heart melt and my poor knees go down—you go now and fight for us!"

The man trembled and could not meet her eye.

A shell exploded near, hurling the dust and gravel in advance clear above them. A piece of iron buried itself in the earth but three feet away.

Angela cried in terror. The man suddenly stiffened, looked into the face of his boy, rose, seized his rifle, kissed his wife and rushed down the red lane of death to the front.

Angela watched him with pride and terror. He was still in plain view in the little valley below when he met the ragged lines of our retreating men. The color-bearer fell. Tommaso seized the flag and called the men to rally.

Through a hell of bursting shrapnel and machine-gun fire he turned the tide of retreat into a charge— a charge that never faltered until the last man fell on the slippery slopes of blood below the trenches of the enemy.

Tommaso staggered to the breastworks and stood one man against an army cheering and calling his charge to the field of the dead.

The enemy rose in the trenches and cheered the lone figure silhouetted against the darkened heavens until he sank at last exhausted from the loss of blood.

CHAPTER XXXII

OUR observers in a captive balloon had made out before sunrise the massing of machine guns in front. They were still coming on in endless procession of swirling auto-transports that lifted clouds of white dust that swept toward our lines in billows so dense at times the field was obscured.

Hood decided to close in on those guns before they could be assembled and mounted.

With a savage yell a brigade of regulars led the charge, followed by ten thousand picked men. Pressing forward before a dust cloud the regulars penetrated within a hundred yards of the enemy's lines before they were discovered. The rush with which they crossed the space was resistless. The splutter of pompoms filled the air and half the line went down. The remaining half reached the first crews. Hand to hand now and man to man they fought like demons—bayonets, revolvers, clubs, fists and stones! Friend and foe mingled in a mad holocaust of death. While still they fought, the second line of our charging men reached the spot and joined the fray. Twenty machine guns had been captured and turned on their foes. An ominous quiet behind the scene of this bloody combat followed the first roar of the clash.

The commander of the invaders, seeing that he had lost some guns, instantly drew back his lines and re-formed them fan-shaped with each gun bearing on the breach.

A tornado of whistling lead suddenly burst on the mass of our victorious troops. Five hundred machine guns had been concentrated with a speed that was stunning.

Our men dropped in platoons. They swayed and rallied and once more faced the foe for a second charge. Machine guns seemed to rise from the earth. They were fighting five regiments of men all armed with them.

The commander of our charging division tried in vain to rally. In thirty minutes there was nothing to rally. They lay in ghastly moaning heaps while whistling bullets sang their requiem in an endless crackle that came like the popping of straw before the roar of flames in a burning meadow. Whole regiments were literally wiped out with every officer and every man left torn and mangled on the field.

The reserves in the trenches saw the hideous butchery in helpless fury. No moving thing could live within the radius of those guns.

When the last man had fallen, the spluttering pom-poms died away and a green billow of smoke began to roll toward our lines. It swept on in a steady, even wave three miles long. The wind was carrying the cloud straight across the trenches in which our men crouched to receive the charge they expected to follow our failure.

The dust clouds had been pouring in their faces all morning. They paid no attention to the changing greenish tints of the new dust bank. The deadly fumes poured over our trenches in silence. The men breathed once and dropped in strangling horror, clutching and tearing at their throats. The guns fell by their sides as their bodies writhed and twisted in mortal agony. The pestilence swept the field scorching and curling every living thing.

Behind it in the shadows stalked a new figure in the history of war—ghouls in shining divers' helmets with knife and revolver to complete the assassin's work.

A thousand fiends of hell charging in serried ranks with faces silhouetted by the red glare of the pit could not have made a picture more hideous than these crouching diving machines as they scrambled over the shambles of the trenches and ruthlessly shot the few surviving figures, blindly fighting for air.

Behind those monsters who were proof against the poison fumes advanced the dense masses of infantry.

The way was clear, the backbone of the defense had been broken. Three miles of undefended trenches lay in front. It was the simplest work of routine to give the order to charge and watch them pour through the far-flung hopeless breach, swing to the right and left and roll the broken ranks up in two mighty scrolls of blood and death.

It was done with remorseless, savage brutality. Our men asked no quarter. They got none.

The leader of the charging hosts had orders to exterminate the contemptible little army of civilians that had dared oppose the imperial hosts.

They were setting an example of frightfulness that would make the task of complete conquest easy.

"Kill! Kill! Kill!" shouted the stout bow-legged General in command of the cavalry. "It's mercy in the long run! Let them know that we mean what we say!"

When our men saw their methods and knew that the end was sure, they sold each life for all it would bring in the shambles. Many a stalwart foe bit the dust and lay cold and still or writhing in mortal agony among the heaps of our dead and wounded before the awful day had ended.

The cries of the wounded were heartrending. A weird, unearthly sound came from the vast field of

groaning, wailing, dying, gibbering men. The most
hideous scenes of all were enacted by maniacs who
laughed the red laugh of death in each other's faces.

The horizon toward Southampton was black now
with the smoke of burning villages. They had set them
on fire with deliberate wanton purpose of destructive
terror.

Would they burn Babylon in the same way? Would
these maddened brutes break into our homes and make
the night still more hideous with crimes against women
and children?

A wave of horror swept Vassar's soul as he thought
of his nieces and the woman he loved. He crept through
the shadows of the woods and hurried toward the Holland home.

CHAPTER XXXIII

THE twilight was deepening on scenes of stark horror in the streets of Babylon when Vassar slipped through the field and along the hedgerows toward the center of the town.

Flames were leaping from a dozen homes along the turnpike. He saw the brutal soldiery enter a pretty lawn, call out the occupants and as they emerged fire in volleys on old men, women and children. They fell across the doorsteps and lay where they fell. A dark figure approached the open door, hurled a quart of gasoline inside, lighted his fire ball, and walked away, his black form outlined in the night against the red glare of hell.

A crowd of panic-stricken women and children with a dozen boys of fourteen rushed down the streets toward the squad of incendiaries. Without a word they raised their rifles and fired until the last figure fell.

A child toddled from the burning home carrying her kitten in one hand and a toy lamb in another. She was sobbing bitterly in one breath, and trying to reassure her kitten in the next.

Vassar heard her as she hurried past on the other side of the hedge.

"Don't you cry, kitty darling, I won't let them hurt you."

Her people were dead. She was hurrying into the night alone. From every street came the shrieks of women dragged to their doom by beasts in uniform.

Vassar set his jaw and crept along the last hedgerow to the gate of the Holland home.

The lights were burning brightly. A sentinel stood at the steps of the porch, his burly figure distinctly outlined against the cluster of electric lights in the low ceiling.

A sentry was on guard at the gate not ten feet away. A battery of artillery rolled past, its steel frames rattling and lumbering.

Vassar saw his chance.

As the last caisson wheeled away beyond the flickering street lamps the guard turned into the hedge out of the wind to light his pipe.

With a tiger spring Vassar leaped on him, gripped his throat, pressed an automatic to his breast and fired.

He took the chance that the passing battery would drown the muffled shot. The sentry crumpled in his arms and he held his breath watching his companion at the house. The steady step showed that he had not heard.

He drew the dying soldier into the shadows inside the lawn and exchanged clothes. He threw the body close under the hedge, seized the rifle and took his place at the gate.

He would side-step the officers, guard the house and make the men who dared attempt to violate it pay for their crime. It was evident that a commander had selected the house for his headquarters for the night. He watched the drunken revelers who passed and wondered what was happening inside.

So long as the officer of high rank remained and was sober the women were safe. He would stand guard until daylight and make his escape.

He watched the figures pass the lighted windows with increasing anxiety. A disturbance had occurred. The sentinel stopped, glanced toward the house, lowered his gun, watched a moment and resumed his beat.

Vassar crawled on his hands and knees halfway across the lawn, gripped his rifle, and waited.

CHAPTER XXXIV

THE orderly who searched the house found two shotguns. The Colonel who had quartered his staff for the night pointed to the two old men.

"Arrest them—you understand."

Andrew Vassar knew what the brief clause with which the order ended meant. He crossed himself and breathed a prayer for the safety of his loved ones.

Zonia and Marya burst into tears. Virginia and her mother drew themselves erect and waited white and silent.

Holland faced the commander, erect, defiant.

"I am a soldier, sir," he began with dignity. "I fought for my country through four bloody years in a hundred skirmishes and twenty-six great battles. I have the right to bear arms. I have won that right with my blood. I claim it before any court on earth over which a soldier presides."

The commander fixed him with a stern look.

"You have disobeyed the proclamation of the Governor-General, the servant of my Imperial Master. You have therefore forfeited all rights."

"I demand a trial by drum-head court martial!" Holland answered.

"You shall have it—you and your companion. Take them away."

Between two soldiers they were marched across the fields.

The children burst into incontrollable weeping.

The Colonel spoke in sharp tones:

"Come, come, my children. It is nothing. I must respect the forms. Their lives are forfeited, but I spare them for your sakes. They will return, both, tomorrow—have no fear!"

Zonia seized the officer's hand still sobbing:

"Thank you! Thank you!"

Marya in her joy kissed him.

The crisis passed, the Colonel turned to the ladies with a courtly bow.

"I am sorry to have to be so rude in your presence, madam," he said, addressing Virginia's mother. "We are soldiers. I must obey the orders of my superiors. I have no choice. We are sorry to put you to the trouble—but we are tired and hungry and we must dine. I will appreciate a good dinner and I shall see to it that your home is safe from intrusion on this unhappy evening."

His heels clicked again and he resumed his seat.

"We will serve you dinner at once," Virginia quickly replied before her mother could answer. "We are sorry that it will be so poor. We have had no market for the past two days—"

"Some good wine will go far to make up for what else you may lack," a Lieutenant interrupted.

"By all means, some wine—" the Colonel added.

The three men were bidden to enter the dining-room with a bow from Peter, the black butler.

"We dine alone?" the Colonel asked in surprise.

"De ladies is feelin' very po'ly, sah—Dey axe to be 'cused—"

"Say to the ladies," was the stern answer, "that we cannot sit down without their presence. We await them. Ask them to come at once."

The request was a command.

The women held a council of war.

"I'll die first," Mrs. Holland calmly answered.

"You will not," Virginia firmly declared.

"We've something big to live for now. Our country needs us. We too are soldiers from tonight. We play the war game with our enemy—come all of you—"

Without delay she forced them to enter the dining-room. Virginia, Zonia and Marya took seats opposite the intruders, the mother, her accustomed place at the head of the table.

The dinner moved with quiet and orderly dignity until the officers' faces began to flush with wine. The Lieutenant's leering eye continually sought Zonia's.

She avoided his gaze at every turn.

"Come, now, you little puss!" he cried at last. "Don't freeze me with dark looks and averted gaze. I like you!"

Zonia blushed and dropped her head lower.

"I suggest, Lieutenant," Mrs. Holland began, "that your remark is a little rude. I trust we are in the presence of gentlemen of culture and refinement."

Virginia held her breath in painful suspense. She saw the Colonel give a wink aside to his subordinate.

The Lieutenant tossed off his glass of wine, rose, clicked his heels and bowed.

"I assure you, madam," he said with a laugh, "you do me great injustice. I have been honestly smitten with admiration for the charming and beautiful young lady. We are enemies, but she has conquered. I acknowledge defeat. To show you my sincerity, I will apologize—"

With a quick swing, his word clanking, he walked around the table and leaned close over Zonia's soulders, his reddened eyes searching her frightened face.

"You will forgive me, my dear!" he drawled.

His head touched the girl's dark hair and she shrank with a little cry of horror.

"Please!"

"So! I'm not to be forgiven!" he growled.

"Please leave me!" Zonia breathed timidly.

"Come now—don't be silly—" he protested. "Am I a leper?"

The girl lifted her eyes to his flushed, lecherous face, sprang to her feet, rushed into the hall and up the stairs. The Lieutenant followed with a loud laugh and oath.

Virginia and her mother leaped from their chairs to follow. The Colonel stood in front barring the way.

"Enough of these high and mighty airs, if you please!" he commanded sternly. "We are the masters of this house. It is a woman's place to obey. Sit down!"

"Colonel, I beg of you—" Virginia pleaded. "I must protect this girl. She is under my care—"

"I will protect her! My officer means no harm. Your suspicions are an insult. He is only having his little fun with a foolish girl. It is the privilege of the conqueror—"

He seized Virginia's arm and forced her into her seat. Marya was sobbing bitterly. Mrs. Holland sank helplessly into a chair where she stood.

291

The Colonel opened the front door and beckoned the guard.

The sentinel entered.

"Attend us. The ladies will not leave this room until our dinner has been properly served."

The man saluted and took his place beside the door.

The noise of a struggle in the room above brought a moment of dead silence. The Colonel smiled. Marya screamed and Mrs. Holland fainted.

"Stop! Stop, I say!" Virginia heard the Lieutenant shout.

A vulgar oath rang through the house and Zonia's swift feet were climbing the second flight of stairs, a man stumbling after her.

Virginia rushed instinctively to the rescue. The guard seized her arms and forced her into a chair.

"My dear young lady," the Sublieutenant cried, approaching her with a leer. "It's only a little fun! Not a hair of her precious head will be harmed. He only fired to frighten and bring her to terms."

The Colonel continued to eat.

Virginia rushed to her mother's aid with a glass of water as her limp form slipped to the floor.

The Colonel bent low over his cups and laughed at a joke the Sublieutenant whispered.

A shot rang out from the wall of the house.

A piercing scream echoed from the tower against the roof.

Something crashed through the vines and struck the stone walk with a dull thud.

"O my God!" Virginia moaned, covering her ears.

Virginia leaped from the floor and heard the quick familiar step of Billy passing the back door.

He was hiding on the lawn, heard Zonia's first scream, and had killed the officer. Virginia saw it in a flash.

Their vengeance would be complete when they knew the truth. She must escape. There was work to be done for her country and she meant to do it. Life was too precious to be thrown away tonight.

She glided silently toward the door, reached the hall, seized Zonia's hand, passed the guard and reached the lawn.

"Follow her!" the Colonel shouted. "Bring her back dead or alive—I'll not be flouted by women!"

The man plunged after Virginia, and called once: "Halt!"

He raised his rifle to fire as she rushed squarely into the arms of the sentry who held the gate.

She struggled fiercely to free herself from the hated uniform and felt his arms tighten with savage power.

Vassar spoke in low, tense whispers:

"Be still, my own!"

She lifted her eyes in joyous terror and saw the face of her lover tense with rage.

"God in heaven!" she cried.

"Sh, still now—on your knees," he breathed.

"Oh, Uncy darling!" Zonia moaned.

Virginia's body slowly dropped as if in prayer that her life be spared.

The sentinel from the house leisurely approached.

"Good work, old pal!" he called.

The Colonel and Sublieutenant rushed from the house, followed by Marya and Mrs. Holland who had revived. The commander blew his whistle and the entire guard who patrolled the grounds hurried to the spot.

Billy stepped from the shadows, and spoke in low tones to Vassar.

"It's all up with me now. I shot the devil who was after Zonia."

"Billy darling!" Virginia moaned.

"Keep still, sis—it's all right!" he whispered.

The Colonel approached the group at his leisure, smoking a cigarette.

He merely glanced at Vassar and began in quick business-like tones:

"Who shot that man?"

Billy stepped forward.

"I did, sir—"

"So?"

"Virginia Holland's my sister—"

The Colonel touched his mustache and looked the youngster over with admiration.

"A boy alone defies a victorious army. I like you. I want you in our ranks—"

He paused thoughtfully as Mrs. Holland and Marya crept close, clinging to each other in dumb misery. Zonia slipped close to Billy—

"My darling boy!" his mother moaned.

"It's all right, mother," he called cheerfully— "What's the odds? They shot John Vassar's father and mine an hour ago—"

A low moan came from Virginia's lips.

The mother was silent. Her eyes were fixed on the rigid figure of her boy with hungry, desperate yearning.

The Colonel caught the look of anguish and felt for a moment the pull of its tragedy. He too had a mother.

He turned to her and spoke in friendly tones:

"Madam, your son is of the stuff that makes heroes. I'm going to spare his life—"

"Thank God—" she sobbed.

"On one condition—I want him in the service of

the Emperor. Frederick the Great called thousands of conquered foes to the colors—they made good. If he will take off his cap and give three cheers for the Emperor—I will place him on my staff and he shall live to find new paths of glory."

Billy smiled.

His mother, Virginia, Marya and Zonia pressed close and pleaded that he yield.

His mother held him in her arms in a long, desperate embrace.

"O my baby, heart of my heart, you must—I command it. Your father is gone. You must live and care for your poor mother—"

"Do it, boy," Virginia whispered, "and give them the slip—fight the devil with fire—you must."

"Please, Billy!" Marya pleaded.

Zonia slipped her arms around his neck.

The boy looked into the wistful face of the girl—bent and kissed her.

"All right, Zonia," he cried steadily.

"I'll do it for your sake and mother's—"

"Sensible boy!" the Colonel cried. "Now attention!"

He clicked his heels as the guard fell in line behind him. With quick wit John Vassar took his place with the others.

"The ladies by my side, please, in honor of the ceremony," the Colonel called.

Virginia, Marya and the mother huddled in a group beside the commander.

"Now, sir," he cried, "we'll have three cheers for his Imperial Majesty, the Emperor!"

The boy's face went white and his voice failed.

"Billy—" his mother pleaded.

"Billy!" Virginia sternly commanded.

"Billy!" Zonia pleaded.

The youngster's body suddenly stiffened and a smile overspread his face. The tense scene was unearthly in the pale moonlight. His voice was quick and rang in deep, manly tones.

"Hurrah for the President of the United States!—to hell with all emperors!"

The Colonel drew his pistol and shot him down before their agonized gaze.

The mother swooned, Marya fled in terror to the woods.

Zonia caught the crumpled figure in her arms.

Vassar with a single leap was by Virginia's side, seized her and rushed toward the shadows of the hedge.

He shouted to the commander:

"She's mine, Colonel—by right of conquest!"

To Virginia he whispered hoarsely:

"Shout, fight, scratch, scream to him for help—"

Quick to catch his ruse, she struck wildly with her hands, and called for help.

The Colonel laughed.

"I had reserved higher honors for you!" he shouted. "You're not worth it—go with your man!"

CHAPTER XXXV

M RS. HOLLAND rallied from her swoon and Marya helped her to rise as Zonia shouted joyfully: "Come quick! He's alive—he's alive!"

Billy opened his eyes feebly and raised his hand to the ugly wound in his breast. Zonia caught it, bent and kissed him.

Mrs. Holland staggered to the group and knelt by their side.

"Oh—my boy—you'll live—I feel it—I know it. God has heard my prayer—"

She paused and turned to Marya—

"Go, darling, quick—bring some water and tell Peter to come."

Marya darted across the lawn, entered the house, summoned Peter and seized a glass of water.

In ten minutes the faithful old butler had carried Billy from the lawn and was leading the stricken group toward the road for New York.

Vassar's trick succeeded. He reached his post without interference, thrust Virginia into the edge of the dense hedgerow and waited until the guards had returned to their places. Not a moment was to be lost.

He seized her hand and rushed down the street lit by the glare of burning houses.

"Play your part now!" he commanded. "It's the only way and it's safe. It's the order of the night's work."

They pushed through mobs of panic-stricken fleeing refugees and groups of drunken soldiers revelling in every excess. Again and again they passed brutes with captive girls as their prey. Some had them tied with cords. Others relied on a blow from their fists to insure obedience.

They waved their congratulations to Vassar and his captive as they passed.

They reached the outskirts of the town without accident and ran into the stream of horror-stricken humanity that was pouring now toward New York.

A great murmur of mingled anguish, rage and despair rolled heavenward. It seemed a part of the leaping flames and red billowing smoke of the burning city behind them.

Lost children were crying for their parents and trudging hopelessly on with the crowd.

A farmer with a horrible wound across his forehead

was pushing a wheelbarrow bearing his mangled child. Beside the body sat a little three-year-old girl clutching a blood-smeared doll.

A big automobile came shrieking through this crowd of misery. Beside the chauffeur sat an officer in glittering uniform, behind two soldiers, their bayonets flashing in the glare of the conflagration. In the rear seat alone, in magnificent uniform with gold epaulets and cords, sat the Governor-General of the fallen nation.

Waldron saw Virginia with a look of surprise and rage and lifted his hand. The car stopped instantly. The guard sprang out and opened the door of the tonneau.

"Quick!" Virginia whispered. "He has seen me. He will recognize you—run for your life!"

"I'll not leave you to that beast's mercy—"

"Run—run I tell you, if you love me!" she cried in agony. "I can take care of myself now. I'll manage Waldron—and I know how to die!"

He gripped her hand fiercely.

With sudden resolution, she tore from his grasp and rushed to meet her rescuer.

Vassar no longer hesitated. She had made it impossible for him to linger a moment. He leaped the fence and disappeared in the shadows.

301

Waldron grasped Virginia's hand in genuine surprise and distress.

"My dear Miss Holland," he said with a touch of royal condescension, "what does this mean?"

"I was a prisoner," she gasped.

"A prisoner?"

"The brute who ran had seized and dragged me from the lawn and through the streets."

"I'm proud and happy in this chance to prove to you my devotion. You have treated me cruelly. I show you tonight my generosity."

"Thank you," she murmured gratefully.

With a lordly bow he handed her into the car and ordered his chauffeur to drive down the turnpike toward the Holland house.

The home was in flames. The Colonel had fired it in revenge for the death of his Lieutenant and sought new headquarters for the night.

Virginia found her mother, Zonia, Marya—with old Peter nearby holding Billy in his lap—standing in dazed horror watching the flames leap and roar and crackle.

Waldron helped the stricken mother and girl into his car.

Virginia lifted her white face.

"My father was shot—"

302

"Tonight?"

"Yes—"

Waldron turned sharply to a guard.

"Find his body. It can't be far and bring it to New York for burial."

"If you will permit me, Miss Holland," Waldron said with a stately bow, "I will take you and your mother to your house on the Square. I fear it has been looted by the soldiery who got out of hand for a few hours. But you will be safe there from tonight. I will place a guard at your door. You are under my protection now—"

"Thank you! Thank you," Virginia answered in low tones.

The Governor-General drove by the army headquarters, spoke for a moment to the Commander-in-chief, arranged the programme for the triumphal entry into the city, secured a cavalry escort and leisurely drove back into New York through miles of weary plodding, stunned and maimed refugees still fleeing before the savage sweep of the imperial army.

He placed Virginia and her mother in their wrecked home and stationed a guard at the door.

With lordly condescension he took her hand in parting:

"Please remember, Miss Holland, that I'm the most

powerful man in America today. My word is law, and I am yours to command."

"You are generous," she answered softly.

He lifted his hand in protest, bowed and took his seat again in his automobile.

Virginia stood beside a broken window and watched the swiftly galloping horses of his escort sweep past the little park toward Broadway.

She walked with wide staring eyes through the litter of broken furniture, a dim resolution slowly shaping itself in her soul. It came in a moment's inspiration—the way of deliverance at last. Her heart gave a cry of joy. The nails of her slender fingers cut the flesh as she gripped her hands in the fierce decision.

"I'll do it—I'll do it!" she breathed with uplifted head and chalk-white face.

CHAPTER XXXVI

VASSAR succeeded in making his way to Fort Hamilton and joined General Hood. He had cut his way through Waldron's garrison which had mobilized in Brooklyn to join its levies with the invading army.

General Hood disbanded the handful of surviving officers and men and ordered each individual to join him at a secret rendezvous on the plains of Texas. He kept intact two companies of cavalry for an escort. He would take his chances with these by avoiding the fallen cities.

He placed final orders to his faithful secret service men in New York in Vassar's hands.

"You wish to stay a few days in New York. All right. Disguise yourself, travel by rail and join me later. Tell our people everywhere to play the fox, submit, take their oath of allegiance, and wait my orders. They'll come in due time. I'm going to retreat to the Sierra Nevadas if necessary and get ready."

Vassar pressed the General's hand.

"You will surrender the forts?"

"Certainly. I shall leave them intact. We'll need them again."

"I could blow them up. It would be foolish. The city they were built to defend is lost for the moment. The submarines are already lying in the harbor and hold the Navy Yard."

With a quick pressure of hand the men parted. The General embarked his cavalry on a small army transport that lay under the guns of Fort Hamilton, slipped to sea at night and sailed for Galveston.

Vassar reached New York disguised as a Long Island truck farmer. He drove a wagon loaded with vegetables, circled Stuyvesant Square next morning and called his produce for sale.

He looked for an agonized moment at his battered house, snapped the iron weight strop on his horse's bridle and rushed up the stairs.

The wreck within was complete and appalling.

He hurried across the Square to the Holland house. He was sure that Waldron would give his protection.

He could kill him for it and yet he thanked God Virginia was safe. Waldron loved her. He knew it by an unerring intuition. He would use his wealth and dazzling power again to win her. He knew that too by the same sixth sense.

He couldn't succeed! If ever a woman loved, Virginia Holland loved him. With her kind it was once for life.

And yet he trembled at the thought of what such a brute might do when every appeal had failed. Would he dare to use his power to force her to his will? Such things had been done by tyrants. A new day was dawning in a world that once was the home of freedom—the day of the jailer, tyrant, sycophant, and soldier who asks no questions.

It strangled him to think that he must leave her here. He wouldn't! He would make her come with Marya, Zonia and her mother into the West and take her place in the field by his side.

The thought thrilled him with new life.

In ten minutes he was holding her in his arms—war and death, poverty and ruin lost in love's mad rapture.

"You must come with me, my own!" he breathed. "I will find a tent for you on the great free plains—you, your mother, and Marya and Zonia. You can follow when I send you the word—"

She shook her head sadly.

"No, my lover, I cannot surrender to our enemies like that—my place is here."

"Your life is not safe in Waldron's hands."

"I'm in God's hands. I have work to do. You shall do yours on the plains training our brave boys for the day that shall surely come. I must do mine here—"

"I can't leave you!" he protested bitterly.

"You must. My mother can't live. I know this. The shock of a journey would kill her. Marya and Zonia shall be my sisters."

For half an hour he pleaded in vain. There was but one answer.

"My work is here. I've thought it out to the end. I shall not fail. I'll tell you when I'm ready and you will come then—"

There was an inspiration, a lofty spirit of exaltation, in her speech that hushed protest.

He pressed her lips.

"I will not see you again," he said at last. "My coming is dangerous to us both. My work is done to-day. We may be watched by other eyes than Waldron's guard on your block—"

"I am grateful for his help. I shall be sorry for him when the day I dream comes. But it must come. I have betrayed my country by folly beyond God's forgiveness. I shall do my part now to retrieve that error—"

Vassar moved uneasily.

308

"You shall know and approve—and I shall not fail!"

She paused and held his gaze with a strange, glowing light in her eyes—the light of religious enthusiasm. It filled him with fear and thrilled him with hope. Her faith was contagious.

"You cannot work here—" she went on, "a price is on your head."

He left her at the door, the same dreamy brilliance in her sensitive face. She stood as if in a trance. He wondered what it meant—what her mysterious work was going to be?

CHAPTER XXXVII

THREE days later the magnificent imperial army entered the fallen metropolis, its scarlet, gold-embossed standards flying, its bands playing.

Waldron marched to meet them at the head of twenty-five thousand picked men of his garrison. His division more than made good the losses of battle.

When the grand march began at the entrance of the Queensboro Bridge—one hundred and sixty-five thousand men were in line. The immensity of the spectacle stunned the imagination of the curious thousands that pressed close to the curbs and watched them pass. When the German army entered Antwerp in the world war, the streets were absolutely deserted save for stray dogs and cats that howled from wrecked buildings. New York was consumed by a quenchless eagerness to look on their conquerors.

All day from seven o'clock in the morning until dark the torrent of brown kahki poured through Fifty-ninth Street and down Fifth Avenue. When the Avenue was filled by the solid ranks from Central Park to the

Washington Arch, the imperial host at a given signal raised their shout of triumph.

"For God and Emperor!"

Until this moment they had moved in a silence that was uncanny. Their long-pent feelings gave the united yell of a hundred and sixty thousand an unearthly power. They shouted in chorus first from every regiment in one grand burst of defiant pride. And then they shouted by regiments, beginning with the first. The shout leaped from regiment to regiment until it swept the entire line far out on the plains of Long Island. Each marching host tried to lift the note higher until the frenzied bursts came with the shock of salvos of artillery.

And then they sang the songs of their grand army on the march. For an hour their voices rang the death knell of freedom while conquered thousands stood in awed silence.

Waldron moved at the head of the column on his white horse in gorgeous uniform. Beside him rode in service suit the Commander-in-chief on a black Arabian stallion with arched neck and sleek, shining sides.

The ceremonies at the City Hall were brief. The grand procession never paused. Timed to a dot, the lines had divided as they passed the cross streets leading to our great tunnels. At Forty-second Street a division swung into the Grand Central Station to entrain for service in the interior. The cars were waiting with steam up and every man at his place under the command of army officers.

At Thirty-fourth Street another division swung into the Pennsylvania Station. At Twenty-third Street another swept toward the Lackawanna and the Erie. At Fourteenth Street another swung toward the Chelsea piers, where transports were waiting to bear them to Baltimore, Norfolk, Charleston, New Orleans, Jacksonville and Galveston.

These transports had been seized in the harbor. The great armada was already loading the second division of a hundred and sixty thousand more men at the wharves of Europe. The imperial army of occupation would consist of a million veterans. They would be landed now without pause until the work was done. A A fleet of a hundred submarines lay in wait for our Pacific fleet in the Straits of Magellan. Its end was sure.

The conquest was complete, overwhelming, stunning. The half-baked desperate rebellions that broke out in various small towns where patriotism was a living thing were stamped out with a cruelty so appalling they were not repeated. At the first ripple of trouble the town was laid in ashes, its population of males massacred, its women outraged and driven into the fields to crawl to the nearest village and tell the story. One short-lived victory marked the end.

The Virginians raised an army of volunteer cavalry, led by a descendant of Jeb Stuart raided and captured Washington. The garrison were taken by complete surprise at three o'clock before daylight. The fight was at close quarters and the enemy was annihilated.

A battle cruiser promptly swept up the Potomac from the Chesapeake Bay, opened with her huge guns and reduced our capital to a pile of broken stone. Incendiary shells completed the work and two days later the most beautiful city in America lay beneath the Southern skies a smouldering ash-heap. The proud shaft of shining marble to the memory of George Washington was reduced to a mass of pulverized stone. A crater sixteen feet in depth gaped where its foundations had rested.

An indemnity was levied on New York that robbed the city of every dollar in every vault and sent its famous men into beggared exile. Waldron's list of proscription for banishment included every leader in the world of finance, invention and industry.

He had marked every man with a genius for political leadership for a term of ten years' imprisonment.

313

Exile was too dangerous an experiment for these trouble-makers. They were safer in jail. Ten years in darkness and misery would bring them to reason.

The world's war had cost the Imperial Federation a staggering total of thirty billions. Waldron promised his royal master to replace every dollar of this loss within five years by a system of confiscation and taxes. His first acts of plunder sent treasure ships to Europe bearing fifteen billions. The revenue from all the confiscated railroads, mines, and great industries taken over by the new government would reduce taxation in Europe to a trifle.

When the conquest was complete the net result was that Imperial Europe had fenced in a continent with bristling cannon. Inside the inclosure were a hundred million of the most intelligent and capable slaves the world had seen since the legions of Rome conquered Greece and enslaved her artists and philosophers.

There was no pause in the ruthless work until the last spark of resistance had been stamped out.

By one of the strange ironies of fate the fiercest of the futile rebellions broke out on the East Side of New York, where the attempt was made completely to disarm our half-baked foreign population. The men who sulked in the tenement districts below the Bowery had been accustomed to fight constituted authority in the

Old World from habit. The first squad of soldiers sent into this quarter to disarm them had never returned. Not one of their bodies were found.

When a regiment with machine guns rushed in they found the side streets below Fourteenth barricaded with piles of trucks and lumber. From every window they received a hail of bullets.

A battery of artillery cleared the barricades and the slaughter began. After four hours of butchery in the streets, the commander discovered that the old Tenth Regiment Armory was crowded. More than a thousand women and children accustomed to attend Vassar's school of patriotism had sought refuge there.

The children had found the flags and their mothers in foolish superstition had pinned them on their breasts for protection—the flag they had been taught to love!

The Imperial Guard turned their artillery on the armory and tore the flimsy front wall into fragments. When the screaming children and frantic women rushed through the breach, a withering fire from the pompoms piled their writhing bodies on the blood-soaked pavements.

Benda had been killed in the second intrenchments on Long Island. Angela faced the storm of lead at the door, holding her boy behind her back to shield him from the bullets.

A shell exploded inside and a fragment buried itself in the child's breast. The mother felt the stinging shock and heard the thud of the iron crash into the soft flesh.

The boy made no cry. The iron had torn through his heart. The little hand was lifted feebly and clutched the tiny flag that covered his breast.

With a cry of anguish she clasped the bleeding bundle of flesh in her arms, ran through the building and found her way into the darkened basement.

When the building was cleared the commander entered with a squad of soldiers, lighted a cigarette and inspected the ruins.

On the blackboards still were standing in clear white chalk the sentences and mottoes Vassar had written:

ALL MEN ARE CREATED EQUAL.

The Commander laughed and wrote beneath it:

BUT YOU COULDN'T STOP A SIXTEEN-INCH SHELL WITH HOT AIR!

The men cheered.

On the next blackboard stood the words:

LIBERTY—EQUALITY—FRATERNITY.

The officer struck a line through each word and wrote beneath:

AUTHORITY—OBEDIENCE—EFFICIENCY.

"A battery of artillery cleared the barricades and the slaughter
began"

Again the soldiers cheered.

Within three months the fallen nation had been completely disarmed and rendered helpless.

The penalty of death was enforced against everyone who dared to conceal a pistol, rifle, shotgun or piece of explosive. The manufacturing plants making arms and ammunition were under the control of the invaders.

They not only controlled these gun and shell factories, they took possession of every chemical laboratory and every piece of machinery that could be used to make explosives. It was no more possible to buy a piece of dynamite for any purpose than to buy a forty-two centimeter siege gun. All blasting for building and commercial purposes was done by an officer, who charged well for his services.

Every street railway and trunk line was manned by the army. The ammunition factories were all working with double shifts of American laborers, compelled by their conquerors to turn out shells for future use against their fellow-countrymen.

Every newspaper, magazine and publishing-house had installed an Imperial censor. Not a line was allowed to be printed under penalty of death except by his order.

Freedom of speech and press was relegated to the dust heap as dead heresies against constituted authority. The people were only told what their masters permitted them to hear. Our press, of course, was unanimous in its praise of the new Imperial régime. "Law," "Order," and "Efficiency" were the new watchwords of America. The people were not asked to do any thinking. Their masters did it for them, their part was to obey.

Waldron determined to make Virginia Holland the leader of a new woman's party to proclaim the blessings of the imperial and aristocratic form of government.

He honored her with an invitation to his palace to discuss his scheme. When Virginia received the perfumed, crested note, her cheeks flushed with joy.

"Thank God!" she murmured fervently.

CHAPTER XXXVIII

VIRGINIA had just dressed in dead black for her visit to the palace of the Governor-General on the Heights. Waldron insisted on sending a state automobile. The machine was at the door with liveried flunkies standing in stiff servant attitudes.

A slender Italian woman passed them with a listless stare and rang the bell of the Holland house.

Virginia answered. She had seen the somber figure from the window.

"Angela!" she cried in surprise.

Si. Signorina, I may see—you?"

"Yes"—was the quick, sympathetic answer.

The drooping figure shambled to a seat and dropped.

"Tell me—what has happened?" Virginia urged.

"You see the papers?"

"About the riots on the East Side—yes—the people were very foolish—"

The woman leaned close—her breath coming in deep quivering draughts.

"They kill my bambino—signorina! The shell tore

319

his little heart all out—see! I bring the flag he wore—
all red with blood. And now I come to you—you
speak so grand, I want my revenge—"

She paused, strangled with emotion.

"I keep this flag and I love it too! I will kill and
kill and kill! You will tell me how? They kill your
father—they kill your brother—you tell me, Signorina!
We fight now—you and me—we fight for this flag—
is it not so?"

She held in her hand the blood-stained emblem.

Virginia took the stricken mother in her arms and
sobbed with her.

"Come with me," she said in low tones, leading
the way to the sitting-room in the rear. She closed
the doors, and pressed Angela to her knees.

Into the ears of the kneeling woman she whispered
an oath.

"You swear?"

"By the mother of God and all the Saints!" came
the quick answer.

For ten minutes Virginia gave instructions in tones
so low that they could not be heard even by the keenest ear at her door.

There was a light of wild joy in the swarthy face
as she rose.

"Now—I live—I breathe—Signorina! Si—si. I

understand! I take the little organ and monkey. I go. I see all the people. I whisper to those I trust. We meet. I go again to West Side and do the same. I go everywhere and I tell you. Si—si. I *live* again!"

She threw her arms about Virginia, held her in silence and left with quick, eager step—the light of purpose flashing in her dark eyes.

CHAPTER XXXIX

THE Governor-General received Virginia in royal state. His manner was gracious and genial. He led her to a seat in his great library and closed the doors. The royal guard took his stand outside.

"I told you, Miss Holland," he began eagerly, "that I had high ambitions. You see that I am a man of my word. Of course, the thing that happened was inevitable. It was written in the book of Fate. Had I not seized the reins—another would. Conditions made my coup possible. For the excesses of the Imperial Conquering Army I have no words in palliation. Such is war. Had I known the peril of your father and mother, I assure you I would have hurried to their rescue—you believe me when I say this?"

"I am sure of it, now," she answered promptly.

"I hurried to Babylon the moment I learned that the defense had collapsed and our troops were victorious—"

He paused and leaned closer.

"I want to apologize for the unpardonable blunder

322

I made the last time we met in this house. I did not realize then how deeply and madly I love you. In anguish I learned it too late. But I have bided my time. I have lived to prove my devotion in the hour of your peril and I have only begun what I wish to do for you—"

Again he paused, his eyes devouring her pensive beauty.

"I had rather win you than rule the Empire that's mine. I would win as a man woos and wins the one woman he loves—you believe me when I say this?"

"Yes," was the frank reply. "I believe now that you are in dead earnest."

"Good. I don't ask if you love me. I know that you do not. I do not ask you to marry me immediately. I know that I must first win your regard. I prize you all the more for this reason—"

"Man-like, of course," Virginia interrupted with a smile.

"First, I wish to pay you personally the highest tribute a man in my position can give to any man or women. I am going to offer you the second highest place in the Empire next to mine. Your fortune has disappeared in the wreck of war. You shall rebuild it tenfold through the work I shall place in your hands.

My first ambition now is really to pacify the mind of the States. It can be done through our women.

"I appeal to your reason. Here is the situation. The last hope of successful rebellion has been stamped out. The millions of America, completely disarmed, are helpless to resist our army of occupation. I wish, not only to complete the crushing of the last hope of insurrection; it is my ambition to convince the people that the central monarchical and aristocratic form of government is the only natural order of life and therefore a divine law.

"The quick intuitions of women have been always more open to this truth than the more brutal and anarchistic male mind. Women have always been the bulwark of aristocracy and imperial monarchy. Man is an anarchist—woman a royalist by instinct.

"The American democracy was only an accident of time and space. The oceans are now the King's highway and he owns them by right of eminent domain. Democracy can never survive this bringing of the ends of the earth together. Democracy cannot live because when brought face to face with the monarchical form it is not worthy to live. The United States of America gave the human race the one supreme example of a weak, corrupt and contemptible government. The like of it was never known before in the history of man.

"Democracy is a disease—a form of crowd ego-mania which drives millions of people mad with the insane delusion that they have been called of God to do something for which they are utterly unfitted.

"All government worthy of the name must be conducted by a few brilliant minds—divine leaders—presided over by a supreme leader whom we call emperor or king. This is true in so-called democracies. The people only pretend to govern—imagine that they govern. They do not. A few master minds and brutal wills do it for them. Hence the system of bosses whose foul record we have ended forever.

"No nation can have an art or literature unless monarchical and aristocratic—America has never had a literature. It will have one only when its conscious life is reincarnated in the soul of a sovereign who takes his crown from God, not man.

"The people of this country were never fit to govern themselves. They got the kind of government they deserved. In Central Europe government has long been reduced to a science. Their cities are clean—their life as orderly as the movement of the stars.

"The monarchical form of government only can answer the questions of Socialism. Germany did this a generation ago. When the world-war came the

Socialists were as loyal to the Emperor as the proudest prince of the blood.

"The conquest of America has been the best thing that could have happened. Its battles were of minor importance. Had not a powerful Imperial government come to our rescue we would have been deluged in blood by a second French Revolution within this generation.

"The noblest minds in this country have felt this for years. They have gradually been turning in disgust from our corrupt legislatures, our corrupt courts, our corrupt municipalities, our rotten boroughs, our corrupt Congress. I tell you this to show you that I have been led by no weak or vulgar ambition into a betrayal of the liberties of a people. I believe in what I have done—believe in it with every ounce of my manhood. We owe the progress of the human race to aristocracy, not democracy. Democracy is the great leveler of the world—the destructive force that presses humanity downward and backward. Aristocracy is the inspiring power that leads, uplifts, creates and beckons onward and upward.

"All the achievements of thought and science are by the chosen few. The herd merely eats and sleeps and reproduces its kind. But for the pressure from their superiors the masses would all lapse to elemental savagery within a few brief generations—"

326

Waldron stopped suddenly and gazed on the placid waters of the Hudson.

Virginia watched him with genuine astonishment. He had revealed a new side of his strong character. She had not dreamed that his philosophy of life had been so logically wrought. She had not believed since his betrayal of his country that he had a philosophy of life at all.

"You astonish me beyond measure," she said at last.

He smiled coldly.

"I understand. You did not think me capable of such sweeping thoughts or such close reasoning—confess it!"

"It's true, I didn't—"

"You know now that I am in earnest in my political ambitions also?"

"I'm thoroughly convinced—"

"Good! You are a woman of rare intelligence and high ambitions. It is therefore easy for me to speak, now that you know that I am sincere—"

He held her gaze in a moment's searching silence.

"I may trust you now I'm sure with a secret that is not a secret if I should be accused. *You* will know that I mean something very definite when I say that this nation is too great, its resources too exhaustless to remain forever a conquered province of Imperial Europe. Am I not right?"

"At least I hope so," was the diplomatic reply.

"Exactly," Waldron answered confidentially. "In other words the day will come when a political leader of supreme genius will win the utter loyalty and confidence of the soldiers who hold these millions in hand. The man who does that will ascend a throne in Washington in a palace worthy of a Continental Empire washed by two oceans—you understand?"

"I see!" Virginia breathed.

"Remember then, dear young lady, that I am your servant from today. If I have high ambitions and glorious dreams for my people and my country, I dream new glories for you—"

"And the commission you would offer me?" she asked steadily.

"That you organize the women of America into loyal legions who will sustain the government against the possible forces of anarchy and rebellion. If you will consider the offer I will place unlimited money at your command. The old régime is gone forever. You can help me now to organize a nobler one on its ruins."

"And my reward?"

"I shall lay at your feet all that I am and have and

328

ever hope to be. I offer it now without condition if you will accept my hand in marriage—"

"Your commission I accept at once," was the prompt reply. "If I succeed we shall meet on terms more nearly equal."

Waldron sprang to his feet, seized her hand and kissed it.

Could we have seen the expression of her white face when his lips touched her flesh he would not have smiled as he led her to the waiting car.

CHAPTER XL

THE jails were crowded with our leading states-
men. The President and his Cabinet had been
transferred to Fort Warren at Boston before
the Capitol was destroyed.

The Honorable Plato Barker, for reasons deemed
sufficient by the Governor-General, was placed in the
United States penitentiary at Albany. In spite of his
mania for peace, Waldron thoroughly mistrusted him.
His passion for oratorical leadership he knew to be in-
satiate. What fool scheme he might advocate in secret
could not be guessed. In vain Barker offered to take
the iron-clad Imperial oath. Waldron was deaf to all
entreaties even when the petition was borne to him by
the officer of the army who had captured the silver-
tongued leader and made him a scullion. Villard, the
Commanding General, had allowed Barker to deliver
Sunday lectures to his soldiers on harmless themes of
Chautauqua fame. The Commander had grown to like
the orator as a harmless sort of court jester. He was
particularly fond of his illustrations and jokes. He
declared that Barker had missed his calling—he should
have been an evangelist or a clown.

Failing to release his favorite captive the General interceded to save his reason.

Barker could not endure the silence to which he had been doomed. His mind began to break under the strain. He was saved from madness by an order which permitted him to preach to the prisoners on Sunday.

His first discourse was on "The Extraordinary Food Value of Grape Juice."

The men who were living on bread and water didn't like it.

The lecture was interrupted by an incipient riot. He was compelled to drop the subject and stick to historical religion. He switched to a discourse on Saul of Tarsus, which was well received. It in no way mocked the appetites of his hearers.

Pike proved to be another proposition for his captor. He became so peevish and sullen that his taskmaster went out of his way to make his life unendurable. The bow-legged Commander not only continually repeated Pike's former expressions on the dangers of being armed and the wickedness of being prepared for defense in the presence of the preacher while he danced attendance as a waiter at his headquarters, but he added insult to injury at last by forcing the advocate of peace to become an expert shot by daily target practice.

When Waldron ordered the doughty cavalry leader to St. Louis, he dragged Pike with him to continue his systematic torture. He piled the last straw on the little man's back the day after their arrival in the new quarters by ordering him to don the uniform of the Emperor, join a firing squad and shoot a deserter.

The preacher refused point blank. To have his fun the General ordered two guardsmen to bring the rebel to his room and force him into the uniform —his horse was standing at the door saddled and ready to gallop to the field and watch Pike faint at the ordeal.

The General roared with laughter when he finally stood forth arrayed in the brown uniform of the army. The guardsmen in their shirtsleeves were laughing too. He had struggled manfully to prevent the outrage and they had only drawn the clothes on him by main force. It took the hostler at the door finally to win the contest.

"Cheer up, Cuthbert, you'll soon be dead!" the officer cried.

The boys roared.

With a sudden panther leap Pike was on the General, snatched his automatic from his belt, shot him dead and killed the three men before they recovered from the shock.

With a second leap he was on the waiting horse and calmly galloped through the camp before the guards discovered the incident.

He found his way to General Hood's headquarters in the Sierra Nevadas and reported for duty.

"Keep your uniform!" Hood laughed. "We'll need it for scout work."

"Sure I'll keep it," the preacher snapped—" and use it myself, sir! I'll show them that my name's Pike —not Piker!"

The General despatched him to the Coast on an important and dangerous mission.

CHAPTER XLI

VIRGINIA HOLLAND'S conversion to the open advocacy of the principles of monarchy and aristocracy was Waldron's first sensation in the campaign in which he began to destroy the American conception of liberty.

Her confession of faith was a liberal outline of the ideals which the Governor-General had proclaimed in his library. Waldron was elated at his complete triumph.

Her brief statement and appeal to the women of America to support her movement of loyalty he ordered printed in every newspaper in the country. It duly appeared on the front pages, accompanied by a portrait of the distinguished young convert.

Her first year's engagements in organizing the Woman's Imperial Legion of Honor covered the principal cities of every state.

Her appeal had been received by the women of America with secret rage, amazement and horror. The Government had commanded their attendance on her lectures. Her reception at first had been cold and formal. But her magnetic personality turned the tide. Within a month there was no hall large enough in America to hold the breathless throngs of women who hung on her words. And strangest of all, they cheered her with an enthusiasm that amazed Waldron.

His agents reported this enthusiasm with oft-repeated praise of her uncanny genius.

The secret of her popularity they had not dreamed. In each town she took into her confidence but one woman on whose love for country she could depend with absolute certainty. This woman she swore in secret to organize an inner circle whose name to them was the Daughters of Jael. The spies who followed her tour to report to the Governor-General never reached this inner circle. In it were taken under solemn oath those whose love for liberty was a religion.

The Daughters of Jael comprised only the wisest women leaders, and with them the strongest and most beautiful girls in the glory of youth from twenty to thirty years of age.

They were taught in secret two things—to keep their lithe young bodies hard and sun-tanned and learn to wield a steel knife whose blade was eight inches long, slender and keen. When a million had been sworn and trained the order would come to strike for freedom. The rank and file knew nothing of this purpose. Only their leaders knew. Each had sworn to lay their souls and bodies a free offering on their country's altar and to obey their commander's word as the law of God.

It was two years from the beginning before Virginia ventured to meet her lover in a deep mountain gorge of the inner Sierras.

Their embrace was long and silent. They spoke at last in low, half-articulate sounds that only love could hear and know.

When the first wave of emotion had spent itself, she asked him eagerly:

"Your last invention—the aerial torpedo?"

"A failure like the rest!" he answered sadly. "Great inventions that revolutionize warfare have all required years to perfect—the ironclad a generation, the submarine ten years, the aeroplane ten years. They required the genius of hundreds in their experiments and the lives of thousands. The hope of miraculous inventions in an hour of crisis is only the vain dream of the novelist. We have ceased to hope for such deliverance. We are training men to master the already perfected mechanism of the submarine—thousands of them. Lake, the inventor, is an admiral. We have a model at work six thousand feet above the sea. I command the Eagle's Nest, the camp on a great mountain plateau where we are training thousands of aviators. On another peak among the stars we are teaching men to use the range finders and swing big guns to strike a target at twelve miles. Most important of all we are teaching each and every man how to use cold steel at close range—"

"You fully accept my scheme then?" she interrupted.

"As an inspiration of God! The staff has tested it with a hundred hostile suppositions. It is sure to win if you can train a million girls to co-operate with us in the uprising, win to our cause one man in ten in the Imperial Army, and wield a knife with deadly power. The only question is, can you get those girls?"

"I have them already—"

"A million?"

"And more—I had to stop. I could have sworn another million."

"We will be ready in three months—"

"You can have four—"

"You have fixed the date?"

"Yes. There can be but one—the Emperor's birthday—"

Vassar clasped Virginia in his arms.

"Dearest—you're inspired—I swear it!"

"I have positive assurance," she went on eagerly, "that our girls have already won more than two hundred thousand soldiers of the enemy who will join us the night we strike. Every officer will be in his cups that night. A Belshazzar's feast, with Waldron as their toastmaster!"

"And not merely in New York—" he added, "but in every city in America—on every ship—in every aviation hangar and on board every submarine—once their guns are in our hands—!"

"We'll take them—never fear—" she cried.

"If we can only get our hands on half their rifles, half their machine guns, half the ships and half the aircraft we'll win! The fiends of hell never fought as we shall fight! We'll get them too—" he stopped overwhelmed with emotion. "It's the knife at close quarters in the dark, man to man, muscle and steel, and dauntless hearts, that will turn the trick. How little we've traveled after all our boasted science! All your girls will have to do is to get them drunk that night, rally your converts, strike down the outer guards —smuggle in a few guns and we'll do the rest.

"We'll give your men more than half their rifles," Virginia promised. "And what's more we will put their trained artillerymen, aviators and submarine experts out of commission to a man that night. We will detail two girls for each of these men—there'll be no blunder—"

"There's just one thing I don't like—" he broke in with clenched fists.

"Yes, I know, my lover!" she smiled.

"You've got to make love to those brutes, flatter and cajole them for weeks. You are risking what we hold more precious than life—"

"We have sworn to give as God has given us—all—"

"I don't like it—I don't like it!" he protested bitterly.

She slipped her arms about his neck. Her eyes sought his with yearning in their depths.

"Never speak or think that thought of me again, my own," she whispered. "I, too, know how to die as well as you. This is the third and last lesson we shall teach the Daughters of Jael before the Day dawns! Those who give their honor will scorn the cheaper gift of life. The new sun will rise on a clean and glorious womanhood, redeemed by sorrow and humbled by a divine passion for country we could learn in no other school but this."

She held him at arm's length and slowly slipped her hands from his and waved him back.

"No more—until the Day dawns!"

"Until the Day dawns, my love!" he breathed tenderly.

She leaped on her pony and galloped into the solemn night alone—to deliver her orders to the Daughters of Jael for their third and final lesson.

CHAPTER XLII

THE preparations for the grand celebration of the Conqueror's birthday by the people of America were complete to the last detail at noon on the day preceding.

The Governor-General was determined to make this event an example in promptness, glorious display and perfect efficiency. How prompt and efficient its real managers were going to make it he could not dream!

Every suspicion of disloyalty had been put at rest by the eager enthusiasm with which the Woman's Legion of Honor, with its five thousand chapters, had taken the lead in preparation under Virginia's brilliant direction. For three months the most beautiful girls in America had vied with one another in courting the favor of the army for the approaching festival. From the Governor-General down to the sailors of the fleet our girls had eyes only for the Imperial Army uniforms.

The artillerymen, the aviators, and the submarine experts were the favorites. The conquerors began to feel a contemptuous pity for the poor native devils their charms had put out of the running.

Even the chauffeurs and railroad officials were everywhere courted and fêted by the fair ones. Every railroad agent, conductor, dispatcher, and superintendent was an officer in the Imperial Army. These men, who had rarely shared the glory of the regular army, were particularly elated over their triumphs with the girls.

When the Day dawned every terminal and every train in America was decorated with the royal flags. The spirit of abandonment to joy in a strange, subdued mania swept the nation. Beneath it beat the throbbing hearts of a million Sons of the New Revolution and a million Daughters of Jael who had offered their souls and bodies a living sacrifice for the glory of the Day. The contagion of earnestness from these eager millions of young men and women set every heart to beating with expectant awe.

Angela received her final instructions at the Holland house at six o'clock. The magnificent display of fireworks would begin at eight-thirty, the dancing at nine-thirty, the banquet at eleven-thirty.

"You have a girl with every chauffeur?" Virginia asked sharply.

"Si, signorina—" Angela paused and smiled.

"And they have learned to drive, too—yes—they have had some fun these three months!"

"At the Seventy-first Armory, a girl for every sailor of the fleet?"

"For every one—"

"At the Twelfth Regiment?"

"For the birdmen's chauffeurs—I have two—very prettiest girls—two for each—"

"At the Seventh Regiment?"

"A girl for every waiter to help them serve. My girls they help the waiters everywhere—"

A look of fierce triumph overspread the dark features of the little mother. Her eyes grew misty. She fumbled in her bosom and slowly drew out the blood-stained flag her boy had worn on his breast.

"And I have the flag, signorina! When I tear the red crown from the staff I wave this one and shout for my bambino."

Virginia merely nodded. Her mind was sweeping the last possibility of accident.

"You haven't been able to reach a single man among the wireless operators of the Woolworth tower?" she asked dreamily.

"Not one, signorina. The old devil up there don't like the girls. He is not human—"

"There's no help for it then," she answered. "We'll

try another way. When all is ready attend me at the palace of the Governor-General. When the signal flashes from the Metropolitan tower I want the car I always drive at the door instantly—"

"Si, signorina—my chauffeur he like me very much —I must think of my bambino when I strike!"

"You will not fail?" Virginia sternly asked.

Angela touched the little flag and shook her head.

"Do not fear—I shall not fail!" She paused, bent close and whispered, "My chauffeur join our men, signorina—the Sergeant of the big guns, too. He swear to me the guns shall be ours!"

With a quick pressure of her hand Virginia hurried to enter the car of state which was already standing at the door.

The streets were thronged with thousands who talked in subdued tones. They had felt the iron hand on their throats too often during the past three years to abandon themselves to the occasion.

There were no screeching horns, no riotous boys and girls hurling confetti. Such crude expressions of liberty were forbidden.

Beneath the outer quiet slumbered the coming volcano.

Virginia drove to the Waldorf-Astoria, sent her card

to a distinguished guest and was ushered into his parlors.

The dark foreigner with a Van Dyke beard bowed over her hand.

"Your Lordship had a pleasant trip across I trust?" she asked.

The door closed and they were alone.

With a smothered cry she was in Vassar's arms murmuring foolish, inarticulate sounds.

She freed herself with quick decision.

"There's not a moment to be lost," Virginia whispered. "I've failed to reach a single man in the Woolworth tower."

"It must be taken then!" he answered firmly. "I have ordered the other stations destroyed. We must hold that before we strike in the banquet halls. I've made my plans to call our cavalry and automobile orders from there. Our first line of men must mobilize and be on their way within five minutes after the searchlight signals from the Square—"

He paused thoughtfully.

"There's not a moment to be lost. I'll take that tower myself. Send three of your girls to meet me there at nine o'clock dressed as country folks on a sight-seeing trip to the city—"

"Armed of course?"

"Yes—with automatics if you have them—I'll find a way to get them up to see the fireworks."

At nine o'clock a noisy group of country louts succeeded in reaching the room that led by a narrow winding stairs to the upper room of the Woolworth tower. They were singing loyal songs for God and Emperor! Their pilot was drunk but good-natured and determined to show them the pinnacle.

The cautious red-faced Captain in charge of the wireless, who had been celebrating a little on the quiet, had thawed to a genial mood.

"T'ree cheers for Zemperor!" the jovial pilot from the country shouted.

The Captain laughed and joined the chorus. He glanced contemptuously at the giggling girls.

"Say, Cap," the leader cried, leaning heavily on his shoulder—"my girls gotter see the fireworks—from the top—tip top! I promised 'em I'd take 'em to the very tip top—gotter make good—"

His legs wobbled and his breath was heavy with beer.

The Captain laughed.

"Think you could climb these winding stairs?"

"Surest thing you know."

The drunken man staggered to the steps, rushed half way up, slipped and fell, sprawling to the floor.

The Captain roared.

345

"Try again!" he shouted. "I'll let you go but not these women!"

The girls joined in the laughter while he made another ludicrous effort and slipped again.

The two operators left their instruments and peered down the shaft.

"Go back to your places—this is my show!" the Captain called.

The drunken countryman watched them withdraw with wagging head but keen eye. He saw there were only two. He knew his task now.

He made another desperate effort to climb the spiral, turned a complete somersault and came down headforemost.

The Captain slipped to a sitting posture weak with laughter.

"Shay, pardner, help me!" the drunken one pleaded.

"No—this is my show—it's too good to lose—I'm the audience—help yourself!"

The drunken countryman tried it backward this time, holding first to the rail.

The Captain wiped the tears from his eyes and bent again to laugh as the fool reached the last step and waved in triumph. He turned and staggered against the wall feeling his way to the door beyond.

346

The girls crowded about the Captain.

"Please let us go too!" they chimed in chorus.

The Captain was adamant. They kept up their parrot cries until the crash above came. They heard the blow that felled the first operator—the shuffle of feet, the tiger spring, the smothered cry.

It was all over with the Captain before the cry. Three fierce, athletic girls bore him to the floor and held his writhing body until it was still.

"All right!" Vassar called. "Stand guard now at the door leading from the elevator—inside the door. Let no one pass!"

The leader of his guard touched her hat in salute. He took his place at the operator's table and answered a call from the tower of the Governor-General's palace.

"Your wireless stations have all answered?" the machine sang.

"All"—was the brief answer.

"I'll give you the signal for the Emperor's toast on the stroke of twelve."

"Good!" Vassar answered with a grim smile.

CHAPTER XLIII

BEFORE eleven o'clock the Daughters of Jael, accorded the place of honor at every banquet hall, had succeeded in slipping from drunken soldiers and sailors thousands of arms. Swift automobiles, commandeered by their persuasive voices, or taken by direct attack from maudlin chauffeurs, were speeding with these guns to the appointed places. More than two hundred thousand soldiers of the Imperial Army have deserted to our colors.

Ten thousand rough riders from the Western plains had been smuggled into the suburban districts of New York since the embargo on horses had been lifted. They were armed with lances and only awaited the advent of revolvers to lead the attack.

Each soldier from the Far West had reached the Eastern seaboard as an individual and reported secretly to his commander. They were in their brown kahki suits tonight stripped for action, awaiting the signal to strike.

Billy Holland, a captain of infantry, had been chosen by Vassar to lead the assault on Waldron's place. His sweetheart and sister were behind the walls of the Governor-General's magnificent house and the division leader knew the boy's mettle. That he would give a good account of himself Vassar was absolutely sure.

As Waldron entered the grand ballroom, accompanied by Virginia, Marya, Zonia and a group of young admiring officers, Billy led his men cautiously through the underbrush toward the house.

On the signal of the toast to the Emperor, the Daughters of Jael had agreed to join their lovers, extinguish the lights, strike down the sentinels and the rest would be easy.

The men in the palace were joyously drunk before eleven. Only a few officers survived the siren call of the cup urged by the charming girls in their white and gold uniforms.

Waldron led the dancing with Virginia Holland. He moved with the easy grace of a master, never missing for an instant the perfect rhythm of her lithe, graceful body.

The surprise of the evening for the Governor-General had been the appearance of every American woman wearing the shining helmet of the soldier of the ranks in token of their full surrender to Imperial authority.

"A beautiful idea—those helmets!" he whispered as they swept through the throng.

"You are pleased?"

"I am more than pleased, I am happy tonight. I know that only your brilliant imagination could have conceived so graceful a tribute to my Imperial Master—"

He paused.

"You are closer to me tonight than ever before," he said softly. "I feel it, I know it."

She turned her head and breathed her answer:

"Yes—"

The dancing ended at eleven-thirty. Waldron gave his arm to Virginia and led the way to the banquet tables. A band of stringed instruments, concealed in bowers of roses, filled the room with exquisite music. The waiters moved with swift, noiseless tread.

The revelry steadily grew faster, the drinking deeper, the dancing more exciting.

Billy's men had dropped flat and were crawling toward the open space in front of the palace when a light footfall was distinctly heard approaching. Billy lifted his head and saw Zonia. She halted with quick precision and gave the countersign.

In a moment she was in his arms.

"What on earth's the matter, little girl?" he whispered excitedly.

350

"Virginia fears that Waldron suspects," was the quick answer.

"Nonsense"—

"He has doubled the guard—Virginia says you'd better retreat until a full division comes up—"

"I'll not do it," Billy broke in. "Four to one, or ten to one, I'm going to take that house—"

"She'll give the signal if I don't return," Zonia warned.

"All right—I'm ready," was the firm response. In quick business fashion Billy led Zonia back of his lines. "Wait here and report if I fail"—

The young Captain crept back to his place and watched for the flash from the Madison Square tower and the signal of lights out from within.

On the stroke of twelve, Waldron rose, lifted his glass and gave the toast—the exact form of which he had sent to every toastmaster in America:

"To the Lord of War—master of the world—the Emperor!"

Virginia's left hand clasped the glass, her right was lifted with nervous intensity giving the sign of the Daughters of Jael to Marya whose hand was on the electric switch. The searchlight on the Madison Square tower flashed and every whistle in the city and harbor screamed its tribute.

With a sudden click the lights went out. In total darkness again and again the blows of the dagger found their mark on the sentinels at the door. Over the curses, groans and shouts rang the shrill battle cry of the Daughters of Jael:

"For *our* God and country!"

Waldron's keen eye caught the tremor of Virginia's fingers as she gave the sign to Marya. The uplifted glass came down with a crash and his iron fist closed on her right hand.

"So!" he growled.

She fought with tigress strength to free her hand and reach the knife concealed in her bodice.

Waldron shouted through the darkness, "Lights! Lights!"

His servants threw the switch in vain. The current had been cut.

With muttered curses he choked Virginia still, carried her in his arms into his library, tore the knife from her bodice and flung her across the room.

"Move a muscle now—damn you! and I'll blow your brains out." He had found a pair of automatics in his table drawer.

He called from the doorway and two guards who had rushed in from the lawn answered.

He pointed to Virginia.

"If she moves, shoot her dead in her tracks. Stay until I return."

He sprang up the narrow steps to the wireless tower. His operator sat lifeless in his chair.

He seized the keys and called central in the Woolworth tower.

"The Garrison to arms! At once—every man to his place and every ship's deck cleared!"

The tower answered O. K.

Vassar sprang to his feet trembling with alarm.

She had failed at the Palace. What did it mean? Her life was in peril. There could be no doubt of it.

He called every wireless station of the enemy on the North Atlantic. Not one answered.

"Good!" he muttered.

He summoned the nearest operator to his relief in the tower:

"Come, for God's sake, quick," he called to Brooklyn, "and bring me a car—there's trouble at the Palace—"

"Coming!" the answer sang.

In fifteen minutes an automobile dashed across the bridge and drew up on the curb at the Woolworth building.

The new operator took his instructions and Vassar turned to the chauffeur:

"Quick now—to the *Sixty-ninth* Regiment Armory. We have men and guns there."

Angela had waited in the machine for her leader to leap from the Palace and drive to the first cavalry rendezvous in Westchester. Her chauffeur sat by her side, smiling, his belt and automatic about her waist.

She heard the shout of Waldron for the guards and knew that the complete plan had failed. Billy's men had been crushed by superior numbers and driven to the foot of the hill. The great man's servants were trained soldiers. They would fight like devils inside.

With quick wit she threw in the clutch and the big touring-car shot down the road and flew over the smooth open way of Riverside Drive. In fifteen minutes she overtook the first division of horsemen on the outskirts of the city galloping to their appointed rendezvous.

"To the Palace of the Governor-General! Quick!" she shouted to the Captain. "Take my car—I can take your horse—quick! Quick! Our leader's a prisoner—or dead—they fight and fight. Quick!"

The Captain sprang from his horse, called to the chauffeur, leaped into the car and gave his horse to Angela. She had learned horsemanship too in these two years of training.

"You know the rendezvous?" the Captain called.

"Si, signor!" Angela answered. "I know. I have been to every spot. I was to drive my leader there. I go! I tell them. You go to her quick—for God's sake—quick!"

Urged by her low, nervous voice the horse dashed down the roadway through Yonkers and on to summon the men.

Waldron returned to the banquet hall—an automatic in each hand. He was a man of dauntless courage. The lights were on again. His assistant engineer had found the break and hastily repaired it.

The magnificent hall was deserted. Only the dead sentinels lay in pools of blood on the slippery floor. The Daughters of Jael had done their work and gone —their task to disarm the enemy and deliver the equipments to our waiting men. Every sword and automatic had fallen into their hands except those worn by the sleeping guard in their quarters and the half-dozen men who were scattered over the lawn.

Waldron quickly brought order out of chaos, barred his doors and found that he held his castle still with eighty faithful soldiers and a dozen wounded servants.

He entered the library and took his place as the special guard of Virginia.

He deliberately took her in his arms and kissed her lips. Her mind was still stunned by the anguish of her failure. There was no longer feeling in body or soul. Nothing mattered.

"You're mine!" he cried fiercely. "I hold you Cossack fashion now!"

He paused in breathless rage, stepped close and struck her a stinging blow with his open hand. She fell across a divan and he stood over the prostrate body with clenched fists.

"To think," he growled, "that I made this idiotic blunder to win your smile! Well, it's mine! I've won it—do you hear? You've failed! My men are coming—do you hear?"

The slender, graceful form lay limp and still—the face chalk-white. She had swooned at last. The blow was more than unconquered pride could endure.

He gazed a moment with bloodshot eyes, dropped suddenly on his knees and took her in his arms.

"I love you—I love you—and you're all mine now —all—all mine, body and soul! My Lucretia Borgia —eh? Well, you've found your master. And you're worth the fight!"

CHAPTER XLIV

WALDRON left Virginia to recover, as he knew she would, and hurried again to the tower to rush his garrison. The answer came at once:

"The men are on the way, sir."

They were! Ten thousand cavalrymen with guidons streaming from their lances! A thousand automobiles were sweeping with them in companies of twenty— each machine packed with sturdy infantrymen, their battle standards flying from speeding cars.

The first division of cavalry which Angela had summoned rescued Billy's hard pressed men, wiped out his opponents, and reached the shelter of the porte-cochère before Waldron's guard inside realized their presence.

Supposing the Imperial troops had answered the summons the big doors were opened. The entrance was forced before Waldron saw they wore the felt hats of the United States Army.

He slammed the massive doors of the library, dragged Virginia through another exit and reached the upper story by the rear stairway.

The Captain held the lower floor. Waldron's guard with their rifles and automatics commanded the landings of the two stairs. Vassar found his men holding a council of war when he leaped from his car and entered the blood-stained doorway of the banquet hall.

Vassar had just formed his men in solid mass to rush the stairway and batter in the door above, when the big elevator shot down the shaft, showing Waldron with Virginia under guard. In a flash he recalled that the entrance from the Drive passed through the hill to this shaft. If Waldron could reach the pier he might yet escape on his yacht.

Vassar rushed to the window and looked toward the river.

The yacht lay beside the wharf, her portholes gleaming, her funnels belching flame and smoke. The engineer had gotten the signal. He was using oil to force the steam.

With a fierce cry of rage Vassar called to Billy and a dozen men leaped after them.

They reached the foot of the hill as Waldron emerged from the tunnel to dash across the fifty-yard space that separated him from the Drive. The yacht was but a hundred yards beyond the road.

The Governor-General formed a hollow square with

his faithful guard—Virginia a prisoner within their circle of steel.

Waldron shouted to his men:

"A fortune and a title for every man who fights his way to the water's edge!"

The guard fired a volley at Vassar's approaching men and dashed for the roadway at the moment Angela rounded the curve, riding furiously at the head of a company of the Daughters of Jael.

The white-robed girl riders charged straight for their foes. Waldron, taken completely by surprise, raised his automatic to kill Virginia. His finger was pressing the trigger when Angela swept close, thrust a revolver into his face, fired and circled to fire again.

The Governor-General crumpled in his tracks and his men surrendered.

Virginia threw herself into Vassar's arms.

"I fear I have failed, my love!"

"Your army has not failed, dear heart!" he answered. "You have lifted a fallen nation from the dust!"

It was true.

A hundred cities ran red with blood—but day dawned with the flag of freedom flying from every staff save in Norfolk and Boston.

In both those important ports the plot had been

betrayed, hundreds of suspected women arrested and imprisoned. The serious part of it was in these two harbors were stationed four huge dreadnaughts and forty submarines with accompanying hydroplanes.

In New York the insurrection had swept all before it. The crews of the submarines were wiped out. Of all who had gathered at the dance and banquet halls —Angela's work had been perfect—not a sailor from the fleet set foot again on their decks. Our boys, dressed in their uniforms, had captured every ship before day—hand to hand, muscle against muscle, with six inches of cold steel!

The aviation corps had been practically wiped out. Their machines were circling the skies at dawn passing the signals to our commanders. Every arsenal fell and every ammunition factory.

When the sun rose on the harbor of New York the Stars and Stripes flew from every ship and every fort and an army of five hundred thousand men, half of them with the best rifles in their hands and big guns lumbering in their lines, were mobilizing under General Wood to capture Boston and Norfolk.

The battles that followed were brief, bloody and glorious in their end. Norfolk they abandoned and their fleet was concentrated on Boston.

The Imperial Army and Navy fought with reckless

"Angela swept close . . . . fired and circled to fire again"

bravery, but the end was sure. They were outnumbered now, two to one. Their submarines stayed with superhuman courage and sent six battleships with five thousand of our bravest men to their graves before they went down.

The captains of the dreadnaughts, when they saw the end had come, swung their prows into the teeth of our fleet and sank with colors flying.

On the day our army marched into Boston with bands playing "The Star Spangled Banner," three hundred thousand Bostonians stood in silence and tears and watched them pass the old State House, along Columbus Avenue, up Tremont Street and through Beacon to the steps of the Capitol. There they stood for hours and sang

> "My Country, 'tis of thee,
> Sweet land of Liberty,
> Of thee I sing."

The President and his Cabinet, released from Fort Warren, reviewed our victorious fleet the following day.

There were no vulgar cheers. Their souls were stirred to greater depths.

When the triumphal procession swung past the old Armory on the East Side of New York, Virginia Holland, with Zonia and Marya, rode at the head of a division of fifty thousand Daughters of Jael. The orderly outrider on her left was a slender Italian mother, on whose breast was pinned a tiny blood-stained flag of the Republic.

Congress met in December. The Senate used the East Room of the Executive Mansion, the House of Representatives met in the Belasco Theater. These two buildings stood intact.

John Vassar was elected speaker of the House without a dissenting voice. His bride from her seat in the gallery watched through tear-dimmed eyes as he took his seat on the dais, and two wistful girls, with smiling faces, sat beside her.

The first bill for consideration was passed without debate in just the time it took to call the roll—the bill which Vassar had introduced five years before—providing for a mobile army of citizen soldiers of a million men with heavy artillery and perfect equipment.

The cost of our defeat and humiliation with two years of slavery had been more than thirty billions of the wealth of the people. This fabulous sum could have been saved by a paltry half billion invested in a navy.

Taught wisdom at last in the school of defeat, a mighty nation lifted her head and girded her loins for a glorious future.

(1)

www.ingramcontent.com/pod-product-compliance
Lightning Source LLC
Chambersburg PA
CBHW011350010726
47494CB00008B/2240